A BRIGHTER DAY TOMORROW

When they're not working in a West London munitions factory, Liz Beck and her best friend Marg find time for fun and laughter at the local ice rink. Then a couple of handsome American servicemen sweep them off their feet and Marg's dream of becoming a GI bride looks like it might come true. But tragedy strikes and Liz makes a discovery that causes a rift in her family. With almost nothing left to lose, she finds love and support where she least expects it and, as the war comes to an end, she hopes for a brighter day tomorrow...

A BRIGHTER DAY TOMORROW

A BRIGHTER DAY TOMORROW

by

Pam Evans

Magna Large Print Books

Anstey,
Leicestershire

British Library Cataloguing in Publication Data.

A catalogue record of this book is
available from the British Library

ISBN   978-0-7505-4769-7

First published in Great Britain in 2018 by
Headline Publishing Group

Cover illustration © www.headdesign.co.uk

The right of Pamela Evans to be identified as the author of this work
has been asserted by her in accordance with the Copyright, Designs
and Patents Act 1988

Published in Large Print 2019 by arrangement with
Headline Publishing Group Ltd.

Magna Large Print is an imprint of Library Magna Books Ltd.

Printed and bound in Great Britain by
T.J. (International) Ltd., Cornwall, PL28 8RW

Many thanks to my editor Clare Foss who continues to be a joy to work with, always enthusiastic and warm hearted. To all the team at Headline who make my manuscripts into such lovely books. Thanks also to my agent Barbara Levy who continues to work on my behalf.

Chapter One

Having had a brief, whispered conversation at the filing cabinets with a friend and fellow clerk in the offices of a West London munitions factory, Liz Beck felt the weight of an admonitory hand on her shoulder.

'How many more times must I remind you that this office is not a social club, Miss Beck?' roared the fearsome head of the department when Liz swung round to face her. 'You are here to work, not to chatter at every conceivable opportunity.'

'Sorry, Miss Banks,' said the young woman, with instinctive respect for her superior.

'Yes, you always claim to be sorry when I catch you slacking,' said Beryl Banks, a formidable woman of middle age. Plain in appearance with greyish hair clipped back behind her ears, she had a pale, cosmetic-free complexion and the brightest blue eyes Liz had ever seen. 'But that doesn't seem to stop you doing it again, does it?'

'It was only a few words, Miss,' said the indomitable Liz, a sociable seventeen-year-old blonde with greenish eyes and a sunny smile. 'Marg and I both just happened to be filing some papers ... we carried on working while we were talking, though.'

'You can't work properly and talk at the same time,' the older woman pointed out. 'That's how mistakes are made.'

'We are both very particular about our work,' insisted Liz. 'And we could have been talking about the job.'

'Now I've heard everything,' said the older woman irritably. 'This conversation, which apparently can't wait until after office hours, would have been about your social life, if I'm not very much mistaken.'

Liz bit her lip. 'Well, yeah,' she admitted. 'She was telling me about this...'

'Spare me the sordid details, please.'

'Nothing sordid...'

'I don't want to hear anything about it and neither do I want to catch you idling again.' She waved a hand in the vague direction of the factory. 'In case you've forgotten, this country is at war and on the factory floor of this building there are many people working at machines for long and arduous hours to make munitions with which our soldiers can fight to make us free again. It is our responsibility, as office staff, to back them up by looking after the administration side of things in an efficient manner.'

'I wouldn't mind working in the factory,' mentioned Liz, who had heard that you could earn more money on the machines. 'But I was sent into the office and told not to argue.'

'The people at the Labour Exchange obviously thought you were more suitable for clerical work and we must do as we're told in wartime,' said Miss Banks. 'Now back to work please and if you want to chatter do it in your own time in future.'

'Yes, Miss,' she said, closing the filing cabinet and going back to her desk, her thoughts returning to her pal Marg and her suggestion for an outing which sounded as though it might be a lot of laughs.

A sociable girl, Liz could endure the war and all its hazards, the inconveniences and long working hours, the bombs and shortage of absolutely everything, so long as she could have some fun when she was off duty.

'Ice skating,' said Violet Beck over dinner that night when her daughter Liz mentioned that she was going to the rink nearby with her friend Marg. 'But I thought they closed the place when war broke out.'

'They did but it's open again now apparently and has been for a while,' said Liz. 'And all thanks to the Americans.'

'How's that?' asked her mother.

'The American Embassy persuaded our government to re-open it because the Yanks like ice skating and ice hockey and there are a lot of American servicemen stationed close to London now.'

'So, they've opened it for the Yanks then,' said Liz's father George with more than a hint of disapproval.

'Apparently,' Liz confirmed. 'But the rest of us benefit from it because we can buy a ticket to go in as well.'

'That's good of them,' said George sarcastically. He was a large, handsome man from whom Liz had inherited her colouring, but his blond hair was thin now and white in places.

'They've done us a favour, Dad, so I don't think it's very nice to criticise them,' said Liz heatedly. 'Anyway, they are here helping us to win the war so welcome to Britain, I say, to each and every one of them.'

'All right, no need to go on about it. Of course, they are welcome,' said her father. 'They are different to us, though. From what I've heard they are very full of themselves.'

'They're probably just confident and why shouldn't they be when they are from a country like America,' she said. 'We can't expect people from other places to be as modest as we are. That wouldn't be any fun at all.'

'I suppose not,' grunted George. 'You need to watch yourself around them, though. They have a bit of a reputation as regards women from what I've heard.'

'Yeah, I know about that too. But it isn't all down to the boys. Some girls are all over them because they want nylons and all the other goodies they are so generous with,' said Liz. 'No one forces these women to go out with them. Anyway, I don't know any Americans so I'm not in a position to judge.'

'Why the sudden interest in ice skating?' asked her sister Dora. 'Dance halls and the cinema are more your sort of thing.'

'You know me, I'll have a go at anything,' said Liz. 'But it's Marg's idea. She fancies giving it a try and I thought it might be a laugh. It will be a change anyway.'

'If they opened it for the Americans, the place will be full of Yanks,' said her mother, a small woman who wore her brown hair in a hairnet. 'And you'll get yourself a bad name hanging around with them.'

'You shouldn't judge them when you've never even spoken to one, Mum,' she said. 'I'll be busy learning to skate anyway.'

'You don't have any skates,' said her mother.

'We can hire them there.'

'Can I come?' asked Dora, who was a year or so older though usually behaved like the younger of the two.

Liz's heart sank because her sister had spoilt more social events than she cared to remember. 'But I'm going with Marg,' she explained.

'Dora can go along with you, surely,' said their mother predictably.

'She'll keep an eye on you,' added George. 'Make sure you don't get mixed up with any Yanks.'

Liz felt a dull pain in the pit of her stomach as yet again her parents took her sister's side against her. She should be used to it after a lifetime of favouritism towards Dora, but it still had the power to hurt.

'I'm not planning on doing that anyway, Dad, and I certainly don't need my sister looking over my shoulder.'

'It will be nice for you to go out together,' said her mother, hoping, like most parents, for family unity.

Liz wished her sister had some friends of her own to go around with, but she never seemed able to keep any, which wasn't surprising as she was so difficult to get on with, being argumentative and overly fond of her own way.

'I don't want to go where I'm not wanted,' said

Dora, her voice trembling on the verge of the tears she could produce at will. 'You go with your friend. Don't worry about me.'

'Now see what you've done,' said Violet. 'You've upset your sister.'

Liz felt as though the walls of the living room were closing in on her. This small terraced house in Hammersmith was the only home she had ever known. She lived here with her father, an engineer in a factory, and her mother who was a housewife, despite the fact that it was illegal for women without dependants not to take a job because of the need for war workers. Mum had had a weak heart as a child so managed to get around the rules that way, keenly encouraged by her husband who hated the idea of his wife going out to work. Dora was on an assembly line in a factory.

To a casual observer, the Becks might seem to be an ordinary, happy family. But it wasn't all blissful for Liz. Dora had always been the favoured child, which was surprising considering how badly she treated their parents with her rudeness and temper tantrums. Yet still they let her have her own way. Liz had always felt like an outsider and had learned to accept it, but at times like tonight, when something she was looking forward to was under threat, it made her angry. If Mum and Dad were to support her just now and again, it would mean so much. But that obviously wasn't going to happen on this occasion and Dora was determined to go skating with her tonight, so she turned to her sister and said, 'All right then, you can come.'

'That's better,' beamed Violet. 'But come

straight home if the siren goes.'

'We haven't had an air raid for ages,' Liz reminded her.

'That's true but it doesn't mean that we won't,' said Violet, though now, in the summer of 1943, they had had a long period of calm. 'The war isn't over yet.' She turned her attention to the meal in progress. 'Now eat your food so that I can get cleared up and listen to the wireless.'

Liz looked at the sausage and mash on her plate, recalling the days when swede wasn't added to everything to make it go further. She was too hungry to leave so much as a morsel, but vowed never to eat the watery vegetable when the war was over and they had a choice.

Liz was laughing so hard her stomach hurt as the three of them clung to the sides at the ice rink, unable to move forward and stay vertical without help.

'How does anyone manage to stand up on these blades, let alone dance about?' she wondered, as seasoned skaters sailed by with apparent ease. There were even a couple of girls in proper skating skirts, looking very pleased with themselves.

'Practice, I suppose,' said Marg, also very amused by their own lack of competence.

'They've all had special lessons, I reckon,' said Dora, who wasn't blessed with a sense of humour so spoke in a tone of complaint. 'Show-offs, the lot of them.'

'I think they're just enjoying themselves and good luck I say,' said Liz as some really competent girl skaters whizzed by looking very graceful. 'So come on you two, let's get practising so that we can learn to skate like them.'

Giggling, Liz and Marg slid forward, still hanging on to the sides, while Dora said she wasn't going to make a fool of herself any longer and limped off the ice.

'Have you noticed those American soldiers in the café?' asked Marg as the two girls took a break, still clutching the sides.

'Not really,' said Liz, glancing across at the open-style cafeteria at the side of the rink. 'I've been too busy trying to stand up to pay much attention to anything else.'

'Some of them are gorgeous, like film stars,' enthused Marg, a brown-eyed brunette with a beaming smile and dimples. 'Smart uniforms, good looking and plenty of dosh. One of them will do me nicely and I aim to get one.'

'Marg, that is very manipulative.'

'A girl has to make her own chances in life. No point in waiting for something to happen,' she said airily. 'We're young and so are they so why not give nature a helping hand?'

'Is that why you wanted to come here tonight, because you knew there would be Americans around?'

'Maybe, yeah,' she admitted.

'Oh Marg. There's a name for girls like you,' said Liz. 'My dad would have a fit if he knew.'

'He doesn't though, does he, so let's make the most of our opportunities,' she said. 'We've been sent enough bad stuff because of this rotten war. When we get something to brighten up our lives, why not take advantage of it? The Yanks are like a breath of fresh air around the place. They are the best thing that's happened to this country since before the Germans marched into Poland and boy am I going to make the most of it.'

'If your mum could hear you she'd go mad.'

'She would an' all, but she isn't here is she? And what the eye doesn't see...'

The conversation came to an abrupt end when Liz lost her balance and landed on her bottom on the ice and they both erupted into laughter.

'Thanks for leaving me on my own for so long,' said Dora sarcastically when Liz and Marg eventually went off the ice and found her sitting on a bench, scowling.

'Sorry, sis, but we did come here to skate, not to sit watching other people doing it,' said Liz. 'It's a waste of money if we all come off the ice.'

'You came here to skate. Huh, that's a joke,' she said nastily. 'You spent all your time on your bottoms on the ice from what I could see.'

'It's our first time,' Liz reminded her cheerfully. 'We can't expect miracles.'

'You made complete idiots of yourselves.'

'So what if we did?' said Liz. 'There are several other beginners here and they are all finding it hard to stay on their feet. You didn't give it a chance, going off like that. Falling over is all part of the fun at first.'

'I didn't want to show myself up.'

'Why did you come then?' asked the outspoken Marg. 'Surely you didn't think you would go to an ice rink for the first time and whizz around like a professional?'

'I didn't really think about it.'

'No, I don't suppose you did,' said Liz, disappointed because once again her sister was trying to spoil things. 'You wanted to come because you can't bear to miss anything that I do.'

'Calm down, girls,' said Marg. 'We've come for a laugh so let's have one.'

'Sorry, Marg,' said Liz. 'Let's have a break and a drink of something then have another try.'

'I'm all for that,' agreed Marg, glancing towards the objects of her admiration in the café. 'Are you going to brave the ice with us again, Dora? You might enjoy it second time around.'

'No. I'm going home,' she said and limped off towards the changing room.

'Hi, girls,' said one of two American soldiers. 'Can we get you something to drink?'

'Yes, please,' said Marg without hesitation while Liz stood by looking embarrassed, unaccustomed to such bold behaviour from strangers.

'Coffee?' asked the second man, looking at Liz.

'Tea, please,' she said politely, surprised there was coffee available and wondering if perhaps the Americans had supplied it as their troops were such regular customers here. 'Thank you very much.'

'You're welcome.' He ordered her drink and said, 'We know how much you British like your tea.' He introduced them in a strong American accent. 'I'm Vic. My buddy here is Joe.'

Marg completed the introductions and when they were all seated at a table with their drinks

Vic said, 'We noticed that you gals could probably use a little help with your skating.'

'I think we might be beyond help,' grinned Liz, beginning to relax.

'We've only been this once,' Marg pointed out.

'You can't expect miracles first time,' said Vic, who had dark, cropped hair and eyes the colour of coal. 'You'll get better with a bit of practice.'

'Are you two experts then?' Liz enquired.

'We've been skating since we were kids and we skate for our ice hockey team,' replied Joe, who had hazel eyes and mid-brown, army-style hair.

'Oh well,' said Liz. 'You're well out of our league then.'

'We ain't wanting to compete with you,' said Vic in his slow drawl. 'But we'd be happy to help.'

'And we'd be happy to let you,' said Marg, smiling and flashing her eyes at Joe.

The chemistry was tangible and Liz felt drawn to Vic while the other two got together. After a few instructions and a couple of tumbles, Liz's confidence improved so much she found herself moving along the ice with one hand attached to Vic while the other clutched the side.

'Next time we'll get you to let go of the side and rely on me for support,' said Vic later when it was time for the girls to hand their skates back.

'Sounds good to me,' said Liz.

'Joe and I have to stay on here for team practice after the rink closes to the public, but maybe we could see you here another night,' said Vic, addressing Liz in particular. 'Maybe tomorrow if you're free?'

A look passed between them that melted her young, eager heart and it seemed to her as if something really special had happened here tonight.

'We're free,' said Liz.

'Not half,' added Marg.

'You do realise that we've allowed ourselves to be picked up by a couple of Yanks, don't you?' said Liz as she and Marg got on the bus to go home.

'Yeah, brilliant, wasn't it?' said Marg laughing. 'It's what I've wanted ever since they arrived on our shores. It's no different to meeting blokes at a dance anyway.'

'I suppose not,' said Liz. 'It just feels that way.'

'It feels lovely to me and don't tell me you didn't enjoy it because I won't believe you.'

'Vic is rather gorgeous.'

'So is Joe.'

'I can't wait for tomorrow night.'

'Me neither,' said Marg and they were both laughing as they took their seats.

'Oi oi! Somebody has had a good night,' said the female conductor as she took their money.

'I'll say we have,' said Marg. 'One of the best ever.'

'I wish I was young again and know all I know now,' said the conductor who was one of the breed of older women working on the buses because of the shortage of men due to the war. 'Oh yeah, I'd have a lovely time the second time around.'

'Sorry, Missus, but you only get one crack at it

and we're making the most of ours,' laughed Marg.

'I don't blame you either, girls,' she said and moved on, smiling.

Liz's mood of elation immediately evaporated when she arrived home to find herself in trouble.

'How could you let your sister go home on her own?' demanded her mother while Dora hovered in the background looking forlorn.

'It was her decision to leave,' said Liz.

'You should have gone with her,' Violet declared. 'It's what we do in wartime.'

'There are no bombs around, Mum,' she reminded her. 'Haven't been for ages.'

'Even so, it isn't nice for her to be out on the streets on her own, especially in the blackout.'

'We are all used to the blackout,' Liz pointed out. 'Anyway, Dora is the elder. Maybe she should look out for me every now and again.'

'You should look out for each other,' said Violet.

'Your mother is right,' added George, always game for an argument. 'And you shouldn't answer her back.'

'Dora could have waited instead of marching out in a mood,' said Liz.

'Don't answer me back either,' roared her father, a very domineering man.

'You were ignoring your sister, apparently,' Violet chipped in. 'Too busy with your friend to take any notice of her.'

Liz knew from experience that there was no point in continuing to defend herself because her parents' allegiance was firmly set in Dora's corner.

'Whatever I've done to upset all of you, I'm sorry,' she said, speaking directly to her parents. 'But I'm going to bed now. G'night, all.'

There was a muttered response and Liz headed upstairs with tears in her eyes.

'Why do you always drop me in it?' Liz asked her sister later when she met her on the landing on her way to the bathroom.

'I didn't do it deliberately,' denied Dora, who was taller than Liz and had similar colouring, though her hair was a few shades darker. 'Mum noticed that I came home on my own and asked me why. I had to tell her.'

'And as usual you made up a story so that I would be in trouble,' she said, angry because Dora seemed to delight in her sister's distress.

'I only told the truth.'

'And the rest,' Liz retorted. 'It wasn't true about Marg and me ignoring you. You wouldn't join in.'

'How could I when you two are so close?'

'We are friends; of course we're close,' said Liz, biting back any comment about her sister's lack of friends because she saw no point in hurting her unnecessarily. 'Anyway, we enjoyed the skating even though we couldn't do it. You didn't like it so it's best not to go again.'

'I won't, don't worry.'

That was a relief to Liz because she didn't want her sister tagging along tomorrow night. Neither was she going to tell her that she and Marg had a date with a couple of Yanks, which she would immediately pass on to their parents and all hell would break loose about the boys being Americans.

'Do you want to use the bathroom first?' asked Liz. 'I want to get washed and go to bed.'

'You can go first,' said Dora, and Liz knew that it was her sister's attempt at an olive branch, a rare thing indeed from her. She was a very strange girl. Over the years, Liz had repeatedly offered her friendship and company, but it had never worked because Dora had such a nasty streak.

While Dora headed for her bedroom, Liz went to the bathroom, all thoughts of her sister pushed aside by memories of Vic and excited anticipation for tomorrow night.

Unfortunately the excitement kept her awake for most of the night, which caused her to oversleep and she was late for work the next morning. She tried the old trick of leaving her coat on the hook in the cloakroom and walked into the office as though she had been in for ages, but Miss Banks was far too savvy to fall for that.

'You were twenty minutes late this morning, Miss Beck,' she bellowed, having called Liz into her office. 'What do you have to say about that?'

'I'm very sorry, Miss Banks.'

'I should think so too,' said the other woman. 'What is the reason for it?'

'I didn't sleep well and when I did go off I couldn't wake up because I was so tired.'

'You should go to bed at a reasonable hour when you have to get up for work the next morning,' lectured the older woman. 'Never mind all this gadding about you young girls feel compelled to do of an evening.'

'Yes, Miss.'

'You can make up the time in your lunch hour.'

'Of course,' she agreed. 'And I really am very sorry.'

Miss Banks nodded and Liz left her office feeling thoroughly deflated after the excitement of last night. She always seemed to be in trouble with someone lately. Either her parents, her sister or the head of the department.

'Miss Banks is a miserable old cow,' opined Marg when Liz joined her in the canteen to eat her sandwiches after making up the time she owed the company. 'Everyone knows that. So take no notice of her.'

'She's the department head so of course I have to take notice of her.'

'Don't worry about it though.'

'She's only doing her job, Marg,' said Liz. 'And I suppose I shouldn't have been late.'

'Maybe not, but she could have let it go,' said Marg. 'But no, not her. I reckon she loves it when one of us steps out of line and gives her the chance to dish out one of her punishments. She's a dried-up old prune who's never had a boyfriend. She's jealous of us young ones.'

'We don't know that, Marg,' said Liz. 'We know nothing about her except that it's her job to run the department and keep us all in order.'

'I don't know why you're defending her when she's been so nasty to you. But let's forget about her and talk about tonight,' suggested Marg excitedly. 'We'll have to wear trousers as we're going

26

ice skating, but I've got a nice blouse I can put on and I managed to get a lipstick in Woolworth's the other day.'

'I've got some lippy too,' said Liz.

'We want to look as good as we possibly can.'

'Not half.'

'Oh and Liz,' began Marg. 'Don't bring that sister of yours, will you? We don't want any odd numbers.'

Liz nodded, confident that Dora had had more than enough of ice skating.

The evening went with more than a swing. It was pure magic. Vic gave Liz so much confidence on the ice that she was even able to let go of his hand as well as the sides, briefly, by the time they took a refreshment break.

'We've got the next women's champion here,' joked Vic as the four of them sat around the table in the café.

'Now you're just being ridiculous,' she said modestly, but she enjoyed the compliment.

They laughed and joked and skated some more. When they were taking a breather towards the end of the evening, Vic said to Liz, 'We're having a dance at the base next Saturday. Do you fancy coming along? Joe is going to ask Marg so the four of us will be together.'

There was nothing she would like more, but there were practicalities to be dealt with, not least the fact that he was stationed outside of London somewhere.

'I'd love to, but isn't the base a long way out?' she said. 'I'm not sure how we'd get there.'

'Transport will be supplied by the army,' he said. 'We need girls to make the dance worthwhile so if you've got any friends that would like a night out bring them along. Everyone will be welcome.'

'My sister might like to come,' she said, much against her better judgement. Despite everything she did want things to be good for Dora.

'Bring her with you,' he said. 'The more the merrier.'

A frown creased her brow.

'Problem?' he asked.

'My father,' she said. 'We'll probably be quite late back, won't we?'

'I'll come and see him,' he said. 'See if he's okay about it. I know some people think us Americans are all sex maniacs, but we really aren't.'

She laughed. 'I wouldn't go that far, but there is a certain rumour about you.'

'Let's go now and see your folks,' he suggested. 'I was going to ask if I could see you home anyway. If we go right away it won't be too late. Will it?'

She had a worrying image of her mother in her curlers and dressing gown being suddenly confronted by an ebullient American soldier. 'I think they'll probably be in bed by now,' she said. 'But thank you for offering.'

'Oh, well tell them from me that you and your sister will be in safe hands.'

'I will.'

'The transport will be outside the rink,' he said. 'Six thirty. All welcome. So, shall we get you home now?'

'Don't you have to go back to camp?'

'No, we have an overnight pass, and don't have to be back until tomorrow morning,' he explained. 'We're staying at the American Services club in town. They do cheap rates and have all our home comforts.'

Very nice too, she thought, wondering if British troops had such accommodating facilities, but just said, 'I'd better see Marg before we go.'

'Sure,' he said.

As it happened Joe was seeing Marg home too, so they all got on the bus together and went their separate ways closer to home. Vic told Liz he was twenty-two and from a small town in New York State, which meant nothing to Liz but sounded glamorous. He lived with his mother and sister, apparently.

'I'm an engineer,' he told her as they walked to her house. 'Trained for three years.'

'So were you very annoyed that you had to leave that job to go to war after all that training?'

'I volunteered before they called me up,' he said. 'It seemed no more than my duty. Besides I liked the idea of travel, but I didn't know all that much about England. I'd heard of it, of course. It's the Mother Country so we all know about it.'

'What do you think now you're here?'

He would never forget his first sight of England; the shabbiness around the dock area, the bomb damage and the smallness of everything. The bomb craters and the rubble in particular had upset him. To think that these people had to live with the threat and reality of bombs and still went

29

about their daily business. As he had travelled inland to the camp, the countryside dotted with cute villages had captured his heart, and he'd loved the special buzz of London's West End from his very first visit.

He'd been told by his superiors that the British didn't like to be told how big and colourful everything was in America. As a nation, their hosts tended to be rather self-effacing and expected other people to be the same. He wanted to tell Liz about the glorious hugeness of his homeland, of their big modern buildings, bright stores and sunny landscapes. But he said truthfully, 'I like it fine here.'

'That's good,' she said. 'It would be awful for you if you hated it.'

'It couldn't be awful now that I've met you.'

She laughed. 'I've heard that you Yanks know how to sweet-talk a girl.'

'Just speaking the truth, honey,' he drawled.

She liked it. He could say nice things to her for as long as he liked.

When they reached her gate, he said, 'Are you sure you don't want me to tell your folks about the dance?'

'It's sweet of you to offer, but it really will be better coming from me.'

'Okay. I'd better head off then,' he said. 'I'll take a Tube ride into town.'

'Thank you for seeing me home.'

'A pleasure,' he said and kissed her lightly on the lips. 'See you on Saturday. Don't forget, the transport will be at the rink at six thirty. I'll be waiting for you at the base when you arrive.'

'Goodnight, Vic,' she said and watched as he strode off into the night, a dim figure in the light of a half moon. But it wasn't too dark to see his swagger and she found that attractive.

'Over my dead body,' declared George Beck, having been told of his daughters' plans for Saturday. 'Have you lost your mind or something? An American army camp out in the wilds somewhere. That is just asking for trouble.'

'It's all above board, Dad,' said Liz. 'It's being put on by the American army and they are providing transport. All completely free of charge.'

'I told her it was a silly idea,' said Dora, always keen to stay the right side of their parents.

'You were all for it when I told you about it,' said Liz, glaring at her.

'You're not going and I don't want to hear any more about it,' said George.

'If they are getting taken and brought back, dear, it might be all right,' suggested Violet meekly.

'All wrong more like,' said George. 'Taking a load of young girls out to the country. It doesn't take a genius to know what they have in mind.'

'It's a properly organised event, Dad,' Liz tried to assure him. 'There will be officers in charge. They won't allow the boys to misbehave.'

'Why are they bringing in women from London? That's what I want to know.'

'Because you can't have a dance without girls and there aren't enough local ones where the base is. Vic wanted to come into the house and tell you about it himself the other night, but I thought you would be rude to him so I asked him

31

not to.'

'So, I'm in the wrong now?'

'You're being unreasonable, Dad,' said Liz. 'Dora and I are young. Of course we want to go out and have fun.'

'With Yanks?'

'Yes with Yanks if they ask us, or with Poles or Canadians or people from Australia.'

'Now you are being facetious.'

'And you are being unreasonable,' said Liz heatedly. 'Some women are married at our age.'

'At seventeen, not many, but I wish you were,' he said. 'Then I wouldn't have responsibility for you and it would be a load off my mind.'

'We're old enough to earn our own money and pay for our keep so we should be allowed to do what we like in our spare time, within reason, which this is.'

'She's right, George,' said Violet nervously.

He puffed away on his Woodbine. 'All right, go to the bloody dance, but don't come running to me when you're in trouble, because the door will be firmly shut,' he said.

'It's a dance, Dad, not an orgy,' said Liz.

'That's enough backchat.'

'We'll behave, Dad,' said Dora, keen to stay on his good side as usual.

'You'd better,' he said.

'Roll on Saturday,' whispered Liz to her sister as the girls bounded up the stairs, giggling.

Chapter Two

There was a queue of excited young women waiting to climb into the back of a US army truck parked outside the ice rink on Saturday evening when Liz and the others arrived.

'Welcome aboard the Passion Wagon,' said one of the female passengers as they clambered in.

'Are you speaking from experience?' said Liz, smiling.

'I wish,' laughed the young woman. 'But I'm only joking.'

'Have you been to one of the American dances before?'

'You bet I have,' she replied with enthusiasm. 'A friend of mine is going out with a GI so I get to know what social events are coming up at the base. The Yanks certainly know how to treat their visitors. You wait and see. The Palais won't seem the same after you've been to a dance at the base.'

'I can't wait to get there, then,' said Liz eagerly.

'Me neither,' added Marg.

Behind the dismal exterior of the blacked-out building, all was magical inside the hall. The place resonated with the cheerful clamour of voices while the dance floor was crowded with couples doing the quickstep and jitterbugging to upbeat music played by a small band made up of men in

US military uniform. There were coloured lights along the edge of the stage, bunting strung across the ceiling and at the end of the hall a table spread with snacks and soft drinks.

'You Americans certainly know how to roll out the welcome mat, don't you,' Liz said to Vic when they were taking a break between dances. 'I haven't seen a party spread like this one since before the war.'

'We like to do our best for our visitors,' he said. 'The only thing we don't have is liquor, which is strictly prohibited at our dances. I guess the army doesn't trust us to behave around girls if we've been drinking.'

She thought how wild it might get with alcohol to add to the high excitement already here, but she said, 'They don't have booze at ordinary dance halls so we won't miss it. We don't need drink to have a good time.'

As the band struck up with Glenn Miller's 'In The Mood' he led her into the jiving crowds on the dance floor.

'Do you realise that you've helped me to learn two new skills in the short time since I've known you?' Liz said to Vic as they tucked into hot dogs and sandwiches in the interval. 'Ice skating and the jitterbug.'

'And you're beating me at both already,' he joked.

'That isn't true and you know it, but by the end of the night I'm hoping to match you at the jitterbug,' she laughed.

'We'll see about that,' he said, smiling. 'I'm

pretty good.'

'Modest too,' she teased.

They were both laughing when Marg and Joe appeared looking happy together. 'Enjoying yourself, Liz?' Marg enquired.

'You bet.'

'Marvellous, isn't it?'

Dora appeared and proceeded to flirt embarrassingly with Vic. 'I am going to have the next dance with you,' she said in a silly, girlish voice as she took hold of his arm. 'And no argument.'

He looked uncomfortable for a moment, 'I think you should wait for a lady's invitation dance,' he said. 'And I might consider it then.'

There was an awkward moment, but Liz wasted no time. Excusing herself from the company, she took her sister by the arm and led her forcefully to the door.

'Don't you dare try to ruin things for me with Vic,' she said, outside in the cool summer evening.

'I was only being sociable.'

'No you weren't,' said Liz. 'You were throwing yourself at him and deliberately trying to spoil things for me. You do it all the time at home with Mum and Dad. But I'm not going to let you do it with Vic. Find your own man and keep away from mine.'

'I'm not interested in him.'

'Probably not, but you'd still love to ruin things for me just for the hell of it,' said Liz. 'I don't know what I've ever done to you but for some reason you seem to enjoy making my life difficult whenever you possibly can.'

'Oh, for goodness' sake, stop making a drama out of nothing,' she said.

'Look, Dora,' Liz began in a more persuasive tone. 'I really like Vic so I'm asking you to stop trying to mess it up for me.'

'Are you that unsure of him that you have to warn me off?'

'It's very early days so of course I'm not sure of him.'

Dora shrugged. 'That's your problem, nothing to do with me,' she said.

'Find a fella of your own. There are enough of them here tonight.'

'I might prefer Vic.'

'He's made it clear he isn't interested so back off.'

'Don't tell me what to do.'

'Let me put it this way,' began Liz. 'If you try anything like that again, you and I are finished, Dora, and I mean it. Living in the same house will be the only thing we'll have in common. I will never let you go out with me socially again.'

'Oh.' She was clearly rattled by this. 'All right,' she agreed swiftly, because Liz was often her only chance of a night out. 'It was just a bit of fun.'

'You don't know how to have fun, Dora,' Liz retorted, then turned and went back to the company, hoping that her warning had had an effect. Over the years she had tried many times to be kind to her sister and would love it if they could be friends, but Dora was far too self-absorbed for any such arrangement.

The second half of the dance was even livelier as

people got to know each other and the girls got better at the jive and jitterbug. The band played a few slow numbers towards the end and most couples smooched around the floor. Liz noticed her sister was dancing and was instinctively relieved, hoping that would stop her making a nuisance of herself. As for herself and Vic, they had their arms wrapped round each other while Marg and Joe were looking happy together too.

'It's been a lovely evening, Vic,' said Liz.

'For me too,' he said. 'I can't wait until we meet again, but I'm not sure if I can get to London next weekend. Depends if the army has other plans for me. They're pretty good with weekend passes, but we can't take anything for granted. If you give me your phone number, I'll call you.'

'Phone number,' she repeated in surprise. 'Oh no, we don't have a phone.'

'At work?'

She could just imagine Miss Banks' reaction to a personal phone call for one of the staff. 'We're not allowed phone calls,' she told him.

'Oh, okay.' He mulled this over. 'Shall we say then that I'll come to your house on Saturday night if I can make it? I won't know until late on in the week so a letter wouldn't reach you in time. I can't promise to be there though and it isn't fair to keep you hanging about.'

'I don't mind waiting in.'

'Well, if you're sure,' he said. 'So, let's say if I'm not there by about seven, you'll know I can't get away, but if I don't manage it I'll get in touch as soon as I can after that.'

'Okay, Vic, and when I see you next I'll have the

number of the telephone box at the end of my street. We can keep in touch through that by prior arrangement if the occasion ever arises. And meanwhile this evening isn't over yet.'

'It sure isn't,' he said, drawing her closer to him.

Liz spent the whole of Saturday in a state of nervous anticipation. Whilst she was longing to see Vic and hoping with all her heart that he made it, she was dreading him meeting her parents, her father in particular, because of his outspoken nature and the prejudiced opinion he had about the behaviour of American servicemen.

'He might come and he might not,' George said in a disapproving manner, having been told of the situation. 'What sort of an arrangement is that? It doesn't sound like a decent way to treat a girl to me.'

Unlike her mother, who allowed herself be bullied by him, Liz wasn't afraid to talk back. 'He's in the army, Dad,' she reminded him. 'He can't just do as he pleases. He has to hope he gets a weekend pass and sometimes doesn't know until the last minute.'

'There is that, I suppose.'

'Anyway, I told him I don't mind waiting in,' she said, her voice rising defensively. 'He didn't try to force me into it.'

'All right, there's no need to get on your high horse with me, young lady.'

She was so churned up she didn't want her tea, but it was bad form to waste anything in wartime so she forced herself to eat it. Then at seven o'clock there was a knock at the door and her heart leapt.

'I'll go,' said Dora.

'No you won't,' Liz was quick to say.

'I'll behave.'

'He's my boyfriend so I'll let him in,' Liz insisted.

'All right, keep your hair on,' said Dora.

'So, you're stationed out in the wilds somewhere, then?' said George by way of conversation when Vic had been introduced and offered a seat.

'Not really the wilds, Mr Beck,' said Vic politely. 'It isn't far from London and there is a village nearby so we're not at all cut off.'

'That's Londoners for you,' said the older man in a friendly manner, his mood having improved with Vic's arrival. 'Anywhere not on the Tube line is the back of beyond to us.'

'I can understand that, but we can get pretty much all we want in the base,' he said. 'And we don't mind travelling further afield to find entertainment.'

'They even provide that for you at the camp, though, don't they?' Violet remarked. 'The girls had a lovely time at the dance there last week.'

'Yeah, the army dances are good, but they don't lay on entertainment every week,' he said. 'We like to get out of there when we can anyway.'

'Only natural,' Dora chipped in.

'Do you live in a built-up area at home in America, Vic?' asked Violet sociably.

'A small town, Mrs Beck.'

'With your parents?'

'Just Mom and my sister,' he said. 'Dad died

when I was little. An accident at work.'

'Oh, what a shame.'

He nodded.

'Shall we go then?' said Liz, wanting to bring an end to the stilted conversation.

He looked at her and smiled and she was over-whelmed with love and desire for him.

As Liz was keen to improve her limited skating skills, they joined the queue for the bus to the ice rink. She asked if they were meeting Marg and Joe there. 'I know she was hoping he'd get to see her tonight.'

'He is seeing her but Joe and I decided to split up this time,' he said. 'He fancies the movies, I think. Anyway, I wanted us to be on our own for a change.'

'I thoroughly approve of that,' she said, de-lighted by his enthusiasm.

They exchanged more personal details, both eager to get better acquainted.

'I was sad to hear about your father,' she said.

'Yeah. I was only little when he died so I don't remember him, but everyone says he was a great guy.'

'So, it's just you, your mum and your sister,' she said. 'Are you close?'

'They don't come any closer than us three,' he said. 'Mom is great. There ain't a thing she wouldn't do for me and Rose. It couldn't have been easy for her, raising us on her own.'

'She didn't marry again, then?' she asked. 'She was probably still quite young when she lost your dad.'

40

'No. She never seemed interested in anything like that,' he said. 'Still isn't. I wouldn't mind if she found someone else. At least I'd know she had someone looking out for her and Rose while I'm away.'

'Yeah, I can see why you might feel like that,' she said as the bus arrived and they climbed aboard.

Although it was usual for the man to pay the expenses on a date, not many were as generous as Vic. Not only did he pay the bus fare, the entrance fee, skate hire and drinks in the café when they took a break from skating, he also dipped his hand in his pocket and handed her a pair of nylons and a bar of chocolate.

'Oh my,' she said. 'You are so generous.'

He shrugged, smiling. 'The army looks after us really well. We do better than your guys, so I've heard,' he said. 'So we can afford the odd little treat.'

She was very well aware of the connotations associated with girls taking presents from Americans, but was too thrilled with her gifts to worry about it. Nylons! Blimey!

As they took to the ice again she insisted he go off on his own for a proper fast skate while she slithered around near the sides rather gingerly. But he didn't stay away long.

'Come on, Liz,' he said, returning quite soon and taking her hand. 'Enough of all this beginner's rail-hugging. Let's see you doing some real skating.'

She clung on to his hand as though her life depended on it as he guided her round the rink. It was frightening and exhilarating simultaneously, but her confidence began to grow. She was so happy to be with him she believed there was nothing she couldn't do with him by her side.

'How are things going with you and Vic?' asked Marg a few weeks later as they were on the way to the canteen for their dinner break. 'You two seem to be very close when the four of us go out together.'

'We are. I'm absolutely mad about him,' she admitted. 'How about you and Joe?'

'Head over heels,' she replied. 'So much so I've decided that I'm going to be a GI bride.'

'Does he know about it?' asked Liz, grinning.

'Not yet,' she laughed.

'Seriously though, you wouldn't really want to go to America and leave your family, would you?' Liz questioned. 'Your mum would be broken hearted.'

'I'm one of six kids,' she said. 'One fewer won't make much difference.'

'You don't mean that.'

'No, of course I don't, but it isn't as if I'd be leaving Mum all alone. I really want to go to America with him when he goes back,' she said. 'It's a wonderful place. They have everything there.'

'But you wouldn't be going for the place, surely,' said Liz. 'You'd be going to be with Joe.'

'Of course I would,' she said with feeling. 'But it's all part of the same thing really. I adore Joe and I also love all things American. I've had a passion for it since I first saw it at the pictures.'

'I don't suppose it's all like we see on the films,' said Liz, though the United States had a kind of magic for her too. 'There'll be parts that aren't so good I expect, like all places.'

'It's nice where Joe lives,' she said. 'He's told me all about it. Anyway, nothing would put me off.'

'You'll have to wait for the war to finish,' said Liz. 'And there is also the little matter of getting a proposal.'

Marg laughed. 'I can't do anything about the war, but I'm working on the proposal.'

'How?'

'By being my most irresistible self,' she grinned. 'So that he won't want to go back without me.'

Liz laughed. 'Honestly, that is so devious,' she said.

'No, it isn't,' she denied. 'You and I both know that if people like us want something, we have to go all out to get it because no one is ever going to hand us anything on a plate. Anyway, I love him and I will be good to him.'

'Yeah, I know you will,' said Liz. 'But America is such a long way away and everything is so uncertain at the moment because of the war.'

'Mm, I know. But there's nothing uncertain about my feelings for Joe.'

'There's talk about some sort of an allied invasion in the offing, the second front they're calling it,' Liz mentioned. 'The boys will probably have to take part in that. Who knows what might happen to them?'

'Ooh, cheer me up, why don't you?' she said, laughing.

'Sorry, I'm just trying to be realistic.'

'That's okay. Anyway, what about you?' began Marg. 'In the event that we all live through the second front and the war finally ends. If Vic were to ask you to marry him and go back to the States with him, would you go?'

'I haven't known him long.'

'Based on how you feel now, at this stage in your relationship, would you?'

Liz thought about it. Being brutally honest, she didn't think she would be missed by the family. Mum and Dad didn't have much time for her and Dora would be glad to see the back of her so that she didn't have to share any of the limelight. Liz had never been truly in love before – there had been the occasional crush but nothing like what she felt for Vic.

'Yes, Marg,' she said. 'I do believe I would.'

Marg smiled. 'There you are,' she said. 'You're just as smitten as I am.'

'I sure am, as the boys would say,' she agreed, smiling.

They were interrupted by their department head on her way out of the canteen. 'Oh. So you're only just going in for your meal,' observed Miss Banks in a critical manner.

'Well, yes,' replied Liz.

'You'll have to get a move on or you'll be late getting back to the office.'

'Yes, Miss,' they chorused and as soon as she was out of earshot they went into fits of laughter. They were seventeen and thought the world belonged to them.

Violet was in the queue at the greengrocer's, hoping that the cabbages didn't run out before her turn came.

'There's quite a few in front of us,' said the woman behind her who happened to be a neighbour. 'Not sure if we'll be lucky.'

Violet nodded. 'They've got potatoes and swede and I need those, but a cabbage would be nice.'

'Not half,' said the neighbour. 'Trouble is all those in front of us are probably after one too.'

'Oh well, fingers crossed.'

'Still, I expect you get some nice little extras in your house now, don't you?' said the neighbour.

Violet stared at her blankly. 'No. Why would we? What do you mean?' she asked.

'Well ... now that your Liz has become a Spam Basher,' she replied.

'What on earth is that?'

'Ask your daughter.'

'I most certainly will.'

'I've heard the Yanks have all sorts of nice things and they're very generous with them.'

Vic did give George cigarettes and quite often brought chocolate for the family and they were very grateful, but she didn't care for the other woman's tone. 'Vic is a kind-hearted boy, as it happens, and very good to Liz...'

'Nothing comes from nothing, though, does it,' she went on regardless. 'I expect the girls have to return the favour ... if you know what I mean.'

Violet's eyes popped. 'No, I don't as it happens,' she said furiously.

'Oh, don't give me that,' said the neighbour

cynically. 'Everyone knows what goes on with the girls and the Americans. Randy young sods most of 'em. I must say I was surprised to see your Liz had got mixed up with them, though. I saw her walking down the street with one the other day, arm in arm and as bold as brass.'

'What's wrong with that?'

'Well, she doesn't seem the type.'

'She's a respectable girl. Both my daughters have been brought up properly. What of it if Liz has an American boyfriend? He's very nice as it happens.'

'I'm sure he is,' said the woman. 'I'm only saying what everyone else says about girls who hang around with Americans.'

'She doesn't hang around with them as such,' said Violet. 'She has a boyfriend who happens to be an American and there's nothing wrong with that.'

'I bet you've got plenty of chocolate in the cupboard though, haven't you?'

'No, we haven't and it would be none of your business if we did have.'

'All right for some, though.'

'I am not going to say another word on the subject and I'll thank you to do the same,' said Violet, turning her back on the woman and moving forward with the queue. She was trembling because she wasn't normally outspoken. In fact, she was usually rather timid after so many years of living with a bullying husband.

Unfortunately, Violet's confidence drained away and by the time she got home she was trembling

46

and agonising over being the talk of the neighbourhood. When Liz got home from work she took her into the kitchen and shut the door.

'Everybody is talking about you,' she said.

'Really?'

'Yes, really,' she confirmed. 'They are calling you a Spam Basher, whatever that means.'

'It means a girl who goes out with Americans only for what she can get because the boys have nice things and are generous with them. Obviously, I am not one of those women, but people who know nothing about my private life draw their own conclusions when they see Marg and me with Vic and Joe. Forget about it. It isn't worth another thought, Mum.'

'You can't just brush it aside like that,' said Violet, genuinely distressed. 'It will affect the whole family. We are getting a bad name and we've never had anything like that. We've always been thoroughly respectable.'

'And we still are,' said Liz. 'You've got it out of all proportion, Mum.'

'Maybe I have, but I can't let it carry on, Liz, so you'll have to get rid of him.'

'Oh, Mum, how can you suggest such a horrible thing?' she said, shocked.

'He's a nice boy and all that but I can't cope with people gossiping about us.'

Liz took a deep breath. 'I won't give him up, Mum,' she told her firmly.

'You'll have to because I can't be doing with our family reputation being put into question.'

'So, because of a few mean-minded people and some good-time girls who hang around with the

47

Americans just for what they can get out of them and give the rest of us a bad name, you want me to ditch my boyfriend?'

Put like that it did seem extreme, even Violet could see that. 'Perhaps you could meet him in town instead of him coming to the house, so that the neighbours are none the wiser,' she suggested hopefully.

Liz stared at her in disbelief. 'Absolutely not,' she said. 'I will not keep him hidden away and neither will I give him up. I'm proud to be seen on his arm.'

Violet chewed her thumbnail anxiously. 'But what about our family reputation?' she said.

'It will just have to take its chances,' Liz replied. 'Does it really matter so much to you what people say about us?'

'Yes, I'm afraid it does. In fact, it makes me feel quite ill,' she admitted. 'Silly, I know, but there it is. I've never been good with any suggestion of scandal.'

Having an American boyfriend was hardly scandalous, thought Liz, but her mother did seem genuinely distressed and Liz could see that she was trembling. Part of her hated her mother's slavish dedication to public opinion, but she'd never been blessed with courage. Liz had grown up watching her being brow beaten on a daily basis by her husband and elder daughter. Liz had longed for her to stand up for herself, but she supposed people couldn't help the way they were.

'Mum,' she began in a gentler tone. 'What people say doesn't matter when it's just malicious gossip. Vic and his pals are here to help us. We need them and most people realise that and are glad that they are here.'

'And so am I. It isn't Vic or any other member of the American services that I'm worried about,' she said. 'It's the reputation their girlfriends have. I just can't cope with any sort of bad talk about my family.'

'Well, you'll have to toughen up because I'm not going to give him up or meet him in town. I wouldn't insult him that way. Even if I wanted to do as you ask, I wouldn't, because it would be wrong to pander to silly people who have nothing better to do than gossip about their neighbours.'

'Oh,' said Violet dully.

'Can't you just ignore it, Mum?' she said. 'Sticks and stones and all that.'

'I suppose I shall have to,' she sighed. 'But don't mention any of this to your father.'

Liz thought he would probably get to hear about it anyway at the pub or the allotment, but maybe he wouldn't be so affected by it as his wife.

'I won't say a word,' she promised, but she wasn't happy about it. She didn't want anything about her relationship with Vic to be secret or tainted.

As the soft summer evenings sharpened and became shorter, Liz's relationship with Vic flourished under cover of the blackout. The US military were more generous with passes than their British counterparts so she saw him most weekends. On Saturday night they went dancing with Marg and Joe followed by Sunday morning at the ice rink. Vic usually had tea at the Becks' and he and Liz went out for a walk to have some time alone before the boys went back to camp. Being together on their own was precious as they became increasingly close.

'You two are getting proper soppy lately,' said Marg one Sunday at the ice rink. 'You're all over each other. I sometimes think you don't even notice that we are here.'

'We have to make the most of the time together,' said Vic. 'We never know when we might be shipped off somewhere or moved to another camp.'

'Is that likely, then?' asked Liz.

'Always a possibility, I guess,' said Vic. 'And with this second front in the offing we just never know what's going to happen.'

'Cheer us up, why don't you?' laughed Liz.

'Yeah, you're a proper misery guts tonight,' added Marg.

He laughed. The English way of putting things always amused him. 'Sorry, honey. Just trying to be realistic.' He paused. 'Anyway, enough of that heavy stuff. Let's plan our next night out. How about the American Services club in the West End? There'll be plenty of jitterbugging there.'

They all agreed and carried on skating, but Vic's serious words lingered in Liz's mind. Up until now she'd managed to live for the moment, but he had become really important to her and she had begun to live for the time they spent together. She made a determined effort to put all dismal thoughts out of her mind and concentrated on her skating. Now that her balance was better she found it great fun – until she got overly confident and collided with the ice – on her bottom.

'The West End on a Saturday night,' said Violet disapprovingly when Vic came to call for Liz and told her parents where they were going. 'I'm not very happy about that.'

'I'll take good care of her, Mrs Beck,' said Vic who was always extremely polite to her parents.

'I know you will, but you get some bad types in the West End at night, especially around Piccadilly.' She gave him a knowing look. 'I'm sure you've been here long enough to know what I mean.'

He nodded. 'But we'll be inside the club,' he reminded her. 'And they always keep good order there because of their reputation. So your daughter will be safe with me.'

'Don't make such a silly fuss, Vi,' snapped George on his way to the living room from the kitchen. 'She'll be perfectly all right with Vic. It isn't as if she's going on her own.'

His sharp tone embarrassed Liz. She hated the rude way he spoke to her mother, never missing a chance to belittle her. If he'd been in a different sort of a mood, he would have been the one to disapprove.

'We'll see you later then, ma'am,' said Vic, ushering Liz towards the front door.

'Enjoy yourselves,' said Violet, having been bullied into submission by her husband.

'We will,' said Liz.

Listening to this conversation in the living room, Dora was irritated by her mother's concern for

Liz. Why was it always her sister who went to nice places? What right did she have to a gorgeous bloke? It was a Saturday night and Dora would be at home with her parents, the ultimate social disgrace for a nineteen-year-old woman. It wasn't that she didn't have chances; she went out on dates. She'd been out a couple of times with the GI she'd met at the dance at the base, but he'd not asked her for a third date. She hadn't been that keen anyway, but it had been someone to go out with to save being at home.

She knew she liked to be the centre of attention and men weren't keen on that. They preferred a date to be all about them, to be an object of adoration. She had never been out with anyone who had inspired that in her.

There had been one boy who had loved her unconditionally for the whole of her life since they were both about three years old. Arthur, the boy next door. As they had grown up, her total lack of interest in him had not deterred him. She believed he would have done anything for her. She had always been really horrid to him, but he still came back for more.

She sighed. Even he wasn't around now. He was away somewhere fighting for his country. She hadn't set eyes on him for years.

Her mother came into the room. 'I wonder what's on the wireless tonight,' she said, picking up the newspaper to check.

So, this was the highpoint of her social life, thought Dora. Listening to the wireless on a Saturday night with her parents. Even Dad would probably escape to the pub later on. Oh well, such is life, she thought miserably.

The West End of London was like a celebration, crammed with people – many of them service-men and lots of Americans. There was only a half moon but Liz could see well enough to be able to discern the smiling faces and feel the party atmosphere here. There was blackout, bomb damage and very little to eat, but there was no shortage of spirit.

'Gee, I love this city,' enthused Vic as they jostled through the crowds. 'There is always so much energy and lots going on.'

'But you are always saying how small every-thing is here,' Liz reminded him.

'It is compared to the United States. We're a much bigger country, it's a fact, not a criticism. But I wasn't talking about size. It's the buzz and the heart. London is so full of life.'

'I'm glad we have something that pleases you,' said Marg lightly.

'You've got lots that pleases us,' said Vic. 'Especially yourselves, even if you are a little too reserved.'

In reply he received a playful slap on the arm and they jostled through the crowds that spilled through the streets and the elegant squares at the heart of London.

The Americans certainly knew how to enjoy themselves, thought Liz. As they went through the swing doors into the club it was as though they had actually entered the USA. Everything here – apart from the visitors – was American, from the aroma of Camel cigarettes to the freshly made doughnuts, and chewing gum.

There were several rooms where the service men on leave in London could write letters and get their mending and laundry done. Vic and Joe led them into a large hall where there was a dance in progress. The dancers here made the jitterbuggers at an ordinary dance hall seem like beginners as they threw themselves around to 'Chattanooga Choo Choo'.

Liz was in her element; she twirled and twisted, leaped and let Vic throw her over his shoulder. In the interval they had coffee and doughnuts.

'Enjoying yourself?' asked Vic as she sipped her coffee.

'I sure am, as you would say,' she said with a mock drawl, laughing.

He enjoyed the joke and as he grinned in approval she noticed again how handsome he was with his dark looks and square jaw.

'Your accent is a little too reserved,' he said, teasing her. 'It needs more of a drawl. I shooor am.'

She gave him a playful shove and then became serious for a moment.

'You are so generous, Vic,' she said as she finished her doughnut. 'And I really do appreciate it.'

'Aw, it's nothing,' he said. 'We have the things that you don't. The least we can do is spread them around a bit.'

'Thank you anyway.'

He looked serious suddenly and their eyes locked. There was a moment when nothing else

54

seemed to exist; just them and a force drawing them together.

'You're welcome,' he said and the moment passed, but she knew it had happened. She would always know that.

'They're getting all soppy again,' said Marg, laughing.

'Yeah. Cut it out, you two,' added Joe. 'We're supposed to be out in a foursome.'

The music started up again and they finished their coffee and headed back to the dance floor.

Towards the end of the evening the band played a slow number 'I'll Never Smile Again' and most of the couples got close. Vic had his arms around Liz, but he pulled back and looked into her face.

'What's the matter?' she asked.

'Nothing.'

'Why the serious face, then?'

'I love you,' he said.

'Oh.' They were the sweetest words she'd ever heard and she'd longed to hear them. 'I love you too.'

'Oh no,' came a cry from Marg who was dancing nearby. 'They're at it again.'

Liz was far too busy to reply.

Weekend passes were less easy to get as winter set in, but Liz and Vic kept in touch by letter and also over the phone by pre-arrangement at the telephone box at the end of the street. It wasn't at all satisfactory because there were usually people waiting to use the phone which meant an abrupt ending. But at least they were able to hear each other's voices, however briefly.

'Joe doesn't seem to know why the passes aren't available so frequently,' Marg said to Liz over lunch one day in the factory canteen.

'Even if they did know they have to keep army matters to themselves, I should think,' said Liz. 'But I expect it has something to do with the invasion we are always hearing about. Something like that would take a lot of training.'

'When is it, I wonder,' said Marg.

'Nobody knows,' she replied. 'Obviously, something like that has to be kept secret.'

'You don't think the boys are just putting us off and have found another couple of girls?'

Liz was shocked by the suggestion. She was so deeply immersed in her feelings for Vic that such a thing hadn't even occurred to her. 'No, I don't think that. Absolutely not!' she said. 'I don't know how you could either.'

'It does happen,' said Marg. 'They are good-looking blokes with plenty of dosh. They can have anyone.'

'But they want us,' said Liz.

'How can you be so sure?'

'I can't about Joe but I am sure about Vic.'

'Not a good idea to be too sure of yourself.'

'It isn't in my nature to be pessimistic so such a thing hadn't even entered my mind,' she said. 'He's told me he loves me and I believe him. I speak to him on the phone quite regularly and he seems as keen as ever.'

'How do you know that he doesn't put the phone down from you and go out and meet someone else?'

'I don't know that,' she said, hating the tone of the conversation. 'And I don't even want to think about such things. Anyway, we're not engaged to them, are we? So, strictly speaking, they are free to do whatever they choose when they're not with us. I don't see why he would want to go out with someone else when he has me.'

'He's a man and that's the sort of thing they do.'

'How do you know?'

'Everyone knows,' she said. 'My dad's had affairs. Mum said men just can't help themselves.'

'I refuse to believe that all men are like that,' said Liz.

'Let's hope you're right,' said Marg. 'Maybe I'm just insecure because I want it so much. The whole thing: Joe, marriage, a new life in America.'

'Which do you want the most, Marg, Joe or a new life in America?'

'Joe, of course,' she said. 'What sort of woman do you think I am?'

'Sorry, it's just that you do seem very keen to marry him and go to the States.'

'Most girls want marriage and I'm no different,' she said. 'I admit I do want that, a lot. Don't you?'

'Of course, when the time is right.'

'Obviously, Joe is more important,' Marg continued. 'America is just the icing on the cake. There's nothing wrong with wanting to travel, Liz.'

'It's a one-way ticket, though,' said Liz. 'Too far to come back if you don't like it.'

'You'd make yourself like it, though, wouldn't you, if you went all that way,' she said. 'You'd learn to adapt.'

'Yeah, I suppose you'd have a damned good try,' said Liz. 'There wouldn't be any alternative.'

'Anyway, I don't even know if he's serious about me yet,' said Marg. 'So it's a bit too early to start making plans. I'm just enjoying his company for the moment. Or I was until the army stopped the weekend passes.'

'Yeah, I miss those too.'

'Uh oh, here comes trouble,' said Marg, looking past her friend.

'Don't lose track of time, girls,' said their department head as she swept past. 'Your lunch break is nearly over.'

'We won't be late, Miss Banks,' said Marg.

'We've got our eyes on the clock,' added Liz.

'I'll see you back in the office very soon then,' Miss Banks said and hurried on her way.

'What a bloomin' nag that woman is,' said Marg as soon as she was out of earshot.

The weekend passes resumed in November so fun was back on the agenda for Liz and Marg. The boys didn't manage to get to London every weekend, but often enough to keep everyone happy. They danced on Saturdays and skated on Sundays, laughed a lot and canoodled whenever they could.

The boys spent Christmas Day at the base, but on Boxing Day they managed to get a lift in a Jeep into London and the four of them went to the West End to see *For Whom the Bell Tolls* at the cinema.

New Year's Eve was celebrated at the Hammersmith Palais and was a terrific night for all four of them. Liz was in love, happy and full of hope for the future. Then the nightly bombing returned to London...

Chapter Three

'You seem a bit quiet tonight,' Joe mentioned to Vic as the two of them stood up in the crowded train on their way to London one Saturday evening in January. 'You okay?'

'Sure,' he said absently.

'The crowds are enough to give anyone the blues,' said Joe, referring to the huge number of people crammed together in the railway carriage. Movement was barely possible and the air was suffocating with the stench of cigarette smoke and sweaty clothes.

'They don't bother me,' said Vic. 'I'm used to life in England now with the crowds and the queues.'

'It will be nice to be back home again, though, won't it?' mentioned Joe.

'I'm happy enough here for now,' said Vic.

'Yeah, me too,' said Joe. 'It's just as well, I guess, as it'll be a while before we go back to America. There's more fighting to do before this war is done. But there's no place like home when we do eventually get there.'

Vic nodded absently, his mind on other things.

They fell silent until Vic said, 'Would you mind

if we cut the foursome for tonight, Joe? I'd like Liz and me to be on our own for the evening.'

'Okay,' he said with a knowing grin. 'It can cramp your style with four of us.'

'Actually,' Vic began, looking serious, 'I am going to propose to her.'

'Aw, gee, that's great,' said Joe in surprise. 'Congratulations, pal!'

'She hasn't accepted yet.'

'She will though.' Joe was confident. 'Anyone can see she's crazy about you.'

'It's mutual.'

'How will that work later on though?' wondered Joe. 'When we go home after the war.'

'I hope she'll come with me,' he said. 'It's a big thing to ask, though, so I'm nervous about proposing. She might turn me down because of it.'

'Some girls can't wait to nab a Yank and get to the States because they've heard so much about it and think it's some sort of paradise,' said Joe. 'But Liz is different. She seems quite level headed.'

'It depends how strong her feelings for me are,' said Vic. 'I'm a little scared. I know she loves me, but it's a huge decision for her to make and she'll have to decide right away. There's no point in getting engaged if she isn't prepared to come to America as my wife after the war.'

'Wow, that's some piece of news,' said Joe, grinning. 'Good luck, buddy.'

'Thanks, pal,' said Vic as the train rumbled into the station.

Liz was in her bedroom getting ready to go out for the evening with Vic when Dora appeared.

'Can I borrow your rouge?' she asked. 'I've run out.'

'I don't have any,' said Liz.

'Oh, now what am I gonna do?'

'Give your cheeks a rub or pinch them; either will brighten them up.'

'It isn't the same as something out of a pot,' said Dora. 'Not so glamorous.'

'It'll have to do for now, though,' said Liz. 'Where are you going, anyway, that you are making such an effort to look good?'

'The Palais with some girls from work,' she said. 'I'm hoping to meet someone nice.'

'There'll be plenty to choose from there, especially on a Saturday night.'

'The blokes do the choosing though, don't they, and there'll be lots of competition. Some of the best-looking girls in London go there.'

'There'll be no shortage of glamour, that's for sure, even though clothes and make-up are so short. Still, you're a match for all the others.'

'Where are *you* going?' asked Dora without acknowledging the compliment.

'I'm not sure. We'll decide when the boys get here, I expect,' she said. 'It'll probably be dancing somewhere.'

'Might see you there then.'

Not if Liz had anything to do with it. She didn't need one of Dora's dramas on a precious night out with Vic.

'Maybe. But we've heard it's good at the Lyceum on the Strand so maybe we'll go there.'

'When is he calling for you?'

'He should be here quite soon,' she replied,

excited at the prospect.

Vic and Joe were in the queue waiting for a bus to Hammersmith when the air raid siren sounded and the crowd dispersed, people heading for the shelter or the Tube station.

The two men were just deciding whether to take their chances or head for the shelter when there was an incident close by. A young woman with a small boy was having a problem with the toddler, who was screaming and refusing to move, obviously upset by the noise and the sudden rush of movement. 'He isn't used to being out during an air raid and he wouldn't be normally,' she explained, sounding worried. 'He isn't well so I've just taken him to the doctor's. I have to get him to the shelter and he won't move.'

'I'll take him,' said Vic.

'He won't let you pick him up,' she said.

'You wanna bet?' said Vic, sweeping the screaming child into his arms and heading off with the woman and Joe following. 'Come on, kiddo, let's head for the Tube station.'

'You must have the magic touch,' said the woman coming up behind. 'He's stopped crying.'

'The shock probably did the trick,' said Joe and even as the three of them reached the station entrance, the roar of approaching German bomber planes could be heard.

Inside the crowded Underground Station, they were on the way to the platform when the toddler started to cry again and call out for something.

'It's Bertie, his toy rabbit,' the young mother explained. 'He must have dropped it on the way.

Oh dear, I'll never get him to sleep without it. What a day this is.'

'I'll go back and see if I can find it,' said Vic.

'No. I can't let you do that. Absolutely not!' said the woman quickly. 'It's dangerous up there. We'll manage, don't worry about it. It's just a soft toy.'

Vic turned to Joe. 'You wait here with them and I'll go and look for the rabbit. I'll be back in a couple o' minutes,' he said as the woman continued to protest.

'Don't worry, I'll just have a quick look,' he said. 'I promise not to hang about so I'll be fine.'

'He had it in the bus queue,' said the woman, 'so it must be somewhere between there and here, unless someone's nicked it and I doubt that because it's a scruffy old thing. It would only be of value to my boy.'

'I'll see what I can do,' he said. 'I'll be back in no time. Stay with these two, Joe.'

'Okay, we'll wait here,' said Joe, while the young mother tried to pacify her little one.

The streets were emptying as people took shelter, which made it easier for Vic to look for the rabbit. Eyes to the ground he retraced their steps and found the toy close to the bus stop which was now deserted.

The woman was right; it really was a scruffy old thing, but clearly important to the child. Vic felt an unexpected rush of pleasure at having found the article and was looking forward to giving it to the boy.

Rain was lashing across the street as he hurried

back to the station. As if this country didn't have enough problems, it had foul weather too. He quickened his step as the roar of a bomber grew louder and seemed to be overhead.

He had almost reached the station entrance when the explosion knocked him off his feet, smashing his head on the edge of the kerb as he came down, still clutching the scruffy old rabbit.

It was nearly half past eight and there was still no sign of Vic at the Beck house. Dora had gone out saying that it would take more than an air raid to keep her indoors when she had the chance to go dancing. Mum and Dad were still in the Anderson shelter and Liz was at the front window staring out into the dark in the hope of seeing Vic. He must have been delayed by the air raid. They did cause havoc on public transport.

The 'all clear' sounded but Liz barely noticed. Where was that man of hers? He was never late so something must have happened to him.

At last someone was approaching the house; she could just make out the uniform and felt weak with relief. She rushed down the path, her smile fading when she saw that it was Joe with Marg following behind him.

'Where's Vic?' she asked, waving them inside.

The silence thundered around them.

'Where is he?' she asked. 'Come on. Don't mess about. You're scaring me.'

'I think you'd better come indoors and sit down, Liz,' suggested Joe.

'It's probably no comfort to you right now, but

he died helping someone,' said Joe, having told her that Vic had been killed by the force of the blow to his head when it had hit the edge of the kerb. 'He would be alive now if he hadn't gone out of the station to find the kid's toy.'

Liz was silent and as still as stone.

'Do they know if he had any pain?' she asked eventually.

'They think not,' he said. 'He would have died instantly with the force of the blow.'

'That's something to be thankful for,' she said, though she wasn't feeling grateful about anything just now.

'I don't know any more details,' said Joe. 'When he didn't come back into the station I went looking for him and the medics were with him, but there was nothing they could do.'

Liz's stomach was tight and the pain was hardly bearable, but she couldn't shed a tear. Vaguely she was aware that her parents had come up from the shelter and been told what had happened. Mum was giving her a cup of tea. She took it and managed a sip, the cup rattling on the saucer.

'Anyway,' Joe was saying. 'I called the base from the phone box and they'll come to London to collect him and let his family know. All of that stuff.'

The room resonated with words of sorrow and sympathy. 'Are you all right, Joe?' asked Liz.

'No, not really. He was my best buddy and I shall miss him like hell,' he drawled, sounding shaky. 'We're trained for this sort of thing, but it doesn't seem to be helping right now.' He gave a helpless shrug. 'I wasn't prepared. I never imagined losing my pal on the street ... on the battle-field maybe, but not on an ordinary street when we were off duty.'

'Of course you didn't, son,' said Violet while Marg held his hand supportively.

'Bloody bombers,' said George.

'You guys have to live with them all the time,' said Joe. 'It can't be easy.'

'It isn't,' Violet confirmed. 'And something like this really brings it home to us.'

Joe seemed thoughtful for a few moments, then he turned to Liz and said, 'There is one thing I think he really would want you to know.'

She looked up, trying rather unsuccessfully to take an interest. 'Yeah. What's that?'

'Vic was going to ask you to marry him to-night,' he told her. 'He was going to propose.'

Her bones were suddenly warmed and tears filled her eyes. 'Really?' she said.

'Yeah, he told me about it on the train on the way to London. He wanted you to go back to the States with him after the war, as his wife.'

Despite everything, Liz felt a thrill followed im-mediately by even deeper sadness.

'Aah,' said Marg tearfully. 'That is so sad.'

'I don't know if it's any help for you to know, but you would have been on his mind when he died,' said Joe.

'It's all such a bloody waste,' said Liz, tearful but angry too. 'A young man with his whole life ahead of him. We would have been happy to-gether and it's all ruined.'

'Yes, it's tragic,' said Violet. 'But at least we get to keep you here.'

Liz supposed people said all sort of things they didn't mean at times like this. She had never felt particularly valued by either of her parents and hadn't thought they would care if she went away. Still, they were only trying to be nice at this sad time and she was grateful for that.

'I think it's time I put the kettle on again,' said Violet.

Liz was still feeling knotted up and shaky and didn't know how to ease her grief, but when Marg and Joe said they thought they should leave she said she would walk to the end of the road with them, hoping that some fresh air might help. It was raining heavily, but she barely noticed.

'Sorry to be a gooseberry,' she said. 'I just had to get out of the house.'

'I'll tell you when you're being a gooseberry and that time definitely isn't now,' said Marg, linking arms with her in a friendly manner.

That small gesture of friendship loosened the tension and Liz started to cry.

'You two go,' she said as Marg went to comfort her. 'I need to be on my on.'

'But Liz...' began Marg. 'We can't leave you like this.'

'Yes, you can if it's what I want,' she said through her tears. 'There isn't a raid on and I need to be by myself for a while. I'll see you soon.'

Leaving them somewhat bewildered she hurried away into the night.

She had no idea where she was going. All she knew was that she needed to be out of the house and on her own. It didn't help, of course. Indoors or out, alone or with company, Vic was still dead and she was devastated.

The rain was steady and there was no moon, but she was so accustomed to the blackout she could find her way even though she was walking blindly. There were few people about in this awful weather. Everyone was inside. She walked to the river, stood a while on the bridge looking blindly at the water and was then driven home by the rain blowing into her face and the damp seeping into her bones. She didn't feel any better for the fresh air and didn't think the pain would ever go away.

Liz was in bed with the light off when Dora came into her room. Not a keen observer of subtlety, she switched on the light and said, 'Are you awake, Liz?'

'Yeah.'

'Mum's told me about Vic. How terrible.'

Turning over, Liz said, 'Very.'

'I'm ever so sorry,' she said.

'Thanks.'

'Killed in the street, just like that,' Dora went on, sitting on the edge of the bed as though settled for a long chat. 'Blimey, what a turn up for the books.'

'Mm.'

'Do you know any details?' asked Dora, eager to hear the awful facts.

'No. Only what happened.'

'I suppose that's all you need to know for now.'

'Could you go to bed please, Dora. We'll talk about it tomorrow,' said Liz.

'Yeah, o' course,' said Dora, unhooking her stockings and rolling them down. 'Mum said he went to find a toy some kid had lost and that's why he got caught by a bomb.'

'Apparently, yes.'

'I bet you're cursing that kid, aren't you?'

'I'm trying not to,' said Liz. 'Vic did what he thought was right and I'll always think well of him because of it.'

'I don't think I'd feel so kind about it.'

'You and I are very different,' said Liz. 'Can you turn the light off on your way out, please.'

'Yeah, sure,' she said breezily. 'So, you'll have to find someone else now won't you?'

'Oh, for goodness' sake, Dora. Of course, I won't,' she said. 'Have a little respect for Vic, please.'

'Well, there's no point in looking for someone up the Palais,' she said as though her sister hadn't spoken. 'There's plenty of blokes but even more competition.'

'Will you please stop talking and go to bed,' said Liz, desperate for darkness and quiet.

'Just trying to cheer you up.'

'I'm going to sleep,' said Liz, turning on to her side away from her sister.

'G'night then.'

'Goodnight,' said Liz. She knew she wouldn't sleep, but she couldn't stand any more of her sister's empty chatter.

As well as the pain of losing Vic, which ached in the pit of her stomach without respite, Liz was imbued with a feeling of not having meant anything now that he wasn't around. Because she wasn't married to him or even engaged, she had no status and wasn't invited to the funeral that the army arranged, so she couldn't say a proper goodbye. She couldn't even send her condolences to his family because she had no address for them.

'Maybe Joe can get Vic's mother's address from the army if you want to write to her,' suggested Marg when they were discussing it in the dinner hour in the works canteen. 'I doubt if he'll have it himself because they didn't know each other before the army.'

'The army won't give that sort of information to anyone.'

'You're not just anyone, are you?' Marg reminded her. 'You were his girlfriend. He was going to propose to you.'

'As far as anything official is concerned I'm no one. Just a girl he went out with.'

'I suppose so, but it seems a shame.'

'But it's a fact,' said Liz. 'It feels odd, almost as though Vic and I never happened.'

'You've got me to remind you that it did,' she said.

'I have my heart to do that, Marg,' she said. 'But thanks a lot anyway.'

A stern voice interrupted their conversation. 'It's time you two weren't here,' said Miss Banks on her way out. 'Your lunch break has finished.'

Liz was about to assure Miss Banks that they were on their way when Marg leapt up and confronted the older woman. 'Have you no heart?' she demanded. 'Liz's boyfriend was killed the other day and I'm trying to give her some comfort.'

'Oh dear, I'm so sorry, I didn't know,' she said, looking at Liz remorsefully.

Ignoring her, Marg stabbed her finger at the clock on the wall. 'There's still a few minutes to go until we are due back so I'd be grateful if you would leave us alone until then.'

Miss Banks looked at Liz and seemed about to say something, but then went on her way.

Touched by her friend's loyalty, Liz said, 'Thanks for standing up for me.'

'That's all right. That's what friends are for,' she said. 'The old bag needed telling. That was harassment. There's life beyond this factory and her flamin' rules and regulations. Just because she isn't a part of the world outside, that doesn't mean it doesn't exist for the rest of us.'

'We don't know anything about her outside of this office,' Liz pointed out. 'She might do all sorts of interesting things. Art, classical music, that kind of thing. She might even have had a busy love life in her youth for all we know.'

'That old crow, not a chance,' said Marg and the two of them headed back to the office.

'Do you fancy going out somewhere, Liz?' asked Dora one evening after dinner a week or so later, when the women of the family were relaxing. George was working late.

'No. Not really,' Liz replied.

'You're doing yourself no good sitting about indoors every night,' admonished Dora, who saw her sister's loss as an opportunity for a companion for her to go out with in the hope of meeting a man.

'Maybe not, but it's what I want to do,' said Liz.

'It isn't good for you.'

'I am not going out man hunting with you so you can forget it,' said Liz.

'Please yourself,' she said huffily.

'Strictly speaking your sister is in mourning, Dora,' their mother remarked.

'How can she be when she wasn't even related to him,' said Dora rudely.

'She can because she was very fond of him,' said Violet.

'Mourning is for relatives only, isn't it?' stated Dora.

'It's a state of mind and it isn't quite as cut and dried as you seem to think,' said Violet in a tone of defiance. Dora had an argumentative streak in her when she was in the mood. It was usually easier to agree with her rather than have another one of her exhausting scenes. But not this time.

'I'm not interested in the details,' said Dora. 'So let's drop the subject for goodness' sake.'

'Don't be so rude to Mum,' said Liz.

'Oh, I see. Trying to get in her good books, are you?' Dora accused.

'You're being really childish, Dora,' said Liz. 'And I'm not in the mood for it.'

'This house is like a ruddy morgue.'

'Why don't you go out then, dear?' suggested Violet.

'Because I've got no one to go with as my sister has turned into an old lady and wants to stay at home.'

The sound of the air raid siren cut into the conversation. 'There you are,' said Liz with a wry grin. 'You can go for a walk down the garden to the shelter. Problem solved.'

Dora wasn't amused, but Violet exchanged a smile with her younger daughter.

'Do you fancy going skating tonight, Liz?' asked Marg a few weeks later as the two of them walked to work. 'It'll be a bit of fun and it might do you good.'

'Not another one trying to get me out,' said Liz. 'My sister keeps trying to persuade me. But in her case, it's in her own interests rather than mine.'

'She's got nobody to go out with, I suppose?'

'Exactly,' replied Liz. 'But Vic's death seems to have sapped all my energy and I don't want to go anywhere when I get home from work.'

'You sound about sixty,' she said.

'And you sound like my sister.'

God forbid, thought Marg, but she said, 'I just thought it might cheer you up. It's where we first met the boys and we had a lot of fun there with them. You might enjoy the memories and if not we'll leave.'

'Okay, as the boys would say,' agreed Liz.

Vic was everywhere at the ice rink. He was the steady hand guiding her around on the ice and the voice telling her to carry on when she wanted to cry her heart out and go home and hide away under the bedcovers. He was the sweet taste of the coffee and the sound of laughter as people socialised. She was very glad she had come, but

73

knew she never wanted to do so again.

When the air raid siren sounded, they headed off the ice, handed their boots in and got ready to go to the shelter. On their way to the exit they saw the most extraordinary sight. A bomb came through the ceiling and landed on the ice. People stopped in their tracks for a moment and watched as it slid along the ice and went into the machine room. Expecting an explosion, there was a sudden rush for the exit and panic everywhere. But all was silent; nothing happened.

The next day they heard that the bomb didn't go off and was made safe by experts. In Liz's rational mind she knew there was a reasonable explanation for the bizarre happening. In a flight of fancy, she wondered if Vic had been looking out for them.

The recent spate of air raids which was referred to as 'The Little Blitz' continued and as people grew increasingly keen for an end to this dreadful war, the eagerness for the second front to begin grew. It was generally believed that this would be the final act that would end the war.

'It's another invasion, is it?' Marg said to Liz one day as they walked home from work.

'Apparently,' said Liz. 'A big one.'

'I suppose Joe will have to go then.'

'I should think so.'

'That's a bit scary.'

'You don't have to go into battle to get killed. We know that only too well,' Liz reminded her.

Marg halted in her step and squeezed her friend's arm. 'I know how you must be feeling,' she said kindly. 'You're coping ever so well. Or is it all an act?'

'Mostly an act,' she said. 'You can't go around with a long face when so many people are getting killed every night in the air raids. But I still have this awful pain, eating away at me. I miss him so much, Marg.'

'Ah,' said Marg, slipping a comforting arm around her friend's shoulders.

Marg was ecstatic when she called to see Liz at home one Sunday night a few weeks later.

'Oh Liz,' she began. 'I hate to have such good news when you're suffering, but I just had to come and tell you. And I know you'll be happy for me.'

'What's happened? Has Joe proposed?'

'Yeah, that's exactly right,' she said, beaming. 'How did you know?'

'Because that was the one thing I knew would make you so happy.'

'He's just gone back to camp and I couldn't wait for you to know.'

Liz hugged her. 'I'm really pleased for you, kid,' she said and meant it. 'I know how much you wanted it.'

'It's like a dream come true,' said Marg, waving her left hand at her friend to show her the ring, which was highly praised.

'So you will get to be a GI bride.'

'Yeah, I know, isn't it great?'

'It really is,' said Liz.

'Apparently, Joe was deeply affected by what happened to Vic. It really got to him and made

75

him realise just how short life can be in wartime,' said Marg.

Liz swallowed a lump in her throat and nodded.

'He wants us to tie the knot as soon as possible, too, before this invasion that everybody is talking about. He'll probably be involved in that.'

'I suppose he might be.'

'We're getting a special licence,' she went on excitedly. 'It will only be a registry office do and not a posh kind of a party because it's such short notice. I don't care about any of that, Liz. I'm going to be Joe's wife; that's all that matters to me.'

'That's how it should be.'

'Of course, he has to get permission from the army and that might take a month or so but as soon as that comes through, we'll get everything organised,' she said. 'As I said, it won't be a big do but you have to be there.'

'I wouldn't miss it for the world,' said Liz.

'Oh Liz,' said Marg, hugging her friend close. 'I am so very happy.'

'I know you are,' said Liz emotionally.

Liz stood in the wedding group outside the registry office after the ceremony, delighted for the happy couple and glad that the weather had smiled on them and pale spring sunshine shone on the small gathering. Marg looked lovely despite being dressed in a blue suit that had seen several seasons, but been refreshed with a spray of flowers; Joe upright and handsome in uniform.

Liz couldn't help but think that this could have been her and Vic, but she tried not to dwell on it.

Life happened and couldn't be altered so had to be accepted, no matter how painful. And by God it hurt!

Everything would be a lot different when Marg went to America. Liz felt a sharp pang at the thought because she couldn't imagine life without her friend. But it was what Marg wanted, and anyway, it wouldn't be for a while so Liz had time to prepare herself.

Chapter Four

George Beck's voice was hoarse and trembling with fury as he addressed his younger daughter across the dinner table, following some news she had just imparted.

'Get out of this house before I throw you out.'

'George,' intervened his shocked wife, 'you can't do that to her.'

'I think you'll find that I can,' he bellowed. 'It's my name on the rent book so I get to choose who lives here and Liz is no longer welcome.'

'But I've nowhere to go, Dad,' said Liz, pale with shock. She'd expected a trouncing, not eviction.

'You should have thought of that before you discarded your morals,' he roared. 'You're a bloody disgrace and I'm ashamed of you.'

'You're being very heartless, George dear,' said Violet nervously.

'What else do you expect?' he shouted. 'She's

turned her back on the values she was raised with and I'm not having her and her bastard child living in this house.'

'If Vic was alive I'm sure he would have married her,' suggested Violet hopefully. 'We all know that he intended to propose.'

'But he isn't here, is he? Anyway, that doesn't make her behaviour acceptable. She's gone against everything we brought her up to believe in so I want her out.' He stood up, his braces stretched over his corpulent middle, and addressed his next remark directly to Liz. 'By the time I get home from work tomorrow night I want you gone from this house.'

Ashen faced, Liz stared at him in disbelief.

'What if she were to put the baby up for adoption?' suggested Violet, desperate for a solution that would keep her daughter in the safety of home at this worrying time. 'We could send her away when she starts to show and the baby would be taken soon after the birth. No one need know about it then.'

'I won't do that, Mum,' Liz said firmly. 'Not under any circumstances.'

'It wouldn't change anything anyway,' said George. 'She'll still have let us down.'

'But George...'

'It's all right, Mum, I'll go tomorrow,' said Liz, but she was very shaken.

George dipped his hand into his pocket, took out some pound notes and put them, rather forcibly, on the table. 'That will help you with your initial expenses. When that's gone you're on your own. And don't bother to come visiting because you won't be welcome in this house ever again.'

'That's cruel, George...' began his wife.

'She knows the rules, Violet,' he cut her short. 'We brought her up to know the difference between right and wrong and she's let us down good and proper. I'm not having a scandal destroy the good name of this family.'

Liz wasn't normally devoid of spirit, but this was such a blow and she was at a loss to know how she could find somewhere to live so quickly. She felt helpless and isolated from the family. Already plagued with nausea and exhaustion due to the pregnancy, this setback seemed insurmountable.

'I think you're being very heartless, Dad,' said Dora in an almost unprecedented show of sibling support. 'She *is* your daughter, for goodness' sake.'

'And as such she's let me down.'

'She's only human,' said Dora. 'These things happen.'

'She's done something that would bring disgrace on this family if people were to get to know about it. Let this be a lesson to you too, Dora,' he warned. 'Just in case you've any plans to break the rules.'

'Huh, fat chance of that,' she said. 'As I don't even have a boyfriend.'

'It's just as well if this is the result.' He stood up. 'I am going to the pub to calm my nerves as my evening has been ruined.'

'All right, dear,' said Violet.

When the door had slammed behind him Liz said to her mother, 'Surely you could have tried to get him to change his mind, Mum. This is your grandchild I'm carrying.'

'You know your father; when he's made his mind up about something, there's no shifting him,' she said. 'It's the way he's been brought up. His parents were very strict.'

'So … you'd see me on the streets rather than stand up to him,' said Liz.

'Don't put the blame on me,' snapped Violet. 'You're the one who's done wrong. Surely you must know how serious what you've done is.'

'As it's been drummed into me ever since I had my first period, of course I know it's the worst kind of sin and I'm not proud of myself. But I loved Vic with all my heart so I can't be sorry I'm having his child no matter how hard life gets. This baby will be a part of him and I will cherish it. I certainly won't ever turn my back on it as you are doing to me.'

'You brought it on yourself so don't put the blame on me,' she said, defensive because she was feeling guilty.

'Surely it's a mother's instinct to stand by her child.'

'It is, but I have no influence over your father,' she said. 'You know that very well.'

'Then you should have,' said Liz, her spirit returning. 'It's pathetic the way you let him walk all over you.'

'He's always been the dominant one in our marriage.'

'Why not stand up to him now and again,' Liz suggested. 'You might find you enjoy having a say in things.'

'I doubt it,' she said. That sort of thing just isn't in me. Anyway, I'm more concerned about what's going to happen to you.'

If she was that concerned she would try to persuade her husband to let their daughter stay, thought Liz, but she said, 'Don't worry, Mum, I won't hang around and make things awkward for you. I'll be gone tomorrow morning and I won't be back.'

'Where will you go?' asked Violet, pale with worry.

'I have absolutely no idea,' she said. 'But I'll survive somehow. I don't have any choice.'

'You'll let us know where you are.'

'No, Mum, I won't,' she said bitterly. 'When I leave here you won't hear from me.'

'Oh!' Violet was clearly shocked. 'Well, if that's the way you want it.'

'Seeing as I'm being forced out of my home when I most need it, yes, it is,' she said, gulping back the tears.

'I wish you weren't leaving,' said Dora later in Liz's bedroom as she was gathering some things together ready for her departure in the morning.

'You do surprise me. I thought you'd be glad to see the back of me,' said Liz. 'We've never really got along, have we?'

'No, I suppose not,' Dora agreed with a casual air. 'But there'll be no one young in the house when you leave. And you're better than no company. It'll be just me and those two old fogies. I'll have no one to talk to.'

'You'll have no one to annoy and argue with.'

'That's true,' she said with a wry grin.

In all honesty, Liz couldn't feel sad about the prospect of not being around her sister. Her father had never been close to Liz either. The one who was breaking Liz's heart was her mother because she hadn't stood up for her. Just a feeble protest when he'd first issued his orders, then she'd surrendered. She was completely in thrall to him at the expense of everyone else.

Still, she herself was the one who had done wrong so she was in no position to judge. As sins went, in the Beck household it was seen as second only to murder. Somehow, though, she had to survive this setback and make a life for her child, but God knows how! A pregnant woman without a husband really was considered to be the lowest of the low.

The following night Liz lay on the top bunk in a crowded dormitory in a hostel on the outskirts of Paddington. The noise in here was awful: snoring, snorting, coughing, farting. It smelled horrid too – of unwashed clothes, sweat and a lingering aroma of cabbage from the kitchen downstairs.

But she had a bed and was grateful for it. What a day it had been. First thing this morning she had asked a policeman on the beat if he knew of anywhere she could stay, a cheap boarding house or a hostel. He'd directed her to this place and they had managed to find a bed for her. Some hostels had closed for the duration of the war so she'd been lucky.

Arranging this had made her late for work, which hadn't pleased Miss Banks. 'I'm surprised you've bothered to come into work at all,' she'd blasted at her.

'Sorry, Miss Banks, but I had an important personal matter to attend to,' she'd said.

'Really.' The older woman ran a questioning eye over her. 'Are you all right, Miss Beck? You don't look your usual smart self.'

'Sorry, Miss, I was in a hurry this morning,' she said. 'I'll tidy myself up in my dinner hour.'

'Are you not feeling well?' she asked. 'You are looking a bit peaky.'

Actually, Liz felt dreadful. The nausea was constant and she was tired all the time, but she daren't let the older woman get so much as a hint of this. Liz was on her own now without any support and had to earn a living so needed to seem fit for work. She could just imagine Miss Banks' reaction to the pregnancy. As a very prim lady of a certain age she would be even more disgusted than Liz's parents and that took some beating.

'I'm fine thank you, Miss Banks,' she said politely. 'Probably just need a bit of lipstick.'

'Be sure you eat something at lunchtime, then come back early to make up the time you lost by being so late.'

'Yes of course,' she replied.

'You're staying in a hostel?' Marg said in their dinner break. She had known about her friend's condition since she had first been late with her period. 'So, what happened at home?'

'I told them I'm pregnant and Dad told me to get out,' she said.

'Oh, that's terrible.'

'I didn't expect him to be quite so harsh, I must admit.'

'I'd ask my mum if you can stay with us, but she'd want to know why you'd left home and you'd have to hide the pregnancy. She'd have a fit if she knew.'

'You're already overcrowded in your house, anyway,' said Liz. 'I'll be all right. I can give a hand with the cleaning and other jobs at the hostel to help pay for my bed and meanwhile I'll look for some cheap lodgings. I feel as though this is a challenge I have to get through on my own. I got myself into this mess so it's up to me to deal with it.'

'I wish I could do something to help you.'

'You can. Just be my friend,' she said, tears falling.

Marg reached across the table and took her hand.

At least the bombing had stopped so that was one fewer problem for Liz to deal with. Since her life had changed so dramatically, she concentrated on the positives in order to keep going. Having always lived within a family it wasn't easy to be alone, but she was determined to make a life for herself and her baby, despite everything. She took it one day at a time and daren't look ahead too far. It was hard enough on her own to find accommodation, with a child it would be practically impossible. But she would face every hurdle as it presented itself. She was still in the early stages of the pregnancy.

Despite her determination to be positive, there

was a nasty little ache in the pit of her stomach that refused to go away. For all her faults, she missed her mother.

Still, the hostel wasn't too bad. The facilities were basic; there was a kitchen with a cooker and a sink and communal toilets and a washroom. She registered her ration book in the shops nearby and cooked the most basic of food. There was a community room where you could social-ise, but the residents changed almost nightly so there was little chance to make friends.

Most of the people here seemed sad; like her they were alone. A few young people passed through but the residents were mostly older and often inebriated. To help towards her rent, Liz worked on the reception in the evening and cleaned some of the public areas before she went to work.

She scoured the local paper for lodgings and also walked the streets looking for a sign in a window for accommodation, but everything so far had been too expensive. She was only a general clerk so her salary was modest. She thought of trying for a job in a factory where she could earn more, but having such a sickly pregnancy she knew she wouldn't be up to the demands of the work, which she'd heard were punishing.

Still, at least there was optimism in the air about the war as everyone waited for news of the expected invasion. The skies were rarely empty of allied planes, which people took as a good sign. There were far bigger problems than her own and she reminded herself of this on a regular basis.

One morning after George and Dora had left for work, Violet Beck sat at the kitchen table staring at a letter that had just arrived in the post. It was addressed to Liz and had come by air-mail from America. Must be from a relative of Vic's, she supposed. She would hand it in at Liz's place of work as she didn't know where she lived now. Of course, she could give it to Marg to pass on but she didn't feel comfortable about seeing her daughter's friend, who would almost certainly take Liz's side and see Violet as the enemy for not defending Liz against George. In all honesty, she couldn't really blame her.

It wasn't easy to face the fact that you didn't know where your own daughter was living, especially as she was pregnant and probably in need of some moral support. She saw it as an act of cruelty to force a pregnant daughter to leave home with nowhere to go, but George wasn't the sort of man you could argue with.

She should have tried harder. She ought to have stood up to him. It was wrong what they had done. Yes, Liz had gone against everything they had taught her to believe in, but to turn her out in her condition was cruel. Violet wanted to put things right but didn't know how because George wouldn't have Liz back even if Violet went down on her knees. As he was so keen on pointing out; he was the breadwinner and he made all the rules. So, there was nothing to be done except pass on the letter. She would hand it in at the reception desk at the factory.

Of course, she could wait outside the factory at finishing time and hand it to Liz personally but she couldn't face her; she was too ashamed. Dabbing a tear from her eye, she got up and went over to the sink to wash the breakfast dishes.

That night Liz sat on her bed and opened the letter. She'd left it until late because, the way her life was going at the moment, she was expecting trouble of some sort from every aspect of her life. Her hands were trembling slightly. Being riddled with guilt for her wretched situation, she expected everything to be a threat. She was very hurt that her mother had handed the letter in at the desk rather than wait until she finished work to give it to her personally. It twisted the knife even more.

So, it was with some trepidation she read the missive from abroad. Instead of trouble, it was a wonderful letter full of warmth and caring from Vic's mother Jane.

Vic gave me your address when he wrote to me to tell me that he had met a girl he loved and was hoping to marry and I was so happy for you both. Sadly, it wasn't to be...

She said she guessed that Liz was feeling devastated too and hoped they could stay in touch and perhaps be friends, albeit from a distance. She thought that Vic would like that.

Liz read the letter over and over again. She had felt as though she was nothing in Vic's life after he'd died. But she was wrong. She had been the woman he had wanted to marry enough to tell his mother.

These words from his parent refreshed and

strengthened her. She felt wanted again. Her first instinct was to write back as soon as she could. But did she tell her about the baby? Might Jane have the same reaction as her own parents? She supposed that a similar attitude applied in America. Maybe she should wait until after the baby – Jane's grandchild – was born. But that wouldn't be right either.

She decided to write back as soon as she could get hold of some writing paper. She would tell her about her pregnancy and face the consequences whatever they were.

Meanwhile she had to deal with a bedbug on her pillow. There were plenty of those around at the hostel.

Around mid-morning the next day, Liz was busy at her desk when Miss Banks' secretary appeared and said, 'She wants to see you in her office.'

'Oh no, what have I done now?' she said to Marg who was at the next desk. 'I wasn't late this morning so it can't be that. I've obviously upset her majesty somehow, though. That woman really has it in for me.'

'It might not be anything bad,' said Marg.

'This is Miss Banks; how can it not be bad?' said Liz with a wry grin.

'That's true,' agreed Marg. 'So, go and get it over with.'

Liz was asked to take a seat at the desk opposite Miss Banks and she waited for her fate.

'I get the impression that all is not well with you, Miss Beck,' she said.

'You're wrong. I'm absolutely fine,' she responded. 'I was bang on time this morning.'

'Yes, I had noticed.'

'So, what have I done then?' she asked. 'I always seem to be in trouble over something or other.'

'You're not in trouble with me.'

Liz looked puzzled. 'So why am I here?'

'Because I am concerned about you.'

'*You're* concerned about *me,*' she said incredulously.

'That's right,' she confirmed. 'I know that you girls think I am an old dragon who does nothing but crack the whip, but I do actually care about my staff. And at the moment I think you are below par. Added to that, the fact that your mother came here to deliver your mail indicates to me that all isn't well at home.'

Liz's heightened emotions turned to fury. 'All right, you nosy old cow. My parents threw me out because I'm pregnant,' she said, out of control. 'I am living in a hostel. Satisfied!'

The older woman nodded slowly, ignoring Liz's dreadful rudeness. 'And would the father of the child be the young man who was killed?'

'Of course he is. I'm not in the habit of sleeping around. Vic was the only one I've ever...'

'I'm not judging you, my dear.'

'Oh, I thought you were,' she said. 'So now that you know the awful truth, can I go back to work?'

Before Miss Banks could reply there was a knock on the door and her secretary told her that she was needed somewhere, and at the same time the telephone rang.

She wrote something down on a piece of paper

and handed it to Liz. 'It's my address,' she explained. 'Come and see me after work this evening. We can't talk here because there are too many interruptions.' She raised her brows. 'It's in your own time so not compulsory, but if you fancy a chat you'll find me there. It's near the park.'

Liz couldn't imagine what she and Miss Banks could possibly have to talk about, but she said, 'Thank you.'

'I expect she is going to give you a lecture about the evil of your ways. The older generation are obsessed with it,' suggested Marg when they were on the way out of the building.' I should steer well clear if I was you.'

'My thoughts exactly,' said Liz.

'I bet there isn't a thing out of place in her house,' said Marg. 'It'll be dark and dreary and neat as a pin.'

'She probably files all her personal items, her photos and ornaments.'

Marg laughed. 'At least you're getting your sense of humour back. So we can thank her for that.'

'It isn't as if I've got anything else to do, though,' said Liz. 'Just a tin of soup at the hostel for my tea when I've queued up to use the cooker.'

'I bet you miss your mum's cooking,' said Marg.

'I'll say I do.' Her mother's cooking wasn't the only thing Liz missed. She found herself longing for the whole claustrophobic atmosphere of home with all its faults; feeling comfortable, though confined, within those walls and aware of being the second-class sister. Though even Dora seemed to have lost some of her shortcomings in

Liz's current state of mind.

'We'll go to Lyons at the weekend for something to eat if you fancy it,' suggested Marg brightly. 'To give you a break from the hostel.'

'I'd like that, but won't Joe be coming to London for the weekend?'

'I'm not sure, but I doubt it,' she said. 'If he does, we'll all go to Lyons.'

'Thanks, Marg.'

'They are cutting down on leave even more,' her friend mentioned gloomily. 'It's all to do with the bloomin' invasion, I expect.'

'There's plenty of speculation about it, but still it doesn't happen,' said Liz, realising as she spoke that she had been so immersed in her own problems, the rest of the world had been passing her by unnoticed.

'It'll happen when the powers that be have everything in place, I suppose,' said Marg. 'There's nothing we can do about it except wait and hope.'

'Exactly right,' Liz agreed.

Marg lapsed into thought. 'In all this talk of your family problems and accommodation, I haven't asked you if you actually want this baby given all the trouble it's causing you,' she said.

'I've been too worried to think too much about it,' she said. 'But yes, I really do want it. It won't get the best start in life, but I will love it and do my very best for it.'

'It will be lucky to have you as its mum,' she said.

'Thanks, Marg,' she said, tears smarting her eyes. It felt as though Marg was the only person on her side.

Miss Banks' house was on the other side of town to Liz's family home and was in a rather pretty row in a tree-lined street with the park entrance at the end. The area had its share of bomb sites and the buildings could do with a lick of paint like every other property in London. But the houses were attractive and a few spring flowers bloomed in the tiny front gardens which were mostly being used to grow food for the war effort.

Angry with herself for feeling so nervous, Liz walked up the path and rang the front doorbell.

'A letter from America came for Liz today,' Violet told George and Dora over dinner.

'I hope you put it in the dustbin,' said George.

'Of course I didn't,' said Violet. 'She needs all the support she can get at the moment. I took it to her work.'

'Did you see her?' he asked.

'No. I just handed it in and asked for it to be passed on to her,' she said.

'Good, only I don't want her persuading you to let her back into this house.'

'That's the last thing she would want, I should think, after the way we've treated her,' said his wife.

'She got what she deserved,' said George.

'She got pregnant, Dad,' Dora reminded him. 'She didn't commit a murder.'

'Enough of your cheek,' he said.

Dora had never got on with her sister, but she missed having her around. The place felt empty and miserable without her in the house and, having no one of her own generation, it was dismal. She and her sister had argued most of the time, but at least there had been a spark of youth about the place when she was here. Empathy wasn't in Dora's nature, but she couldn't help feeling curious about what had happened to Liz with her having nowhere to live. Maybe, sometime, she would go around to Marg's place and find out, just to satisfy her curiosity.

Liz was perched stiffly on a soft red sofa in an elegant yet cosy sitting room opposite Miss Banks, who was seated in an armchair with a ginger cat curled up on her lap and a fire burning in the hearth. Liz had been given a cup of tea on arrival, which had been most welcome because her mouth was parched with nerves. Even though she wasn't in the work environment, Miss Banks still carried an air of authority.

'So, you're in a bit of trouble, then,' said Miss Banks.

'Just a bit,' Liz replied with irony.

'Why don't you tell me all about it,' she suggested, adding with a wry grin, 'obviously, you can leave out the conception.'

A joke! Surely Miss Banks wasn't capable of humour. But she seemed to be smiling, which encouraged Liz to speak and she told her all about Vic and how much he had meant to her. She described her father's reaction and how she came to be living in a hostel.

'I was very shocked to find myself out on the street,' she confessed. 'I'd always thought I could rely on my family through thick and thin.'

'There's thick and thin and pregnancy outside of marriage,' said Miss Banks dryly.

Liz nodded. 'It seems to be in a class of its own where crime and punishment are concerned.'

'Yes, that is exactly right.'

The conversation halted as the cat stirred, purred, stared at Liz then jumped off Miss Banks' lap and on to Liz's. She was startled because they'd never had any pets at home so she wasn't used to animals.

'Just put her on the floor if you don't want her with you,' said Miss Banks.

Liz was about to do that when the cat settled down, looked up at Liz with greenish-yellow eyes and purred loudly. 'She's fine,' she said.

'Her name is Dolly,' she said. 'She's rather spoiled, I'm afraid, because I simply adore her.'

'I can understand that.' The animal was very handsome with shiny fur and white patches above her paws.

'So,' began Miss Banks. 'Are you planning on staying on at the hostel?'

'I seem to be living each day as it comes at the moment,' replied Liz, finding it surprisingly easy to talk to the older woman. 'The hostel is fine for now, but it's only a short-term thing. Obviously, my choices are limited, but I'm hoping to find lodgings.' She gave a wry grin. 'God knows what I'll do when the baby arrives. No one will rent me a room then. But I'll face that problem when the time comes. I am trying not to look ahead too much because it sends me into a panic.'

There was a silence. Miss Banks seemed thoughtful. 'Have you ever considered giving the baby up for adoption?' she asked.

'Not for a second,' said Liz without hesitation. 'It is part of me and Vic. Our flesh and blood, my responsibility as he isn't around to help. I know I don't have much to offer it, but I shall love it and do my very best for it.'

Liz was quite unprepared for what came next.

'I have a spare room if you're interested,' said Miss Banks.

'What me, live here, with you?' she said aghast.

'Is the idea so repellent?'

'No, of course not,' she said to be polite, though the idea of living with Miss Banks was truly terrifying. 'It was just such a surprise.'

'I inherited this house from my parents so I don't have to pay rent, and I would be able to let you have a room for a minimal amount with a contribution towards household bills.'

'I see,' said Liz numbly.

'I can see that you're hesitant and I don't blame you,' said the older woman.

'It's a bit of a surprise,' said Liz.

'So why not think about it and let me know in your own time,' she suggested.

'Thank you, Miss Banks,' she said. 'And I really am grateful for the offer.'

'If you were to take the room and things work out all right between us, you would be welcome to stay on here after the baby is born.'

This was a gesture of such generosity it brought tears to Liz's eyes.

'Oh, Miss Banks, I don't know what to say.'

'Go away and think about it,' she suggested. 'Take as long as you like; the room will still be there for you if you want it.' She paused. 'And by the way, if I have cause to reprimand you at the office, it will make no difference to the offer of the room. What happens in the office stays in the office and that will apply if you do decide to move in.'

'Thank you so much, Miss Banks,' she said gratefully. 'I will let you know when I've had a chance to think about it.'

'Just put Dolly down on the floor,' she said, as Liz needed to get up.

'I don't like to disturb her.'

'Don't you worry about her,' said Miss Banks. 'She'll soon find another cosy spot. She's an expert in relaxation.'

Liz lifted the cat and almost instinctively kissed her and put her on the floor.

'I see she has another adoring fan in the making,' said the older woman.

'I think she has too,' said Liz and she was smiling as she left the house.

Marg stared in amazement at Liz across the table in Lyons Teashop on Saturday afternoon. 'You can't possibly go to live with Miss Banks,' she said. 'It would be a disaster.'

'She seemed quite different at home,' said Liz. 'Not horrible at all.'

'She would be if the mood took her, though,' she said. 'People are what they are. If you did something that didn't please her, like take too long in the bathroom or come home late one night, you'd really cop it.'

'You get that sort of nagging when you live at

home,' Liz pointed out.

'Mm, I suppose you do,' she agreed. 'But it's different when it's one of the family having a go at you. Having your boss on your back in your own time. That would be hard to take for anyone, I should imagine.'

'Being comfortable at home is a luxury I lost when my dad threw me out,' she said. 'Now a roof over my head is my main concern. Any roof to be perfectly honest.'

'Oh, it's so awful for you,' said Marg, genuinely concerned. 'How quickly life can change. One minute we were all out enjoying ourselves together, happy and laughing with the boys. The next Vic is dead and you are homeless.'

'Mm, I know. Anyway, Miss Banks says I can stay on there after the baby arrives and that's a huge consideration,' Liz told her. 'That's been one of my biggest worries because unmarried mothers are scum as far as most people are concerned. So at least my baby would have a home.'

'I can see she's made it sound irresistible.'

'Why would she do that, Marg?' she asked. 'She has nothing to gain from having me there. Quite the opposite, in fact. She has a lovely home and plenty of peace and quiet. She's only going to charge me a minimal rent so she certainly isn't doing it for the money.'

'Maybe she's lonely.'

'Yeah, it could be that, but I think it is a genuine act of kindness.'

'Kindness? Miss Banks? Now you really are being naïve,' said Marg.

'And you are being very cynical today,' Liz observed. 'That isn't like you at all. Is there something wrong?'

Marg flushed and her eyes shone with tears. 'Sorry, kid. It's Joe. He doesn't know when he'll get another weekend pass and I miss him so much.'

'Oh, sorry about that,' said Liz. 'Maybe next weekend he'll be lucky.'

'I doubt it. It's the invasion we are hearing so much about that's stopping leave and worrying me to death,' she said. 'He's bound to be involved, though he hasn't said anything, of course. I know everybody wants it to happen because it will end the war, but what about all the boys we'll lose because of it.'

'I think you'd better concentrate your mind on the evils of Miss Banks as my landlady,' she said. 'At least it will stop you from worrying about more serious matters.'

'That's true.'

'It isn't as though accommodation options are plentiful for a woman in my position.'

'Mm, there is that,' agreed Marg sadly. 'So, why not give the old trout the benefit of the doubt?'

'You reckon?'

'Yeah. If she gives you any trouble let me know and I'll sort her out.'

They laughed at the ludicrousness of this suggestion because they were both scared stiff of Miss Banks.

Chapter Five

'Beryl,' Liz shouted up the stairs one morning in June 1944. 'Come quick. It's happened. It's here.'

Beryl Banks tore down the stairs to find her lodger sitting close to the wireless set.

'It isn't official, but there are reports that our boys are over there in France; that the invasion has started,' Liz told her. 'It will be confirmed later.'

'Oh, the invasion,' said Beryl with a wry grin. 'I thought you meant the baby.'

Liz laughed. 'We've another couple of months to go before we can expect any action in that department,' she said. 'And I doubt if I'll be that calm.'

'That's true,' smiled Beryl and joined Liz near the wireless. Contrary to earlier expectations, Miss Beryl Banks did laugh, and quite often too as it happened. Liz had been living here for two months and felt very much at home. Her landlady had set out the rules quite clearly at the beginning.

'I will cook for us both and you will take your turn with the washing-up. You can spend your time in the privacy of your room or you can join me downstairs where I usually have the wireless on. Wherever you feel most comfortable.' She gave Liz a key. 'Feel free to come and go as you please, but let me know if you won't be in at meal times as we mustn't waste food in these hard times. I think we should use Christian names at home from now on, but stick to the formalities in the office.'

She went through a list of house rules, all of which were perfectly reasonable, and then said, 'You must treat the place as your home and I hope you will be happy here.'

'I'm sure I will,' Liz had said, although at that early stage she'd had no idea how it would work out.

At first, she'd felt nervous and awkward, but this hadn't lasted long. Somehow, and Liz still didn't know why it worked so well, these two very different women got along. Liz felt completely at ease here with Beryl and the object of their joint affection, Dolly the cat.

'It's a good thing, of course, that the invasion has started to bring this awful war to an end,' Beryl was saying now. 'But how many more lives will it cost?'

'Yes, I was thinking the same thing,' said Liz. 'Marg will be worried. Her husband is involved.'

'Oh, the poor girl,' she said. 'I shall try and take it easy on her today.'

True to her word, Beryl always left the office behind when they were at home. If Liz had been in trouble at work she received the usual reprimand, but at home it wasn't mentioned and there was never any atmosphere.

'I'll go and wash the breakfast things and then get ready for work,' said Liz now.

'Thank you, dear,' Beryl said and as the cat padded in and looked appealingly at them, added, 'I think we can spare a saucer of milk for her Highness, don't you?'

Liz laughed and went to the kitchen with the cat at her heels. She had a huge number of worries; how was she going to pay her way when her pregnancy stopped her working and when she had the baby to look after? Then there was the equipment she would need; a pram and cot and nappies and so on. At present, she was hiding her condition beneath loose clothes, but it would be impossible to conceal it for much longer. Maybe, because they needed workers so urgently, the management would turn a blind eye, especially as she had Beryl looking out for her.

But how would she cope with the responsibility of motherhood and the stigma of being unmarried? The problems were overwhelming and she didn't have the answers, but she did know she would do her best to find a way forward. Knowing that she had a home for her baby was a huge comfort and she was so grateful to Beryl.

'I wonder how Liz is getting on?' said Violet Beck over their evening meal on D-Day.

'I'm more interested in the invasion,' said George.

'You would be,' said Violet. 'Because you are a heartless bugger.'

'What's heartless about being interested in the invasion?' he asked. 'It's of national interest and will help to end the war with a bit of luck.'

'She's your daughter, George,' she said.

'She was my daughter,' he said. 'Not any more. She forfeited that right.'

'I don't suppose Liz wants to be your daughter anyway after the way you treated her,' Dora put in.

'It makes no difference to me one way or the other.'

'She's out there somewhere with no back-up,' said Violet. 'We don't even know where she's living.'

'That's easily solved,' said Dora. 'Pop round to see Marg. She'll know where she is.'

'I doubt if Liz would want to see me anyway.'

'It's Dad she won't want to see,' said Dora. 'He was the one who threw her out.'

'And I didn't do anything to stop him.'

'As if you could stop Dad doing anything he wants to do,' said Dora.

'I could have tried.'

'Will you two be quiet please,' said George irritably. 'I'm trying to listen to the wireless.'

'I reckon Liz is well out of it,' said Dora, lowering her voice.

'Much more of your cheek and you'll go the same way,' said her father.

'You wouldn't do that, Dad,' said Dora. 'You wouldn't want to lose both your daughters.'

'If you give me much more lip, I might.'

'You'll be threatening to throw Mum out next, but you'd never do that because you would lose your skivvy.'

'Stop yacking and let me listen to the wireless.'

Dora sank into her thoughts. She wondered how her sister was getting along, but her sibling concern was very minor and slipped across the surface of her mind, leaving her emotionally untouched. She certainly didn't care enough to want to make an effort to see Liz. She guessed she would be all right anyway because her sister was the type who would cope with any situation.

Anyway, Liz had a baby to look forward to. She was going to be a mother so she would have some purpose in life, albeit that she would be the subject of gossip and scorn. Dora saw herself as a freak because she didn't have a boyfriend and would rather be in Liz's situation than living at home with her boring parents and no man in her life.

But now her mother had set a dish of bread and butter pudding on the table. What an exciting life they led, she thought sardonically.

Beryl was the most brilliant cook. She could do wonderful things with wartime favourites like corned beef and mince. She could even make turnip and swede taste nice.

'Cooking has always been my passion,' she told Liz when the younger woman complimented her. 'I'll be glad when the war is over and we can get some decent food to cook with. I'm really looking forward to that.'

Liz often thought it was a pity the older woman hadn't had a family because she was such a brilliant homemaker. As well as excelling in the kitchen she also had a knack with furnishings and could transform a room with a well-placed ornament or change of cushion cover.

There was sometimes an air of melancholy about her and Liz wondered if she had had an unhappy childhood or a love affair that had gone

103

wrong when she was young. It was hard to imagine her as a young woman because she was so
severe in appearance now. But she had been once
and her brilliant blue eyes must have looked
lovely in a youthful face.

In the office, Beryl was the consummate professional. Severe, loud and articulate. Not afraid to
speak her mind, she did so on a regular basis. She
gave the orders and made sure they were obeyed,
which meant she was unpopular. At home she
was warm and funny and Liz liked her very
much.

On the evening of D-Day there was a feeling of
excitement in the house. The wireless was full of
the events in France. Everyone knew that the enthusiasm was peppered with fear for more loss of
life, but it was a significant sign that things were
moving. Liz, however, had some pleasant news of
her own.

'I had another letter from Vic's mother today,'
she told Beryl.

'And?'

'She's thrilled about the baby.'

'Oh, that's lovely. I'm so pleased.'

'She didn't even comment about the fact that
Vic and I weren't married,' she said. 'She seems
very excited about the idea of being a grandma
even though she's on the other side of the world.'

'It will be lovely for you to keep in touch.'

'That's what I thought.'

They finished their meal and Liz went to the
kitchen to wash the dishes, as Beryl had cooked.
They had slipped into a comfortable routine and

Liz never stopped being grateful to this Jekyll and Hyde of a woman for giving her a home.

A week or so after D-Day the people of London found themselves under attack again. This time by a new kind of bomb. A pilotless aircraft that stopped and dropped from the sky, exploding and causing a huge amount of death and destruction.

'It's the fact that they come down at any time of the day or night that's so frightening. At least with the other bombs we knew they only came at night,' said Beryl. 'I mean, life has to go on and we all have to go to work. We can't spend all day in the air raid shelter.'

'As soon as the engine goes out, dive for cover,' said Liz. 'That's the advice to stay safe.'

'Yes, I know that's what we're supposed to do, but it isn't always convenient when you're on the road on a bike.'

Beryl travelled to work by bicycle, while Liz met Marg on the route and they walked to the office together. Marg was still rather nervous about visiting Liz at their boss's house because she was such a formidable character at work. But once they were in the safety of Liz's bedroom – at Beryl's suggestion – Marg relaxed.

'Heard from Joe lately?' Liz asked Marg one morning in summer on their way to work.

'No, I haven't and I know I can't expect to hear because he'll be busy helping to win the war for us.'

'That's the spirit,' said Liz and they both dived into a shop doorway as a doodlebug came over.

The explosion sounded close, but there was no

sign of any damage so they hurried on their way. Already people were used to the new bombs and took them in their stride as they had during the blitz.

'I suppose Liz will be getting near to her time now,' Violet said to Dora one evening in autumn when they were doing the dishes after the evening meal.

'Mm, I suppose she must be,' said Dora, drying the plates after her mother had washed them.

'I hope she's all right, with all these bombs dropping out of the sky day and night.'

'I thought you were going to see her,' said Dora. 'Didn't you say you were going to get her address from Marg?'

'I did say that, but I didn't do it.'

'Why?'

'Scared, I suppose,' she admitted. 'I mean, what I did was pretty bad. Allowing your father to banish her from the house and not doing anything to try to stop him.'

'Liz knows what Dad is like,' said Dora. 'She won't hold it against you.'

'You think not?'

'Yeah, I do. If it was me I'd never want to see you ever again, but Liz isn't like that. She's only human, though, so she must have been hurt.'

'I know and I feel awful about it.'

'But she is your daughter,' Dora reminded her. 'So, you've got a right to see her.'

'I think I probably lost that right when I failed to support her,' she said.

'Oh well, I don't know,' snapped Dora, bored

with the subject. 'It's up to you what you do about it.'

As autumn progressed and Liz really struggled to hide her condition, she began to tire of the pregnancy and was eager to move to the next stage.

'I feel like a tired old elephant about the place,' she said to her landlady.

'Yes, it does get tiresome at that late stage,' agreed Beryl who was nursing the cat. 'Or so I've heard.'

'As well as being able to bend down and wear normal clothes again, I'm looking forward to meeting my baby too. I do hope it's a boy.'

'A son who looks like his dad, eh?'

'I would love that, but whatever comes will be welcome,' she said with a grin, before the conversation was interrupted by a knock at the door.

'I won't ask you to get out of the chair as it's such a major operation at the moment,' said Beryl, putting the cat on the floor. 'I'll go.'

'Thanks,' said Liz, continuing with the jacket she was knitting for the baby.

'Mum,' said Liz in astonishment when Beryl showed Violet in. 'What are you doing out on the streets at night? It's dangerous out there. You know they are dropping new bombs on us now, the V2s. They're more dangerous than the first robots. I'm sure the siren went.'

'It goes off so often now, nobody takes any notice,' her mother replied. 'I bet you still go to work every day, despite the air raid siren.'

'Of course I do, but being out on the streets at

night seems more dangerous somehow.'

'Anyway, I've come to see how you are getting on,' Violet said moving forward, leaning down and putting her arms around her daughter in a light embrace. 'And you're out at work during the day so I can't come then.'

'I'll leave you to it then,' said Beryl.

'Don't go,' said Liz. 'That programme you like will be on the wireless soon. I'll take Mum into the kitchen.'

Although Beryl argued, Liz insisted because she was always careful not to take advantage. She heaved herself out of the chair and ushered her mother from the room.

'You got my address from Marg, I assume,' said Liz

Violet nodded.

'Did you tell Dad that you were coming to see me?' she enquired.

'Not likely.'

'Then I'd sooner you hadn't come,' she said, sounding prickly. 'I don't want to be some dirty little secret.'

'Liz, I'm working on him,' said Violet. 'I'll win him round in the end and get him to agree to let you come back home.'

'I don't want to come back, Mum,' said Liz firmly.

'Your pride, I suppose, that's understandable,' said Violet. 'Once you're settled back at home you'll get over it.'

'No. I really don't want to come back, Mum, because I am happy living here,' she said. 'Anyway, the time for my living at home has passed.'

'Oh, I see,' her mother said in a tone that indicated clearly that she didn't.

'Surely it's a relief for you that I'm well and happy?'

'Well, yes, of course, but you should be at home with your family.'

'When my baby arrives, I will take it out with pride and know that Beryl will support me all the way. She'll have no qualms about the fact that I don't have a husband,' she told her. 'Whereas you'll want me to hide it away. You'll be afraid of what the neighbours might say.'

'Not once I get used to it.'

'When you can visit me and my baby with pride and you can tell Dad where you're going, I'll be pleased to see you. Until then I'd sooner you didn't come.'

'Well really...'

'You are ashamed of me,' said Liz. 'You've come here tonight to try to ease your conscience because you stood back and allowed Dad to throw me out. I was hurt, Mum, very hurt. I don't hold it against you, but I don't want to see you under those circumstances so I'd rather you stayed away. When you feel able to visit me proudly and to walk down the street wheeling your grandchild, you'll be welcome. Until then please don't come.'

'If that's the way you feel.'

'It is, I'm afraid.'

'I'll be on my way then,' she said huffily and stalked to the front door with Liz following.

'Mum, at least stay until the all clear goes.'

Ignoring her, Violet opened the front door and sailed out.

'Oh, for goodness' sake,' said Liz, following her in the hope of persuading her to come back indoors. 'There's no need for this sort of dramatics. Wait until we hear the all clear.'

But Violet wasn't to be persuaded and was far too engrossed in taking offence to pay any attention to the roaring object in the sky.

'Mum.' Liz tore down the front path and threw herself at her mother, bringing her down and lying on top of her in a protective manner.

When the explosion came, it wasn't near enough to be seen, but the sky was lit up.

'Are you trying kill me or something?' complained Violet, pushing her daughter away and scrambling to her feet.

'I thought it would be closer than that,' said Liz breathlessly.

'Making a fuss about nothing, as usual,' said Violet straightening her clothes. 'You've always been the same.'

And without another word, she headed off into the night.

'Are you all right?' asked Beryl when Liz went back into the house, shaky and holding back the tears.

'I thought the bomb was closer,' she said. 'I was afraid Mum was going to cop it so I brought her down. She wasn't best pleased either.'

'You shouldn't be throwing yourself around like that so close to your time,' said Beryl.

'Oh. Can I do nothing right for anyone,' she said and burst into tears.

110

'Here, drink this said Beryl, setting a cup of cocoa on the table beside Liz's chair.

'It was pure instinct,' said Liz. 'Common sense didn't come into it. I thought Mum was in danger so I did what came naturally. I didn't realise I could run with all my extra weight, but I certainly shifted then.'

'Your mother should be proud of you.'

'Huh, that'll be the day,' said Liz. 'She's ashamed of me. I'm her nasty little secret. The daughter who got herself knocked up and put the family reputation at risk.'

'If she is ashamed it's society's attitude towards these things that have made her that way,' said Beryl. 'We are all products of the world we live in, aren't we?'

'I suppose so. How is it that you're not hostile to a woman in my position when most other people are?' asked Liz.

She didn't answer at once. 'Maybe I'm more broadminded in my views of these things,' she said eventually. 'Now, are you all right? You didn't break any bones or anything?'

'I do feel a bit shaken up from all the sudden exercise,' she said. 'But I'm okay, I think.'

'Thank goodness for that,' said Beryl.

A few hours later Liz was in an ambulance on her way to the hospital. The midwife had been concerned about the way the labour was progressing and the fact that she hadn't gone the full term.

'I can't lose it,' she said to Beryl who had gone with her. 'This baby means everything to me.'

'You're going to be in the best place,' said

Beryl, holding her hand. 'You'll have doctors close by and medical equipment. They might even have an incubator should the baby need a little help for a while at first.'

'I do hope so,' she said, her words turning to a groan as a contraction took hold of her.

'Is he going to be all right?' Liz asked the nurse when she finally gave birth to a son who was immediately whisked away to be put into an incubator.

'It's too early to say, but he's a month premature so he didn't have the time he should in your tum,' she replied. 'But we'll do everything we can. And we have had much smaller ones than him grow into healthy babies. We do have a few incubators now and that will help.'

'Can you tell my friend he's arrived, please?'

'Of course, and she can come and see you at visiting time tonight. But first you need to sleep. When we've cleaned you up you can have a cup of tea and then get on to the ward and let us worry about your baby while you get some shut-eye.'

'Just as if I could sleep while he's fighting for his life.'

'You'll be surprised,' said the nurse.

She was right. Nature took its course and she slept heavily for a few hours.

When she awoke, she felt refreshed and more able to cope, which was just as well because she found herself on the receiving end of hostility.

'We don't want anything to do with mothers of bastards,' said the woman in the next bed when

112

Liz asked if she knew when the nurse was coming around.

'Suit yourself,' said Liz and got out of bed to find the nurse, ignoring the cries of horror because she was on her feet, two weeks' bedrest being the norm after giving birth.

The nurse was equally as horrified see her patient walking about and told her so.

'I want to know about my baby,' Liz said. 'I want to know if he's all right.'

She was bundled into a wheelchair and told she would do herself terrible harm by being on her feet this soon after the birth. But the nurse did apparently have a heart because she wheeled her out of the ward and into a room where they had a couple of incubators.

'Oh, he's so tiny, she said, looking at this pink, mottled fragment of humanity with a thatch of dark hair. 'He's like his father. He has the same colour hair.'

'It may not be that colour when his proper hair comes through,' said the nurse.

'I don't mind what colour it is,' said Liz tearfully. 'Just so long as he stays with us.'

'You really need someone more senior to speak to you about that,' suggested the nurse. 'But he looks in pretty good shape to me.'

'He's the most beautiful thing I've ever seen,' she said and smiling, added, 'equal only to his father.'

Back on the ward, Liz chose her moment and her words carefully. She knew that all these women had had problem births or they wouldn't be here because it was usual for mothers to have their babies at home. But things needed to be said and she was going to say them. Waiting until there were no staff around, she got out of bed and stood at the end of her neighbour's bed in the centre of the ward so she could be heard by the other women.

'Do you know what you do when you call my baby a bastard?' she said.

'Speak the truth,' said one airily.

'You show your ignorance,' Liz corrected her. 'My son's father was killed by a bomb while trying to retrieve a toy for a child. He would be alive today if he hadn't done that act of kindness in the middle of an air raid instead of taking shelter. He was a good man, a brave one and had he lived I would be wearing a wedding ring now.'

'Says you.'

'It does happen to be true, but if it wasn't, you still have no right to judge me. You should be supportive to women like me. As females, we should stick together whatever our circumstances. It's wrong to torment any woman who finds herself in my position just because you managed to drag some man up the aisle.'

'How dare you,' said the woman. 'My husband and I had been courting for years.'

'Lucky you,' Liz came back at her. 'I didn't know my son's father for long, but I was honoured to have found him before he died much too soon.' She paused. 'And shall I tell you something else to make you hate me even more?'

'Not interested,' said the woman.

'But we are,' said someone else. 'Come on, love,

let's hear it. We need something to help pass the time in here.'

'My son's father was an American, a gorgeous, handsome Yank. So, go on, call me Yank meat, easy, cheap, just to mention a few of the most popular ones.'

'I'll call you bloomin' lucky,' said one of the women. 'The Yanks are very easy on the eye and generous to a fault. They arrived here too late for me. I was already married with two kids when they got to our shores. But I wouldn't have said no.'

There was a murmur of assent and some giggling, then Liz continued.

'You can snub me and insult me all you like, but it won't touch me because all I have on my mind right now is my boy who is in an incubator.' She waved a hand towards the room. 'All of this, the chatter that I am excluded from, the name-calling you are subjecting me to, means absolutely nothing to me. So you're wasting your breath.'

She turned around and went back to her bed. Nobody could guess how close to tears she was and how painful it was to be the subject of such vitriol. She turned on to her side and closed her eyes to hide her feelings. Exhausted from the birth and the effect of this spitefulness, she dozed off.

'They've brought some tea round,' said a distant voice. 'She left yours on your locker, but you'll be annoyed if you let it go cold so I thought I'd better wake you.'

Liz opened her eyes to see a woman she recognised as one of the mums on the ward. 'Thank you,' she said sitting up. 'I could do with a cuppa.'

'Don't take too much notice of her in the next bed,' she said. 'We don't all share her views.'

'Most of them seemed to.'

'A few maybe but certainly not me,' she said. 'Sorry I didn't stand up for you back then but it was hard to get a word in.'

'No need to apologise,' said Liz.

'Anyway, I'll bring my tea over and have it with you, if you like,' she said.

'Thank you, I would like that,' said Liz, thinking what a difference a few kind words made.

Beryl came to visit that evening, though it wasn't easy to get past the frontline troops on the staff as visiting was usually restricted to husbands. Using a mixture of the authoritative tone she adopted in the office and her off-duty homeliness she managed it.

'He's a smasher,' she said, having been to look at him in the other room. 'Well done!'

'Well, nature did it, but thank you,' said Liz. 'I really hope he's going to be all right, Beryl.'

'He looked like a proper little fighter to me, just like his mother,' she said with determined optimism. 'I'm glad they have him in an incubator, though. There aren't too many of them around so we're very lucky.'

'I'll feel more confident when he's out of it because it will mean he's all right.'

'They are real lifesavers though,' she said. 'A doctor in America uses them in a side-show in a funfair to popularise them. Mothers of premature babies – some much earlier than yours – take them to him for a fee. I know it sounds barbaric, but he's saved many lives, apparently.'

'How do you know all these things?' asked Liz because Beryl was always a fountain of knowledge.

'Library books, magazines, newspapers, the wireless. I have always had a hunger for inform-ation,' she explained.

'You're a big reader, I've noticed that.'

'Knowledge is power.'

'I suppose it is.'

'Anyway, how are you feeling?'

'Tired, but okay,' she replied. 'And keen to bring my baby home.'

'I'm sure it won't be too long,' said Beryl. 'I can't wait for you both to come home.'

'They won't keep us longer than they have to because I can't pay.'

'I've seen to all that,' said Beryl. 'So you and your baby will be here for as long as you need to be.'

'You've paid...?'

'I've arranged to when you are done here and we know how much we owe.'

'But I will never be able to pay you back.'

'I know that and it won't be necessary.'

'Why would you do all this for us, Beryl?' she asked emotionally. 'You already do more than enough at home. Cheap rent and all sorts of favours. It isn't fair to you.'

'When you and your little one come home and we have a few quiet moments I will tell you a story which will make it easier for you to under-stand.'

Liz was intrigued. 'I can't wait,' she said eagerly. 'Can't you tell me now?'

'I could do, but I'd rather wait until you are home and we have some privacy.'

'I'm dying to know.'

'All in good time.'

'Okay,' said Liz. 'I'll be patient.'

'So, any ideas for a name for the little one yet?' she asked, moving on swiftly.

'Yes, I am going to call him Charlie,' she said. 'Charles was Vic's second name.'

'I really like that,' the older woman approved. 'It's a good strong name for a boy.'

Beryl stayed for the whole of visiting hour and after she had left Liz thought again how very blessed she was to have such a true friend.

'Was that your mother?' asked the vicious woman in the next bed.

'No.'

'Your mum abandoned you, has she?'

'None of your business,' said Liz.

'So, she has then.'

Liz turned to her and gave her a steely look. 'Is your own life really so boring that you need to take such a keen interest in mine?' she asked.

There was a ripple of laughter further down the ward. 'She's got four kids at home besides this new one so she probably needs a distraction,' said someone.

'Her husband needs a flaming distraction or she'll be in here again this time next year with another mouth to feed,' said another, causing more giggling.

'Bloomin' cheek,' said the woman.

'You ask for it,' another piped up.

'Yeah,' added someone else. 'Judging someone you don't even know.'

Liz was grateful for the support, but thought she might have more enemies in this temporary little community. She was well aware of a lot more trouble to come in the outside world when she took her baby home. But she was ready for it.

Despite all the problems she knew she must face in the future, she just couldn't wait to take little Charlie home and be a proper mum.

Chapter Six

Disappointingly, Liz came home from hospital without her baby. He was progressing well enough, but they wouldn't discharge him until they were happy with his weight. She spent all day with him at the hospital, but came home at night.

'Maybe we can take this opportunity to have a chat while it's quiet before Charlie comes home,' Liz said to Beryl one evening over dinner.

'So, what's on your mind?'

'You are very generous to me and I am grateful, but I have to make some arrangement to pay you for the lovely pram and cot and other necessities for Charlie that were here to greet me when I was discharged from the hospital,' she said. 'You know how I'm fixed, that I won't be able to pay it all at once but maybe I can pay in instalments once I'm working again.'

119

'That won't be necessary,' said Beryl in a firm tone. 'The things were a gift.'

'Now come on, Beryl,' she said. 'You know I can't accept such generosity.'

'You can if I insist.'

'Beryl, I am too much in your debt,' said Liz, concerned. 'As well as the gifts, I'm not paying rent while I'm not working and I feel awful about it. I will find work as soon as Charlie is strong enough to be minded. Maybe fewer hours than I was doing before so that I get to see something of him. But I'll make sure I earn enough to pay my rent.'

'It really doesn't matter so stop worrying,' said Beryl.

Something came into Liz's mind. 'You did say you would tell me why you want to do so much for me and now seems as good a time as any.'

'Yes, you're right, dear, so let's finish our meal and go and sit by the fire.'

'When I was eighteen I realised that I was pregnant,' began Beryl as they sat either side of the hearth with the cat snoozing on the mat between them. 'I was desperate to keep the baby but my parents wouldn't hear of it. They told me that unless I gave the baby up as soon as it was born, I was no longer welcome in their home. I'm afraid I didn't have the courage to strike out on my own. So, they packed me off to an aunt in the country as soon as I started to show and I let them take my baby, a little boy, away soon after the birth. It's the biggest regret of my life.'

'Was there no way you could have kept him?'

asked Liz.

'You kept Charlie, so I could have kept my son, but I wasn't as brave as you.'

'I wasn't brave particularly,' said Liz. 'I just didn't have any choice. My father was disgusted with me so he threw me out. There simply weren't any options.'

'You wouldn't have tried to end the pregnancy or considered adoption for your baby if he had given you the choice, though, would you?'

'Absolutely not! I'd already lost Vic so the baby was the most important thing in my life,' she said. 'And as it happened I didn't need to be very brave because you took me in.'

'You'd have managed somehow if I hadn't.'

'Maybe I would, but you have made it a heck of a lot easier for me.' Liz looked at her. 'So, what happened to your boy?'

'He was adopted, but they wouldn't tell me anything about the people who took him,' she said. 'Apparently, it isn't a good idea for the birth mother to know where the baby is placed. It isn't in the child's best interests. The subject was never mentioned again. It was as though it had never happened as far as my parents were concerned.'

'It must have been awful for you.'

'Yes, it was very hard.' She looked stricken for a moment. 'It really was.'

'I was very shocked when my father gave me twenty-four hours to get out,' explained Liz. 'I didn't think he'd take such a hard line. I was scared stiff when I walked out of that house with nowhere to go. I have never felt more alone.'

'You still went ahead though.'

'What else could I do?' she said.

'A lot of girls in that position would have found someone to fix the problem.'

'Not me. I wouldn't consider abortion even if I had had the money. I knew I faced challenges, not least the attitude of people toward the child of an unmarried mother. I had a taste of that in hospital.'

Beryl grinned. 'I wouldn't fancy the chances of anyone who doesn't treat your boy right.'

'You know me then,' said Liz, smiling.

'Yes, I have got to know you pretty well since you've been living with me,' she said. 'And now that I have told you my story, you can understand why I want to help you.'

'I can understand why you are sympathetic to my situation, but not why you are giving me all this help.'

'Because you've done what I didn't have the courage to do,' she said. 'You could say I want to ease my conscience. Maybe there is some of that in it. But mostly I just want to help. It's like doing it for myself all those years go. I still regret giving my boy up.'

Tears rushed into Liz's eyes, but she didn't say anything.

'I'm not rich by any means, but neither am I short of money,' Beryl went on. 'My parents were comfortably off and I was an only child so what they had went to me when they died. I don't have any children of my own to spend it on, do I.'

'Do you not really need to work, then?' asked Liz.

'I couldn't afford not to until after my parents

died and I inherited. But by that time work was such a big part of my life I would have hated to give it up and I'm not filthy rich or anything. The money would soon disappear if I wasn't earning. I have a good brain and it would be wrong to waste it,' she said. 'So, as long as someone has a job for me I shall continue.'

'I don't know what I would do without you, Beryl, but I will never take advantage,' she said. 'I will find work as soon as Charlie is properly thriving.'

'And put him in a nursery?'

'Well, yes, I suppose I shall have to as I need to be earning,' she said. 'Unless I can find someone to look after him at home. But let's not worry about that yet. Let's get him home first.'

'Yes, of course,' agreed Beryl thoughtfully.

On her way to the hospital a few days later Liz called at the family home, knowing that her mother would be on her own.

'You've had it,' said Violet, observing her daughter's slimmer figure.

'You have a grandson,' Liz said proudly.

'Oh, how wonderful,' said Violet, waving her inside. 'Congratulations.'

'Thanks. I've called him Charlie,' she told her as they went into the kitchen.

'Oh,' said Violet, sounding disappointed. 'I thought you would have named him after your dad.'

Liz looked at her in disbelief. 'You really thought I would name him after a man who won't even acknowledge him?' she said.

'Your dad will come around,' she said.

'My son's name is Charlie and it isn't going to change,' she said adamantly.

'All right, don't bite my head off,' said her mother, sounding peeved. 'So, where is he?'

Liz explained.

'Oh my gawd,' she said. 'So, you must have had had him soon after my visit.'

Liz decided to spare her mother from her part in his early arrival. She didn't seem to have linked it with Liz's energetic and unnecessary attempt to save her life so the less said about it the better. 'Yes, I did,' she said. 'He was a month premature.'

'Oh dear, the poor little mite. The sooner you get him home the better.'

'I just can't wait.'

'Make the most of this quiet time, though,' said Violet in a warning tone. 'There'll be precious little of it when he does come home. He'll have you awake half the bloomin' night.'

Liz felt deflated. Her mother had always had the power to do that to her. Any little triumph she had had at school had always been greeted without enthusiasm. When she compared it to Beryl's reaction it brought tears to her eyes. She wished she hadn't come. But Mum had needed to know that she had a grandson. Anyway, Liz was so proud of her son she wanted the world to know.

'I'll face that when it comes,' she said. 'That period doesn't last long, apparently.'

'That's true,' said Violet, pouring some tea. 'It's exhausting while it lasts, though, and no sooner do you get over that, they're running about and

124

causing havoc.'

'Didn't you enjoy Dora and me as children, then?' she asked.

'Oh yeah. Course I did. I'm just saying that kids are a lot of work and worry.'

'And joy too, surely.'

'Of course.'

'I'm sure I'll cope with all the different phases,' said Liz, wanting to escape and aware of a lowering of self-esteem under this roof. It had always been there, but she hadn't fully realised it until she'd moved out. She couldn't wait to get back to Beryl's.

Marg couldn't understand how her friend Liz could live in the same house as the awful Miss Banks. But she seemed to like it there and even got on well with the old witch.

'Daydreaming again, are we?' asked her boss, leaning towards her.

'No, of course not, Miss Banks,' replied Marg.

'What are you doing then?' the older woman demanded.

'Nothing, Miss.'

'Exactly,' boomed Beryl. 'So I suggest you work your way through that pile of filing.'

'Yes, Miss.'

'And don't take all day about it.'

'No, Miss.'

'I really don't know how you can stand living here with that awful woman, Liz,' said Marg in hushed tones that evening, though Beryl was out helping at the Rescue Centre so they were alone.

'She just never stops having a go at me.'

'She's really good to me and I love it here,' said Liz. 'She's a completely different woman at the office. I remember from when I was still at work. I thought she was hateful then too. So, I know exactly what you mean.'

'Oh well, that's enough about the old witch,' said Marg. 'How's the baby?'

'He's coming on a treat,' she said. 'I can't wait to have him home and look after him properly.'

'I bet.'

'Have you heard from Joe lately?' Liz enquired.

'Yeah! I've had a note to say he's all right,' she said. 'Seems like the war might be coming to an end at last.'

'They did say it would be over by Christmas, but it doesn't seem very likely now with bombs still falling on us day and night.'

'Most people think that we're on the right side of it now though,' said Marg. 'The time is coming when we can get on with our lives.'

'Hooray for that,' said Liz. 'Thrilling for you, going to a new life in America.'

'I know. I am so excited about it.'

'Aren't you a tiny bit nervous, though?' asked Liz. 'It's a really big thing.'

'No, not the slightest bit,' she said happily. 'I just can't wait to get there.'

'I'll miss you something awful,' said Liz.

'Yeah, that's the bit I'm not looking forward to.' She sounded sad. 'But I'm keen to get on with it now.'

Liz couldn't help but think that if it hadn't been for Vic's kindness to a child, she might have been

126

going to America too. She hated the idea of life without Marg as they had been friends since infants' school. But she mustn't spoil it for her. She was so keen to go and she and Joe were good together. So, she must try to share her friend's excitement.

A lot of baby Charlie's first night home was spent in the air raid shelter. Since the bombs had become so frequent, most people didn't bother with the shelter, but Liz wasn't prepared to take any risks with her son at this stage.

'It's chilly for him down here,' Beryl remarked.

'He's well wrapped up,' said Liz. 'I think the bombs are a bigger threat than him catching cold.'

'Hmm, you're probably right,' agreed Beryl. 'And while we're here with nothing to distract us I've come up with a plan to solve the problem of you paying your way, which doesn't bother me but I know worries you.'

'Oh yeah, so what is it?'

'You take on the job of housekeeper and I pay you a wage,' she suggested.

'Oh, that sounds promising,' said Liz.

'This way you can stay at home with the baby and still be able to pay your rent with something left over for yourself. It would be an enormous help to me because I find the housekeeping too much while I'm working full time.'

'So, you've created a job for me?'

'No, I'd like to pass one on to you,' she said. 'It's a different thing altogether.'

'Are you sure?'

'Absolutely,' she said. 'I would continue to cook,

as I enjoy that. But it would be such a relief to shed the other stuff. Washing, ironing, cleaning, shopping and general organisation. If you could take the responsibility of that off my shoulders, it would be an enormous help to me. I know it isn't very exciting, but you will get a proper wage and it might suit you for the time being.'

Liz had been worried about leaving Charlie all day with strangers, him being so little, so it was a huge weight off her mind. And she would make sure that she earned every penny of her wages so she would keep her independence.

'When shall I start?' she asked.

'Tomorrow if you're happy with my terms.'

'Done deal,' she said and they were both laughing when the all clear went and they climbed out of the shelter.

'There's something strange happening at work,' Marg told Liz a week or so later.

'What's that?'

'It's Miss Banks,' she said. 'She's been seen smiling in the office and she isn't being so horrid to me.'

'Really?'

'Yeah, when I was late back from lunch the other day, she didn't go off at the deep end.'

'That's better for you all, then,' said Liz.

'Not half,' said Marg. 'I hope it lasts.'

'I think it will.'

'I wouldn't count on anything as far as that woman is concerned.'

But Liz guessed that Beryl was happier at the office because she knew everything was being taken care of at home and she enjoyed her spare time now that she was no longer lonely. She adored the baby and enjoyed cooking because she didn't have to worry about anything else. Liz felt blessed to have such strong back-up. As a single mum, her life could have been very different. How many women in her position had such support? Not many, that was for sure.

In the afternoons, Liz usually took her baby for a walk in his pram and got the daily shopping at the same time. There were always plenty of other pram-wheelers around and she got to pass the time of day with some of the young mothers. It became an established part of her daily routine and she enjoyed it.

So, when her mother came to visit one afternoon, naturally Liz asked her to go with her.

'No, I'm ready for a cuppa and a sit down,' said Violet.

'Did you walk round then instead of getting the bus?' Liz enquired.

'No, I got the bus, but waiting about for it is tiring. Anyway, it's cold out now that winter has set in. The baby needs to be inside in the warm.'

'The fresh air is good for him and he'll be well wrapped up,' said Liz.

'I want a cup of tea,' insisted Violet.

Liz was irritated by her persistence, but put the kettle on. 'It'll have to be a quick one,' she said. 'I need to get to the shops before it gets too cold out for Charlie.'

'Isn't he coming on,' said Violet, leaning over the pram in the hall.

'Yes, he seems to be thriving now.'

Handing her mother a cup of tea, Liz said, 'Could you drink it sharpish, please, Mum, so we can get to the shops. You can wheel the pram if you like.'

Violet looked uncomfortable. 'You go on,' she said. 'I'll catch you up when I've finished my tea.'

Liz's eyes narrowed in realisation. 'Oh, I see. You don't want to be seen with us, do you?' she said. 'You're ashamed of us. It's all right behind closed doors, but not out in public.'

'Don't be so ridiculous,' she said, but her cheeks were flaming.

Liz picked up her mother's tea and emptied it down the sink. 'I'd like you to go, please,' she said.

'What?'

'You heard,' she said. 'Don't you dare be ashamed of my beautiful son.'

'I'm not, it's just that...'

'I know exactly what it is and I don't want you near my son unless you are prepared to take him to your heart.'

'I've taken the trouble to come...'

'Too bad you didn't come with the right spirit, isn't it?' said Liz. 'Now there's the door. Please leave.'

Mumbling under her breath Violet left and Liz was trembling when she closed the door after her. How dare her mother look down on Charlie. She expected it from ignorant strangers but not her own mother!

That evening Violet was agonising over what had happened with Liz. She didn't want to be

130

ashamed of her daughter and that lovely boy of hers. But he had been born out of wedlock and there was no getting around it. She'd been brought up with these views and they were ingrained in her. People loved a good meaty scandal and Liz had provided them with a nice juicy one.

There was nothing she would like more than to push Charlie's pram around the town. But she was sure to meet someone she knew and that would completely blow the story she had invented to explain Liz's absence from home. She'd told people she'd got a fabulous new job on the other side of London.

This woman Liz lived with seemed to give her plenty of support while her own family gave her nothing, which made Violet feel ashamed. If she could afford it she'd help her out financially but George only gave her enough housekeeping money to manage and if she asked for more he'd want to know why. He'd give her nothing if he knew it was for Liz.

At the moment, he was at the pub and she and Dora were listening to the wireless.

'I went to see Liz today,' she said.

'Did you?' said her daughter without much interest. 'Is she all right?'

'She's doing fine,' she replied. 'Will you be going to visit her to see the baby?'

'Not likely,' she said. 'I don't know anything about babies. Messy, noisy things as far as I can make out.'

'You ought to go and see her,' Violet suggested. 'It is usual when someone has had a baby, especially when it's your sister.'

'Hark at you,' said Dora rudely. 'If you and Dad hadn't thrown her out she'd be here with the baby now.'

'What's done is done,' she said. 'I thought you might like to see your nephew.'

Dora thought about it. Liz was an unmarried mum with a kid so there was no way she could make Dora feel inferior because she had nothing going for her. So maybe she would call to see her at the weekend. Make her feel envious because she'd ruined her life and Dora hadn't.

'Yeah, I suppose I should go and see her and the kid,' she said. 'I'll call round at the weekend sometime.'

'Good girl,' said Violet, her conscience eased slightly because at least one of the family was going to visit.

Dora had been expecting to see her sister looking downtrodden and dishevelled. But when she opened the door to Dora on Saturday afternoon Liz was absolutely blooming, which was annoying. Her hair was shiny and her face glowing even though she wasn't wearing a scrap of make-up. She had an air of invulnerability about her, as though nothing could touch her.

Dora dutifully glanced at the baby and said he was lovely. She congratulated her sister on her achievement, gave her the matinee jacket their mother had knitted and said it was from them both. Liz's landlady said hello then went out to the shops so the sisters were able to talk in private.

'How are things at home?' asked Liz as they sat by the fire drinking tea.

'Same as ever,' she said. 'Nothing ever changes there. What's it like here?'

'I love it.'

'Even though you're living with that old crab?'

Liz frowned. 'She isn't an old crab.'

'Your words not mine,' she said. 'You used to call her that and worse before you moved in here.'

'Maybe I did, but things are different now,' said Liz. 'I've got to know Beryl and she's a really nice woman. She is very good to me and I won't hear a word against her.'

'All right, keep your hair on.'

'So, what have you been doing?' asked Liz.

'Nothing very much. Work, the pictures, a dance now and again.'

'Any new men on the horizon?'

'No. Not a single one, I reckon I'll have to wait for Arthur to come home from the war and settle for him.'

'He might not still be interested.'

'He will be,' she said. 'He's always had a thing for me, the daft bugger.'

'He's older now and been abroad,' said Liz. 'He will have matured.'

'He still fancies me, I bet,' said Dora.

'You are so mean about him.'

'Well, he shouldn't be so soft. Surely he must have known that I wasn't interested in him. I made it clear enough. But he still wanted me.'

'Even when you were both adults?'

'Yeah, I could tell by the way he looked at me.'

'Perhaps he enjoys a challenge. Anyway, has his mum said if he's all right?' asked Liz, who had

133

always got on well with the boy next door. 'Not been injured or anything?'

'Not as far as I know,' said Dora. 'She'd have told us if anything like that had happened.'

'Probably.'

The baby woke up and started to cry. Dora was immediately alarmed. 'That's the trouble with babies. They always ruin everything by crying.'

'How else can they tell us they need something?'

'What does he want?'

'Feeding.'

'Ugh.'

'Don't worry, I'm not breastfeeding. There were problems with that so I can't,' she said. 'Could you hold him while I go and make him a bottle?'

'Ooh no, Liz,' she said, looking terrified. 'I don't know anything about babies.'

'I'm asking you to hold him not adopt him.'

'I might drop him.'

'He's a baby not an overactive adder,' said Liz. 'Look, I need you to hold him for a few minutes, that's all. Honestly, what a fuss about nothing.'

So, Liz had done it again. She had made Dora feel inferior. It didn't matter what terrible fate befell that woman, she would somehow manage to come out on top. 'Give him to me, then,' she said and opened her arms to this frightening bundle.

'Sit down with him,' advised Liz and headed for the kitchen.

So far so good, thought Dora, as she managed to get herself and Charlie into the armchair without dropping him. He stopped crying and looked up at her. Only then did she notice the colour of his eyes. They were the deepest brown she'd ever seen and his hair was fine and dark as coal dust. Something stirred deep within her and she felt tears rush into her eyes. He was the most beautiful thing she'd ever seen.

'Okay, give him to me,' said Liz, re-entering the room. 'Let's give you some food, Charlie boy.'

'Can I give him his bottle?' asked Dora.

'I thought you didn't like babies.'

'I like this one.'

'All right then but take it slowly,' she said, handing her the bottle and a piece of clean cloth.

As Dora held the bottle to Charlie's mouth and felt him taking the milk she felt a sense of deep emotion. She didn't understand it, but knew she wanted more of it. She was so proud to have him as her nephew.

'It's too late now,' said Dora as darkness was falling. 'But next time I come can we take him out in his pram?'

'You're not ashamed of being seen out with him in public then?' asked Liz.

'Of course I'm not,' said Dora. 'That sort of thing is for the older generation.'

'In that case I might even let you wheel the pram.'

'I can't wait,' said Dora.

Liz was under no illusions about her sister. Charlie would probably be a five-minute wonder to her until the next fad came along. But she welcomed her affection for him for however long it lasted.

'Well, so much for a peacetime Christmas,' said

135

Beryl when they heard on the wireless that the Germans had made a breakthrough in the Ardennes.

'Yeah,' agreed Liz. 'They got everyone's hopes up by reducing the blackout and all that talk about an early victory. It's very disappointing.'

It was indeed a gloomy December in London with frost and fog and more shortages than ever, especially coal, so people couldn't even get warm at home. The air raid siren still wailed frequently with the usual accompaniment of explosions from the rocket bombs which droned over the house on a regular basis. Liz now deemed it wise to avoid the Anderson shelter because it was too cold for Charlie so they crawled under the table if the bombs seemed very close.

Into this gloom and misery came a touch of magic for Liz and Beryl. Liz received a parcel from Vic's mother Jane in America. There were romper suits and cardigans for Charlie, all in a bigger size so that they got full use, some soft toys, sweets for the adults and a bottle of perfume each for Liz and Beryl, carefully wrapped in cotton wool to avoid breakages.

'Oh my,' said Liz when she and Beryl opened it together. 'What a wonderful treat.'

'Indeed,' said Beryl. 'And how kind of her to send something for me as well.'

'I've told her how good you are to Charlie and me,' she said. 'So she must have thought, very rightly, that you deserve to be included.'

'I haven't had any perfume for years,' said Beryl.

'Me neither,' said Liz. 'It really is a lovely surprise.'

This package of goodies infused them both with the Christmas spirit and inspired them to make preparations. Beryl had already made a wartime Christmas pudding and cake and Liz queued for everything with renewed energy.

On Christmas morning they had a visitor; Dora came with presents for Charlie from herself and her mother. They toasted the season with sherry and Dora made a huge fuss of Charlie, but she left quite soon because some relatives were coming for Christmas dinner and she had to help her mother with the preparations.

'It was nice of her to come,' Beryl said after she left. 'Shame you won't be seeing your parents over the holiday.'

'I'm banished from Dad's life for ever,' she said. 'And Mum upset me the last time I saw her so I told her to keep away.'

'Maybe you can put that right sometime soon,' suggested Beryl. 'It isn't a good idea to be on bad terms with your parents.'

'It all stems from the fact that they won't accept Charlie,' she said. 'My father not at all and Mum only wants to have anything to do with him behind closed doors. She wouldn't be seen dead with him out on the street.'

'With time that might change,' suggested Beryl. 'When they grow to love him.'

'It's up to them,' said Liz. 'I'm very hurt by their attitude towards their grandson.'

Beryl had a way of showing disapproval without saying a word. It was a look in her eyes and an odd little silence. She was doing it now which meant she thought Liz should try to put things right with her parents. But how could she when they wouldn't accept her lovely boy? She changed the subject to pass over the awkward moment.

This was the first Christmas Liz had ever spent away from the family home and it felt odd. She even felt a pang of homesickness but it disappeared as the day got underway with a tasty Christmas dinner made of a small piece of beef Liz had managed to get hold of and Beryl's Christmas pudding.

Noticing again how good Beryl was with Charlie reminded Liz of her friend's own circumstances.

'Have you ever thought of trying to find your boy, Beryl?' she asked when they were relaxing in the afternoon.

'Oh no, I wouldn't do that,' she said without hesitation. 'The adoption laws say you mustn't anyway. The child can look for a parent when it's grown up, but not the other way around. Naturally I've thought about him a lot and hoped he's having a good life. I would love to know what happened to him and if he's all right.'

'Surely when the child has grown up the law doesn't still apply, does it?'

'I think it does,' she said. 'Maybe one of these days he'll come looking for me.'

'What age is he now?'

'Twenty-seven,' she said. 'He's probably away at the war. And that's something I have worried a lot about, that he might have been killed or injured.'

'Mm. I can see that that's a terrible thought,' said Liz. 'Maybe, after the war you may feel you'd like to know what's happened to him and we could try to find out. And if he's all right you might want him to know the truth about why you gave him up.'

'What about the adoption law?'

'We could get around that by not actually dealing with him,' she said. 'Just find out how life has treated him. Without his knowledge.'

'I'd love to know, but I don't think I should.'

'It just seems so sad that you are a stranger to your own flesh and blood. He's old enough now to know what happened and how hard it was for you. It isn't as if you would be going to steal him away from his adoptive parents.'

'He might not have been told that he was adopted, in which case it could hurt him to know that I gave him up,' she suggested.

'He can't be hurt if you only deal with his parents,' said Liz. 'Anyway, I'm sure he would have been told when he was old enough to cope with it.'

'Yes, I expect you're right.'

'It would be nice if you could let him know that you had no choice but to have him adopted.'

'But I did have a choice, didn't I? I could have done the same as you.'

'I know that, Beryl, but society was even less tolerant back then and you genuinely thought it would be better for him and you were under pressure from your parents,' said Liz. 'Not many women in that position have a fairy godmother like I had, do they?'

'You didn't know I was going to help when you left home and you still went ahead with the pregnancy,' she said.

'We are all victims of our circumstances,' she said. 'Dad told me to get out so I had no choice but to do so. Looking back on it I suppose I might have been able to talk him round if I'd agreed to get rid of the baby.'

'I can't even bear to think about that,' said Beryl.

'Me neither,' she said. 'Lots of women try to make a go of it alone with their baby, but then they can't cope without any support at all and they are forced to put the child into care of some sort. Orphanages up and down the country are overcrowded. I've been very lucky.'

'So have I,' said Beryl. 'Because I have you and Charlie in my life.'

Liz swallowed the lump in her throat. 'Anyway, when this awful war is over and the boys are back home, if you ever feel you'd like to try to find out what happened to your son, I'll help you in any way I can. I've no idea how we would set about it but I'm sure we could find out somehow.'

'Thank you, dear, but I doubt if I'll ever have the courage to do that,' said Beryl sadly.

Chapter Seven

Liz was glad that Beryl had retained her role as cook at the house because she was so good at it.

'This is delicious,' Liz complimented her one day in February 1945 as they ate their Sunday lunch at the table while Charlie slept in his cot upstairs. 'I really don't know how you do it with everything being so short.'

'Making the Yorkshire pudding bigger helps,' she said. 'And plenty of roast potatoes. We don't notice how little meat we are having, then.'

'You certainly know how to make a feast out of very little,' said Liz.

'I suppose we've all learned how to make a little go a long way these past few years and we're not as fussy about our food as we once were because we're all too hungry,' she said. 'Hopefully we won't be punished for much longer. The news seems to suggest that the war might really be on the way out at last.'

'It does seem to be hopeful,' agreed Liz. 'It's nice to have some lighting back on the buses and trains. But I wonder why we can't get rid of the blackout altogether.'

'The government is just being cautious, I expect,' suggested Beryl. 'Just in case that slippery devil Hitler has something else up his sleeve.'

'How lovely to think there will be peace again,' sighed Liz. 'Specially to know that Charlie and all the other little ones will be safe.'

'That's all we want, isn't it, to be safe,' said Beryl, who didn't have a materialistic bone in her body.

'And warm,' said Liz. 'We'll be able to get coal again after the war.'

'And everything else we've been missing,' said Beryl.

'I wonder if it will take long for everything to get back to normal,' said Liz.

'It might take a while for the bomb damage to be put right because there is so much of it, but I should think things like coal and food should be available quite soon,' said Beryl.

'Oh, won't it be heaven?' sighed Liz.

'Absolutely!'

The pleasant interlude was interrupted by loud knocking at the front door. It was Dora in dramatic mood.

'Mum has taken to her bed with her usual winter chest trouble,' she announced.

'Have you had the doctor?' asked Liz.

'Yeah,' she said. 'He's given her some medicine and says she must stay in bed for a week.'

'Oh dear, the poor thing. Still at least we know it isn't serious as she gets it every year and it isn't contagious so you and Dad won't catch it.'

'No problem there,' she said. 'But I need your help, Liz. Can you go around there tomorrow while Dad and I are at work? You don't need to stay all day, but she'll need someone to give her some lunch and make sure she has something to drink.'

'I'm willing to do it, but I'm banned from the house,' she said. 'I did go in when I told Mum I'd had the baby but not for long. I don't know how Dad will feel about my spending time there, especially with Charlie.'

'You'll just have to ignore the ban under the circumstances,' she said. 'Dad won't be there anyway.'

'He'll know I'm going though, or who else will look after Mum?'

'Exactly.'

'Not unless you take time off work,' suggested Liz.

'I can't do that,' she said, horrified at the suggestion. 'I'd lose money. You're at home all day anyway so it will make no difference to your pay packet.'

'Talk about double standards,' said Liz. 'I'm exiled from the family because I've disgraced them but the rules are changed when it suits them.'

'I can see your point, but this is an emergency and you'd be doing it for me, not them. To save me losing money at the factory,' said Dora.

'I don't really have a choice do I?' said Liz.

'Not really,' said Dora breezily. 'Oh and by the way, it's Monday tomorrow so you'll have to do the washing.'

Liz tutted. 'Can't you do it today?'

'On a Sunday!' she said, shocked. 'All that steam and wet washing around on a Sunday? Dad would do his nut. So would Mum, truth be told. You know how everything has to be done on a certain day. Washing on Monday, ironing on Tuesday, so you'll have to do that as well.'

'Don't push your luck, Dora,' said Liz. 'You can do that when you get in from work.'

'Dad wouldn't like the ironing board out of an evening, but we'll see,' she said. 'Now, I have to get back so I'll leave you in peace but not before I've seen that boy of yours.'

'He's asleep,' said Liz.

Dora tapped her ear as a sudden noise from upstairs filled the house. 'It doesn't sound like it to me.'

'You've woken him.'

'From this distance? I don't think so,' she said. 'Can I go and get him?'

'Go on then.'

Contrary to Liz's suspicions, her sister's love affair with Charlie hadn't just been a five-minute wonder. She called to see him quite often at the weekends and sometimes went with Liz to the park or the shops, proudly wheeling his pram. For once in her life she seemed to care for someone else at least as much as she cared for herself.

'I'm sure you won't have a mental breakdown if I don't do our washing until Tuesday, will you, Beryl?' Liz asked. 'I won't have time to do it tomorrow as I have to do Mum's.'

Beryl grinned in reply.

'Where's the baby?' asked Violet when Liz appeared at her bedside the next morning.

'Downstairs in his pram,' she said. 'Where I go, he goes. It seems we're only banned from here until you need something. I wouldn't be within a mile of the place if you weren't ill.'

'All right, Liz. I only asked out of interest so there's no need to go on about it,' she said, sounding poorly, her voice almost lost. 'Not when I'm feeling so rotten.'

'Sorry, Mum.'

It's all right but you need to calm down and not take offence every time your boy is mentioned.'

'I need to get cracking as there's a lot to do,' she said quickly. She knew she was being overly sensitive, but she was hurt that her son was treated like an outcast by her parents. 'So, is there anything you want before I get started on the washing?'

'A cup of tea would be nice.'

'Coming up,' she said.

When her mother was settled, Liz got busy with the scrubbing board and Sunlight soap then got the washing into the copper for boiling. By the time she had rinsed and mangled it it was almost time to get her mother some lunch, but the weather was breezy so she took the washing and the wakeful baby in his pram into the back garden and started to peg it out, sheets first. She had just about finished when someone called out to her.

'Hello, Liz. Haven't seen you for ages. How are you, dear?' Looking round she saw their neighbour, Mrs Dobbs, peering at her from over the fence. 'And how is the little one?'

'We're both fine, thanks.' Liz lifted Charlie out of the pram, wrapped a blanket around him and carried him over to the fence.

'Oh what a lovely little chap,' she cooed. 'All that lovely dark hair.'

'Yes, he takes after his father,' she said, pushing some of the escaping hair back under his hat. 'He has the same dark hair and eyes.'

'Is his dad away at the war?'

'No ... he was killed in an air raid.'

'Oh, I'm so sorry to hear that.'

'Yes, it was a terrible blow.'

'So, how are you managing?' she asked, seeming genuinely concerned.

'I'm getting along all right, thanks,' she said. 'You just have to carry on, don't you?'

'Indeed.' She cleared her throat. 'We don't see you around here very often, but I knew you'd had

145

a baby. Some of the neighbours have seen you out with the pram in the town.'

That wouldn't please Mum, Liz thought, noticing that Mrs Dobbs had the courtesy not to mention the fiction that Mum had put out about her daughter's circumstances.

'I live with a friend on the other side of town near the park,' she explained. 'I'm only here today to help out because Mum is ill.'

'Oh, I'm sorry to hear that,' she said. 'What's the matter with her?'

'Some sort of bronchial trouble,' she said. 'She always has problems with her chest in the winter. Nothing serious, but she's had to take to her bed.'

'If there's anything I can do, please let me know,' she said. 'But your mother doesn't seem to like neighbours calling in, so I'm always very careful.'

'Thanks for offering, though.'

'That's all right, dear,' she said.

For the first time Liz saw Mrs Dobbs as a person. She had always just been Arthur's mum, a shadowy figure who appeared at the door to call him in every so often, like all the other mums, when they were children. Now she could see a woman of middle years with greying brown hair, warm dark eyes and a friendly smile. Liz was overcome with a need to talk to someone so out it all came.

'Charlie's dad was an American soldier,' she said.

'I did see an American going in and out of your house,' she said. 'It was a while back, though.'

'Yes, Vic was killed by a bomb in London on his way over to see me before I even knew I was pregnant. He died without knowing he was going to be a dad,' she explained. 'This means that I am one of those most shameful of things – an unmarried mother.'

Mrs Dobbs nodded politely and managed not to look too shocked.

'Mum and Dad were furious with me, especially my father, so I had to leave home,' she explained. 'That's why I don't live here any more.'

'Oh dear, that must have been hard for you,' she said. 'You need your folks at a time like that.'

'Yes, you really do, but it worked out well for me in the end because a friend, an older lady from where I worked, took me in and is very good to me. I'm really happy living there.'

'Thank goodness you have someone looking out for you,' said the older woman. 'I think your parents are very lucky to have a grandchild. I'd love one of those.'

'You'll have to tell Arthur to get cracking when he comes home from the war, then,' she laughed, remembering that the Dobbses had only one child.

Mrs Dobbs chuckled then seemed to lapse into thought. 'It was lovely around here when you were all little,' she said. 'You and Dora and Arthur all playing out in the street with the other kids. They were happy days.'

'Yeah, I loved those times too,' sighed Liz, then moved on swiftly before they both drowned in nostalgia. 'How are the family?'

'Mr Dobbs and I are fine but we have to hope

147

for the best when it comes to Arthur. There isn't much information in his letters and they are quite few and far between.'

'With a bit of luck you'll have him home soon,' said Liz with an air of optimism.

'Yeah, all the signs are good for an end to this terrible war, at long last.'

'I wonder if Arthur will still have his crush on my sister Dora,' said Liz lightly.

'I should think he will have grown out of that years ago,' said Mrs Dobbs, obviously aware of how horrid Dora had been to him and not happy about it.

'Yes, I'm sure he has,' said Liz, regretting her comment which had seemed to upset the other woman. 'He'll have much more important things on his mind.'

'Indeed. I dread to think what he might be going through.'

'Fingers crossed you'll have him home soon.'

'I hope so.'

'Anyway, I'd better get on. Mum will be wanting some lunch,' said Liz.

'Lovely to see you, dear, and don't be a stranger,' said Mrs Dobbs. 'Call in for a cuppa any time you fancy it. I'd love to see you and your little boy. Tell your mum I'm here if she needs me.'

'Thank you, Mrs Dobbs,' she said, feeling much warmed by the conversation but knowing that her mother would sooner die than turn to a neighbour for help.

'I've told Mrs Dobbs next door the truth about my situation,' Liz told her mother a few days later when she was feeling better.

'Oh no, why did you do that?' groaned Violet.

'Because I am not ashamed of Charlie or the situation I'm in,' she told her. 'I hate hiding behind a pack of lies. I shouldn't have to anyway.'

'I won't be able to hold my head up in this street now,' Violet said miserably.

'Of course you will,' said Liz. 'Be proud of us. Charlie and me. Show everyone how happy you are to have us.'

'I am, of course, you must know that,' she said.

'Then be brave and show it.'

'Your father wouldn't like it.'

'Then let him lump it.'

'You know what he's like.'

'I assume he knows I've been here all week with Charlie,' she said. 'And he's aware that it's me who's been preparing his dinner every single day.'

'Of course.'

'So I can be here when it benefits him but I'm not welcome any other time,' said Liz. 'The man is a fraud as well as a bully.'

'Don't speak like that about your father,' objected Violet. 'Have some respect.'

'Sorry, Mum, but it's the truth.'

'Look, I know that your dad is far from perfect,' said Violet. 'But I married him for better or worse so I accept his bad points. Anyway, we didn't invent the rules by which we live.'

'No, but you don't have to be so slavishly dedicated to them,' said Liz. 'All right, so I did wrong, but surely Charlie and me don't have to be punished for ever more.'

'I'm not punishing you.'

'Of course you are,' she said. 'You won't accept my son and that hurts.'

'I came to see him at Beryl's. You were the one who stopped that.'

'Because you were ashamed to be seen out with him.'

'I'm sorry,' she said miserably.

'That doesn't really help, Mum. But anyway, you're back on your feet now so I won't be round again.'

'Oh,' she said, looking dejected.

'I am not going to come around here on the quiet, as though I'm not fit to walk through the door,' she said. 'I'll do it when you're ill but not when you don't need me.'

'I am your mother.'

'Yes, and if you are ill and need me I will do my duty and come and look after you. But only then will you see me,' she said. 'When you are ready to open your heart to my son, you will be welcome in my life. Until then please stay away.'

'You are a hard woman.'

'No, Mum, I'm not, not normally, anyway. I am just a devoted mother and I want my son recognised for what he is, a beautiful human being, not treated with shame.' She got up, swallowing a lump in her throat. 'Cheerio, Mum.'

'Bye, Liz,' said Violet sadly.

'Do you think if it hadn't happened to you, Beryl, you would have the same attitude as my parents towards children born out of wedlock?' Liz asked that evening after dinner when they were sitting in the living room relaxing.

'I have no way of knowing, but I do hope not,' she said, stroking the cat who was on her lap. 'I know I'm a bit of an old biddy and a stickler for things being done properly, but I hope I recognise that we are all only human and likely to make mistakes. Your mother is just responding to the rules of so-called decent society.'

'She's very influenced by my father,' said Liz. 'I'd even go as far as to say that she's frightened of him.'

'He doesn't hit her, does he?'

'I've never seen him do that, but he's very dominating and talks down to her.'

'And she lets him get away with it?'

'Mm. I'm afraid so.'

'I wouldn't have lasted long in a marriage,' she said. 'I'm far too bossy and men like to rule the roost, or that's what it seems like to me.'

'Not all of them, but my father certainly does.'

'There's one thing I would say, Liz, but you can tell me to mind my own business and I will shut up.'

'Go on,' she urged.

'I'm not sure if it's a good idea to ban your mother from Charlie's life altogether until she is no longer embarrassed by the situation,' she said. 'Especially as his other granny is so far away. I mean I'm like a grandma to him but it would be nice to have your mother in his life too. I think she might be more likely to get over her prejudice if she gets to know him better. Especially as he grows up a bit and gets more knowing.'

'It's so painful for me when she won't walk down the street with him.'

'It's perfectly understandable that you would feel that way,' said Beryl. 'But I think she might get over that as she gets to know him and grows to love him. She can't do either of those things if she never sees him. Anyway, it's only my opinion. I might be completely wrong.'

'I will give it some serious thought.'

Something on the wireless caught Beryl's attention and they stopped talking to listen.

Both women were overjoyed to hear that the blackout was to be lifted from dusk on Monday.

'At last,' said the older woman with a beaming smile. 'It's official.'

'Yippee,' whooped Liz, doing a little jig. 'The end of the war is coming at last.'

'It certainly seems that way,' agreed Beryl.

The joy of this news and Beryl's views on Liz's family problems finally put things into perspective for Liz. Her mother would never learn to love Charlie and lose her prejudice if she didn't see him. So Liz needed to give her a chance by welcoming her into his life. They would take it one step at a time from there.

It was Charlie's first birthday and he was beginning to take a few faltering steps.

'He did six that time,' said Violet in delight. 'Oh, you are a clever little boy.'

'He's doing really well,' added Beryl.

'You are the cleverest boy in London,' said Dora sweeping him up into her arms and kissing him.

He was too little to have a proper birthday party so Liz had invited her mother, sister and Marg to tea. Beryl had made him a cake and they were having a small celebration.

It was October and things had gone down to earth with a bump after the magnificent victory celebrations which Liz knew she would never forget. There had been a communal outpouring of joy and love on VE Day with street parties and bonfires and festivities everywhere. Being at peace after nearly six years of war was an indescribable joy.

Of course, there was sadness too for the missing many who hadn't survived, and Vic had been on Liz's mind throughout the celebrations. But to no longer feel under threat of bombs was sweet indeed. The rationing and shortages hadn't eased, which was a disappointment, but everyone hoped it wouldn't be long before they saw the end of ration books.

But now Charlie was thrilling them all by waddling across the floor before collapsing onto his bottom and letting out a huge giggle.

'Oh, he's so gorgeous,' said Marg, enraptured.

'Making you broody is he, Marg?' said Violet lightly.

'Not half,' said Marg. 'I really can't wait to have a kiddie of my own.'

'Any news of when Joe will be home?' asked Liz.

'No. He hasn't been told,' she said. 'He'll just turn up one day soon, I hope.'

'It must be a huge task getting all the troops back home,' said Beryl.

'The sooner he comes home, the sooner we'll lose you to America, though,' said Liz, gloomy at the thought.

'Yeah, there is that,' agreed Marg. 'I'm sad to be leaving you all and my family, but I'm very excited about going.'

There was a murmur of understanding.

'I feel a little bit connected to the States myself because of Vic's mother,' said Liz. 'She sent one of her lovely parcels for Charlie's birthday. A lovely teddy bear and other bits and pieces.'

'That's good of her,' said Violet.

'Very,' agreed Liz. 'I shall make sure Charlie knows all about his American relatives as he grows up.'

The party continued and as they helped Charlie blow out his candle on the cake, Liz thought her heart would break with missing Vic. He would have so enjoyed all of this.

With what Liz earned from Beryl for the housekeeping she was able to manage financially, but it was difficult to find the money for extras and clothes for Charlie because he grew out of everything so fast. She knew that Beryl would give her more if she asked for it but she already gave her a fair wage and Liz didn't want to impose on her generosity. This shortfall was a constant worry, though, especially with Christmas on the horizon when some extra cash would be especially welcome.

So, when she saw an advertisement in the local paper, her interest was aroused. But before she could do anything about it she had to speak to certain people...

'A job at the ice rink,' said Beryl in surprise.

'Just two nights a week and Saturday afternoons.'

'But Liz, dear, you have enough to do looking
after the housekeeping and little Charlie.'

'I need to earn some money,' said Liz.

'But I can...'

'You are more than generous already,' said Liz,
having anticipated the other woman's suggestion.
'And I manage well enough most of the time. It's
just the extras I find difficult. I thought if I had a
part-time job it would ease the problem. It's only
a few hours a week.'

'So long as you're sure it won't be too much,'
she said.

'Absolutely certain,' Liz assured her. 'I'm
young and strong. It will do me good.'

'You'll need me to look after Charlie and of
course I will with pleasure.'

'Only for part of the time,' said Liz. 'I'll have
him bathed and in bed when you get home in the
evenings if you wouldn't mind taking charge
then, though all being well you won't have to do
anything because he'll be asleep. I thought I'd ask
Mum and Dora if they could have him Saturday
afternoons to give you a break. Dad won't have
him in the house, but I don't think he's going to
get much choice with the two of them on to him.
They'll probably take Charlie for a walk in the
pram for part of the time anyway. So that will get
him out of Dad's way.'

'I'd be happy to fit in with whatever you decide,'
said Beryl. 'Looking after Charlie is a pleasure for
me, not a chore. I'll enjoy every moment.'

'He knows all three of you so he should be

155

happy enough without me for a few hours.'

'You get it arranged and let me know,' she said.

'I haven't even applied for the job yet,' she said. 'I might not get it.'

'Fingers crossed then,' said Beryl.

The unsociable hours meant that there wasn't much competition for the job so Liz started work the following week, having put her childcare plan into place. She was in charge of skate hire and there was a very long queue of eager punters waiting when she first went on duty.

It entailed finding the required size and issuing a ticket which had been paid for with the entrance fee at the pay desk. The punter's shoes were taken and put into a slot with the ticket all in numerical order. A simple enough task but, because she was new, it was taking a while and the people in the queue, who were all young, were sighing and tutting impatiently.

She loved the atmosphere, though, and memories of happier times here with Vic overcame her. It didn't upset her now as it had at first. In fact, she rather enjoyed the bittersweet moments of nostalgia. The job wasn't too challenging and by the end of the shift she felt confident about coming again tomorrow.

Beryl had loaned Liz her bike so she had cycled here which saved time and the bus fare. She rode home imbued with a sense of achievement. It was a simple job but she was earning money and there was something extremely satisfying about that. But now she couldn't wait to get home to see her darling boy, who should be fast asleep.

Charlie was indeed asleep, but Beryl was standing beside the cot looking at him. He hadn't stirred all evening which was a pity because she would have enjoyed soothing him. Being so close to this dear little boy had been a constant reminder of her own child and she ached with wondering about him.

She thought about Liz's suggestion that they try to find out what had happened to him and wondered if it would be possible. She was fairly certain that her family knew where he had been placed; however, it was all a very long time ago. Her parents were no longer around but there was an aunt who might know something.

But no. It wouldn't be right. People could get hurt so she mustn't be tempted just to satisfy her own curiosity. Except that it wasn't just curiosity. It was deep maternal love. She needed to know if he was all right. But she mustn't allow herself to be tempted. It wouldn't be fair.

She heard the back door open. 'I'm home,' Liz called up and Beryl hurried down the stairs to meet her with Dolly the cat at her heels.

'What's all this?' demanded George when Dora wheeled the pushchair containing Charlie into the hall, having collected him from Beryl's, just as her father was on his way downstairs.

'It's Charlie, your grandson,' said Dora. 'Mum and I are looking after him this afternoon.'

'Isn't he lovely, George,' said Violet, undoing the buggy straps to get him out.

'I don't want him here,' said George.

'That's just too bad,' said Dora. 'Because he'll

157

be here for the next couple of hours.'

'It's my...'

'Yeah,' interrupted Dora. 'I think we all know that it's your name on the rent book and what you say goes but I also pay rent which I reckon entitles me to have visitors, especially a relative.'

'But...'

'It's happening, Dad, so what are you going to do, call the police?' said Dora.

'Violet,' he began, giving his wife a warning stare. 'Tell her he can't stay.'

His wife stared at him fearfully.

'Mum, tell him you want your grandson here.'

There was a silence and Dora held her breath.

'He has our blood, George, and he's such a dear little chap. He'll be staying here until his mother collects him later,' she said firmly, though her voice was shaking. 'Why don't you go to the allotment if you'd rather not be around while he's in the house?'

'I'm not being turned out of my own house,' he said. 'There isn't much to do at this time of year anyway.'

'Sit in the shed and read the paper, then,' she suggested. 'Like you always do over the allotments when it's raining and you come home complaining about working in the rain.'

'That's a pack of lies.'

'Well, I know you like it in that shed of yours and there's bound to be someone to talk to up there. Anyway, whatever you decide to do, Charlie is staying.'

'Doesn't look like I have any choice,' he grumbled. 'There won't be any peace here.'

'Plenty of time for peace when we're six foot under,' she said and Dora giggled.

During her shift on Saturday afternoon, when it was quiet at the hire desk, Liz was asked to spend some time on the rink with a nervous beginner. At her interview, she had been asked if she could hold her own on the ice at a basic level if it was ever needed.

'Hold on to me,' Liz said to the girl, who looked about fourteen. 'You can grab the bar as well if you'll be more comfortable, just to start off.'

They did a few full turns around the rink and the youngster grew in confidence sufficiently to let go of the rail. By the time Liz had to go back the desk her protégé was doing spurts on her own, interspersed with times when she held on. It had certainly been a pleasant experience for Liz and she hoped she was asked to do the same thing again sometime.

'Hello, Mrs Dobbs,' said Liz when she met her parents' neighbour in the street on her way to collect Charlie.

'Hello, dear,' she said. 'Where's the nipper?'

'I'm just going to collect him,' she said and went on to explain about her part-time job.

'Good for you,' she said.

They chatted for a few minutes then the older woman said, 'We've had a letter from Arthur at last. He doesn't think he'll be back in time for Christmas, but he's hoping it won't be too long after that. It's a massive job for the military, getting them all home and he's in the Far East.

159

So we just have to be patient.'

'I bet you're looking forward to seeing him.'

'Not half,' she said. 'I'm already putting stuff away for his welcome home party. You know, the odd tin of fruit and stuff like that.'

'You'll have the best do in the street, I bet,' smiled Liz. 'There will be plenty of parties as the boys arrive home.'

'I don't know if ours will be the best but we shall definitely aim to enjoy ourselves,' she said. 'You're welcome to join us. You and the family.'

'Thank you. I'll keep it in mind,' she said and they both went on their way.

Her mother was waiting for Liz at the door with Charlie already in his outdoor clothes and in the pushchair, indicating that she didn't want her to go inside. There was something so demoralising about this that a pain nagged in the pit of Liz's stomach. Still, Mum had had Charlie there all afternoon and that must have taken courage, Dad feeling as he did.

'He's been as good as gold,' her mother informed her.

'A little angel,' added Dora.

Liz thanked them both and Dora went to the gate with her.

'Don't mind Mum,' she said. 'She stood up to Dad about Charlie being here.'

'Did he make a fuss, then?'

'You know what he's like,' she said. 'Mum sent him off to the allotment but he's back now and I don't think she wants to push her luck any more than she has already. He's such a bully. I reckon she's used up her quota of courage for today.'

'Thanks for having Charlie,' said Liz.

'Pleasure,' she said and Liz hurried on her way, pushing the buggy.

Although knowing she wasn't welcome in her parents' house wasn't pleasant, Liz was able to take it in her stride. However, knowing that her father didn't want her son there was crippling. She wondered if she'd done the right thing in asking Dora and Mum to look after him and had really only done so for Charlie to spend time with his relatives. She would speak to them about it before next time because she wasn't prepared to have her son looked down on by anyone. Her pleasure in the job was wiped out by the hurt of feeling like an outcast within her own family.

She turned the corner into Beryl's street and as she approached the house she could see Beryl at the window waiting for them. By the time they got to the gate she was hurrying down the path to meet them with Dolly at her feet.

'Welcome home,' she said, beaming.

'Puss,' uttered Charlie excitedly referring to the cat whom he adored.

'How did you get on, Liz?' asked Beryl, taking Charlie out of the pushchair and smothering him with kisses before putting him down so he could stroke the cat, which made a hasty departure on account of the little boy's overly enthusiastic embraces.

'All right, thanks,' said Liz. 'It isn't exactly a dream job but it was pleasant enough.'

'Oh good, I'm glad it went well,' she said, taking Charlie's coat off. 'Supper is ready when you are.'

All the hurt from the family house was washed away by the warmth of Beryl's welcome. This was their home now, hers and Charlie's. This was where they belonged.

Chapter Eight

One evening in the early spring of 1946, Mick Watson headed along Fulham High Street on his way to the pub. After nearly five years abroad in the army he was looking forward to a good old English pint of beer. He'd heard that it was watered down because of the shortage of ingredients, but after such a long time away he was sure it would taste just fine.

Easy on the eye with strong features and bright blue eyes, he had an attractive air of confidence about him. Still in army uniform until after official demob, he was an imposing figure with his upright stance and tough demeanour. Tonight, he was hoping to see some of his mates but wasn't sure which of them were home as the return of the troops from abroad was proving to be such a slow process.

Disappointingly, there was no one he knew in the pub but the bar staff and punters greeted him in a friendly manner because servicemen were popular. In the absence of company, he took his beer over to a table in the corner, deciding to use

162

this spare time to assess his current situation and make plans for the future.

His first priority after demob was to get a job, but he had a decent sum in back pay so there was no need to panic just yet. The other urgent matter was a place to live. He was staying with his parents at the moment but the sooner he was out of there the better. He was twenty-seven and far too old to still be living under the parental roof, especially as he wasn't particularly comfortable around his folks, but it might take a while to find somewhere else. He'd heard that the housing shortage in London was even worse than usual because of the large amount of property destroyed in the bombing.

His parents were good people and had done their very best for him, in that they had given him a stable home, made sure he was well fed, clothed and had a decent basic education, but they had never shown much in the way of affection when he was growing up. His mum had been distant and his dad had been handy with his fists, believing that boys needed a firm hand to keep them out of trouble.

So it had come as no surprise to Mick to find out that he wasn't actually theirs. He'd been about thirteen when they had told him that they weren't his birth parents, that they had adopted him as a baby. He'd wondered why they would want to adopt a child if they weren't prepared to show it much in the way of love. But he supposed it was just their nature and he was grateful to them for looking after him and keeping him out of an orphanage.

Any attempt on his part to find out more about his origins had failed completely because they both clammed up, muttering something about adoption being a very secretive subject and that they hadn't been allowed to know anything about the circumstances of his not being able to stay with his birth mother. He didn't believe a word of it, but what difference would his knowing make? He had been given away and was better off not knowing the details.

Anyway, their rather reserved style of parenting couldn't have been too bad because he had grown up to be strong and self-reliant. He looked out for himself and didn't allow anyone to take advantage. Some people might say he was hard and conceited but that was just a survival technique.

Well, that was enough retrospection. Now was the beginning of the rest of his life so the job and accommodation were his priorities and once those two issues were settled he needed to find a girlfriend to complete the picture. Oh yes, a woman in his life was essential. He might even consider the idea of marriage if he could find the right woman. It was time he settled down.

But finding a job was his first task. He didn't know what the employment market was like. It might be a bit sluggish until things got back to normal after the war. But he had a good trade; he was an electrician, something else he had to thank his parents for. They had encouraged him to do an apprenticeship. Well, pushed him into it really, because they thought he needed a good solid trade behind him. It was as though they had felt it their duty to equip him with everything he needed in life, which he supposed was the job of parents.

A voice interrupted his thoughts. 'Mick, my old mate, you made it back in one piece then.'

'Terry,' he said, getting up and shaking the hand of a long-term friend. 'Good to see you after all this time, mate. I was beginning to think I was the only one who'd made it back.' Mick moved towards the bar. 'What are you having?'

'A pint of bitter, please.'

'Coming up.'

This was more like it, thought Mick. An English pub and a mate to drink with. His plans for the future could wait.

It was Sunday afternoon; the sun was shining and the park was sprinkled with colour from the daffodils and tulips as Liz and Marg walked with Charlie.

'It's a shame there are no swings like there were when we were kids,' said Liz. 'I'd love to give Charlie a go on a swing or roundabout.'

'It would be nice,' agreed Marg. 'Perhaps it won't be too long before we get them back.'

'Park equipment certainly won't be a top priority on the council's list of things to do,' said Liz. 'They need to concentrate on housing and repairs to property. The best part of a year has passed since the war ended and there's not a sign of anything being done. The bomb sites are untouched and the rationing is worse than ever.'

'Oh Liz, you sound about sixty-five,' giggled Marg.

Liz smiled. 'Must be because I'm a mum that I care about such things now. Not like the old days when neither of us had any responsibilities,' said Liz. 'Anyway, none of it need worry you because you're not going to be around here for much longer and there will be plenty of everything where you're going.'

'I'm not that selfish, Liz,' said Marg. 'Of course I'll still care about you all back here.'

'I know that but you won't have rationing and you will have other things on your mind.' Liz rolled the ball across the grass to Charlie and he squealed with delight. He was steady on his feet now and a joy to have around. 'Have you any idea when you'll be going?'

'I'm still not sure,' she replied. 'I've done everything I was asked to do. I've studied all the necessary documents, completed the paperwork and had the interviews so it shouldn't be long. But the Americans check you out good and proper before they accept you and it all takes time.'

'You mentioned that you won't be travelling to the States with Joe.'

'No, I won't, which is a pity,' she said. 'I'll be on the boat with the other GI brides. There are a lot of us apparently. Joe will go back with the army.'

'Where do you sail from?'

'Southampton,' she replied. 'But I'll be staying in a transit camp on Salisbury Plain before we get on the boat.'

'Excited?'

'You bet,' she said. 'But I really hope I don't get there before Joe. It could happen apparently because there are so many of us travelling to America. They can't guarantee that we'll all arrive together.'

'So, you might be staying with his people without him for a while then?'

'Could be.'

'I'm sure they'll make you feel welcome.'

'I've no doubt that they will,' she said. 'But naturally I want to be with Joe, especially as I don't know them.'

'It won't be for long if it does happen.'

'That's true. We are planning on getting our own place as soon as we can so it's all good. You never know, he might even arrive before me.'

'Fingers crossed that he's there to greet you.'

'I hope so, but I'm not banking on it,' she said. 'I'll love it however it works out.'

Liz was feeling extremely sad to be losing her friend of so many years, but thought it best not to emphasise it because Marg was probably feeling emotional even though she was so excited about her adventure. It was a huge thing she was about to do and it was a one-way ticket. 'Of course, it will be good. It's America, the land of opportunity, how can it not be?'

'Exactly.'

They concentrated all their attention on Charlie, who was very easy to amuse at this age. A few funny faces and a game with the ball and he was all smiles.

'Oh, and by the way,' began Marg. 'What's the matter with your landlady?'

'Nothing as far as I know,' she said. 'Why?'

'She's being a real pain at work. She's back to her old ways of being a misery guts,' she said. 'She was all sweetness and light for a while after you moved in with her but she isn't now. She barks at anyone for the slightest thing. I thought perhaps something was wrong at home.'

'Not that I know of,' said Liz worriedly.

'Perhaps she's having her menopause,' suggested Marg lightly. 'I think that goes on for years so God help us all.'

'You'll be leaving before long anyway,' Liz reminded her.

'And it can't come a moment too soon when Miss Banks is in one of her moods.'

Liz felt uneasy. She was very happy living with Beryl and the last thing she wanted was to leave. But maybe the older woman was finding it too much having her and Charlie there. Small boys made a lot of noise and wreaked havoc on the smooth running of a household. Beryl had always struck her as a woman who wouldn't suffer in silence, but she was also very kind and would hate to have to tell Liz to leave. Perhaps Liz had been too wrapped up in her own affairs and hadn't noticed that Beryl was unhappy. She'd keep a closer eye on things in future and if she spotted anything amiss she would ask her outright. The last thing she wanted was to upset the woman who had been so good to her.

Violet and Dora still looked after Charlie on Saturday afternoons while Liz was at work. Nothing had changed as far as her father was concerned. He still hadn't warmed to Charlie and Liz continued to be hurt by it. But her mother and sister enjoyed having the little boy and Dad apparently made himself scarce so Liz allowed the arrangement to continue.

Liz and Dora had been getting along better since Charlie had been around so Liz had almost forgotten how hateful her sister could be at times. Until one Saturday in spring when her true colours re-emerged.

'How is it that you always manage to come up smelling of roses no matter what?' said Dora at the front gate when Liz had been to collect Charlie and was about to leave.

'What do you mean?'

'Well, you get yourself in the family way, the worst disgrace a girl can have, and here you are with a lovely kid and a good life while I am still stuck at home with Mum and Dad and no boyfriend.'

'I don't know what you can do about the lack of a boyfriend but why don't you leave home if you hate it here that much?' Liz enquired.

'How could I afford to, even if I could find somewhere to live?' she asked grumpily. 'We don't all have the knack of crawling around the boss and getting our feet under her table and living for next to nothing.'

'That isn't what happened at all, Dora, and you damned well know it.'

'I know nothing of the kind. All I do know is that you commit the worst sin a girl can and yet here you are living the life of Riley,' she blasted. 'You only work a few hours a week and you have a cushy time.'

'I work for much more than a few hours,' she said. 'I look after the housekeeping lock, stock and barrel. It's no small job.'

'With no one breathing down your neck, and a

nice little number down at the ice rink,' she said. 'Here am I stuck behind a shop counter all day since my factory job finished when the men came home, slicing bloody bacon and fiddling about with ration books. Admittedly it isn't as exhausting as the war work was but it's still tiring and as boring as hell.'

'Why don't you change your job if you're that unhappy?' suggested Liz.

'Because that wouldn't help,' she said, her voice rising along with her temper. 'Don't you understand what I am trying to tell you? Nothing good ever happens to me while you always fall on your feet. It's the way things are; the way it's always been.'

'I haven't noticed it,' said Liz. 'You've always been the favoured child at home.'

'I never wanted to be,' she said. 'I feel stifled by it. Can't bear the way Mum and Dad crawl around me.'

'I'm sure you can cope with it,' said Liz. 'I've seen how horrid you can be to them.'

'Well, they get on my nerves.'

'You could try to be kinder,' said Liz.

'Easy for you to say,' said Dora. 'You're out of it.'

'I was thrown out with nowhere to go, if you remember,' said Liz. 'And that wasn't nice.'

'You landed well and truly on your feet though, didn't you?' said Dora. 'You always do.'

'I don't know where you get that idea from. Anyway, you make your own luck, Dora,' said Liz. 'If you were nicer to people, they'd be nice back.'

'Oh yeah, so you're the expert on human behaviour now, are you?' she snarled.

'Not at all,' she said. 'It's just common sense. I make an effort with Beryl and we get on well. If I took her kindness for granted I'd soon be out of there.'

Hearing raised voices, Charlie, who was in his pushchair, started to cry. Liz soothed him then said to her sister, 'I need to get him home now. If you're feeling so hard done by that you'd rather not help me out by looking after him on a Saturday afternoon, I'm sure Beryl will be happy to step in.'

Dora looked stricken. 'You know Mum and I love having him. Don't take that away from us.'

'You're the one who's being nasty,' said Liz. 'I don't want you taking out your resentment of me on him.'

'You know I would never do anything to hurt him,' she said with genuine feeling. 'You know how much I love him.'

In her heart Liz did know that. She was also beginning to think that Dora's love for Charlie came from a lack of it in her own life. She needed a child of her own to love but as she couldn't hang on to any boyfriend for more than a few dates the likelihood of that happening was remote.

'See you, then,' said Liz and went on her way.

Liz was so immersed in her own thoughts that she almost collided with a soldier coming the other way.

'Liz!' the man said with a wide grin. 'I haven't seen you for years.'

He had changed so much it was a few seconds before she realised who he was. 'Arthur,' she said eventually. 'You're back. It's so good to see you after all this time.'

'You too,' he said with a wide grin. 'And yes, it's been a hell of a long time. I sometimes thought I'd never get home.'

He had changed quite dramatically in appearance. The skinny lad he had once been was now a well-set-up man with broader shoulders than she remembered and a firm jawline, his face matured. He still had a broad smile and warm brown eyes but his appearance was now enhanced by a tan.

He looked at Charlie. 'So, you're married now, then?' he assumed.

She made a face. 'Not exactly,' she said. 'Ask your mother when you get home. She'll fill you in.'

'Oh, okay,' he said, looking puzzled.

'When did you get back?'

'Yesterday,' he said. 'So, I haven't had time to see anyone outside of the family yet.'

'You'll soon catch up.'

'How is Dora?' he asked. 'Married I expect.'

'No, she's still single,' she said, relieved to note that he didn't seem particularly pleased to know that she was still available. She knew just how cruel her sister could be to him, even this more attractive version.

'Mum and Dad are having a welcome home party for me next Saturday,' he told her. 'We'd love it if you fancied dropping in. You and Dora and your mum and dad too, if they'd like to come.'

She looked towards Charlie. 'Not so easy for me now because of him,' she said.

'Well, if you can arrange it we'd love to see you,' he said casually. 'About eight o'clock. All welcome.'

'I'll do my very best,' she said. 'It really is good to see you again.'

'And you,' he smiled and they went their different ways.

What a lovely bloke he was, she thought as she headed home. The party might be fun but she wasn't even going to mention it to Beryl because she would immediately offer to babysit Charlie and she did more than enough for Liz already. Any sort of a social life was just a distant memory for Liz anyway so she certainly wouldn't miss one party.

Liz had underestimated Dora's determination to get her own way. The following Saturday after her shift at the ice rink when she went to collect Charlie, her sister said brightly, 'It's all arranged. Beryl is going to look after Charlie while you and I go to Arthur's welcome home party tonight. I met him in the street and he told me about it so I paid Beryl a visit.'

'How dare you go behind my back,' she said, infuriated. 'I didn't want Beryl bothered with it.'

'She wants to do it,' said Dora. 'Let's face it, she doesn't have anything else to do.'

'How do you know that?' demanded Liz.

'Because she's a dried-up old spinster with an empty life apart from you and Charlie.'

How little she knew about Beryl, thought Liz,

but she wasn't about to enlighten her. 'You've got a damned cheek,' she said. 'And I'm going straight home to tell her that I won't be going to the party.'

'You've got to come.'

'Why?'

'Because I want to go and I'd rather not go on my own.'

'Selfish as usual,' said Liz. 'I might have known.'

'Don't be such a misery,' said Dora. 'There might be some decent blokes there. Arthur's mates.'

'You are unbelievable and I am not coming,' said Liz and stormed off.

But she had a battle on her hands with Beryl too.

'A night out is just what you need,' she said, seeming almost excited on Liz's behalf. 'You're young; you need that sort of stimulation. I shall look forward to hearing all about it and Charlie will be fine with me.'

'I really don't fancy it, Beryl.'

'You'll enjoy it when you get there,' said the other woman determinedly.

And so it was that Liz found herself dancing to 'Sentimental Journey' in the Dobbses' front room, which was decked with bunting, the carpet rolled up.

'So, you're Arthur's neighbour?' said the sailor she was dancing with.

'Not now, but I used to be,' she said. 'I grew up in the house next door.'

'Lucky Arthur.'

'We did have a lot of fun when we were growing up,' she said. 'But my sister is the one he is interested in.'

'He must be mad.'

She laughed. She didn't particularly fancy the sailor, but it was nice to be on the receiving end of a compliment. Just then Arthur's father called for silence and they all drank a toast to Arthur and officially welcomed him home. Throughout the entire evening, Dora was a glutton with the drinks on offer and flirted outrageously with one of Arthur's mates.

'Calm down, Dora,' Liz warned her. 'You're making a show of yourself.'

'Just making sure Arthur gets the message that I'm not interested in him.'

'I think he's been well aware of that for years,' she said. 'So there's no longer any need to rub it in. We're not children anymore. Arthur is a man of the world now. Don't spoil his party by getting drunk.'

'Mind your own business,' she said and flounced off to dance with a soldier.

Liz didn't want to watch any more of Dora's theatrics, but it seemed rude to go home so early so she went out into the back garden for some air, away from the fog of cigarette smoke filling the house.

'It is a bit stifling in there, isn't it,' said Arthur appearing beside her.

'I just fancied a breath of air.'

'Me too,' he said.

'So, what's next for you then, Arthur?' she asked, turning towards him.

'Demob leave then back to work.'

'Did your old firm keep your job open for you?'

175

'Yes they did so I'll be back to a nine-to-five life.'

She smiled. 'You were the only one of us kids in the street to go to grammar school. You trained to be an accountant, as I remember it.'

He nodded. 'I qualified and went into the army almost right away,' he said. 'It will feel strange living a normal life again, going into the office every day.'

'I bet you'll be glad,' she said. 'It must be awful having to fight in a war.'

'Not nice at all,' he said. 'But I had some great mates. Friendship is everything in that situation.'

'I can imagine it would be.'

'You haven't been having it easy yourself, have you. I did what you said and asked Mum.'

'And you are still speaking to me?'

'Of course,' he said with a grin. 'Why would I not?'

'I've had plenty of disapproval.'

'Well, you won't get any from me.'

'That's nice to know,' she said. 'It's ongoing from my father. He still refuses to accept my little boy.'

'Oh, what a shame,' he said.

'Yeah, I shouldn't care but I do, very much,' she said. 'Parenthood makes you incredibly vulnerable.'

'I'm sure it must do.'

The music stopped and the roar of party voices drifted out to the garden, the high-pitched shriek of Dora's laugh rising above the others.

'By the way, Liz,' Arthur began. 'Can you tell your sister that she has no need to put on such a show for my benefit. I know she doesn't fancy me and the feeling has been mutual for *many years*.'

'Oh, I thought...'

'I had a crush on her when I was about eight but I'm a grown-up now and I got over it long ago.'

'I'm pleased about that,' she said. 'I hated it when she was so horrid to you.'

'All part of growing up,' he said. 'And there's nothing like fighting for your country to toughen you up.'

'I suppose not.'

Liz's maternal instincts were beginning to bother her and she wanted to go home.

'I think I'll be on my way soon, Arthur,' she said. 'Would you mind?'

'Of course not.' He looked at his watch. 'It's not far off midnight, but I expect this lot will go on until the early hours. Do you live far from here?'

'Ten to fifteen minutes' walk.'

'I'll go with you,' he said. 'It's too late for you to be out on your own.'

'There's no need...'

'I'll be the judge of that,' he said.

'Hark at you being all masterful,' she said laughing.

'I have my moments,' he told her.

'So, you get to walk the second-best sister home,' she said jokingly to Arthur as they walked through the drab streets, the shabbiness of everything visible in the amber glow of the street lights.

'There's nothing second best about you, Liz,' he assured her. 'And I'm not walking you home in the usual sense. I am just making sure you get home safely.'

'Oh, so you're not going to jump all over me when we get to my gate, then,' she laughed.

'I most certainly am not,' he said, sounding miffed. 'Surely you know me better than that.'

'Just joking.'

'That's all right then.'

She smiled to herself. Arthur was a lovely bloke but he did take life too seriously at times. He always had.

'So ... had you been going out with your boy's father for long?' he asked.

'Quite a while,' she said.

'Mum said he was a Yank.'

'That's right.'

'Did you love him?'

'Oh yeah, very much,' she said with emphasis. 'I wouldn't have got myself pregnant if I hadn't.'

'Of course not,' he said. 'Sorry.'

'No offence taken,' she said. 'I don't regret it; I can't regret it because my boy is everything to me and I wouldn't be without him.' She told Arthur about Vic's death.

'So he didn't even know he was going to be a father, then?' he said.

'Neither did I when he died.'

'You've had a rough time,' he said.

'A bit rocky for a while, but I've been very lucky,' she said and went on to tell him about Beryl. 'God knows what would have happened to Charlie and me without her.'

'You'd have got through it, Liz; you've always struck me as the type to tackle anything,' he said.

'But I'm really glad that you've had some help.'

'I thank God for it every day.'

'So ... will you stay there or do you have other plans?'

'I'm not in a position to have plans,' she said with a dry laugh. 'I just take life one day at a time and thank God that I have my boy and a roof over our heads.'

'I expect you'll meet someone else eventually.'

'It would be nice to be with someone, of course. It's the natural way of things,' she said. 'But I'm in no hurry. I'm not over Vic yet. Anyway, not many men would be willing to take on another man's child.'

'I'm sure there are some out there.'

'Maybe, I don't know. I haven't given it a great deal of thought because I'm happy in my own way,' she said. 'But I'll never forget how alone I felt when I left home with nowhere to go. I was so scared and I didn't see how I would ever find a way through it but I knew I had to somehow because Dad couldn't cope with my situation. He still can't as it happens. But back then I had never felt more alone and frightened. It was awful. Then Beryl, a lady I didn't even like at that time, offered me a home.'

'And you're all right living with her?'

'More than all right; she's little short of a saint,' she said. 'Isn't it funny how some people aren't at all as they seem when you get to know them.'

'Yeah,' he said. 'You learn to get along with all sorts of blokes in the army. People from different places and walks of life. The companionship is everything.'

'I bet.'

'So, this lady you live with is good to you then.'

'Very. She's turned out to be a motherly sort of a friend,' she said. 'She's marvellous with Charlie. She's never been married. The three of us are just like a little family unit.'

'Ooh, you'd better not tell your mum that.'

'She didn't try to stop Dad from throwing me out so she can't blame me for getting fond of Beryl,' she told him. 'I don't think she'd be that bothered anyway. Dora has always been the favourite in our family.'

'I can imagine that,' he said. 'Your sister has always liked plenty of attention.'

'I'll say.'

'Anyway, I'm glad things worked out for you, Liz, as far as they can without your boy's father.'

'Thank you, Arthur,' she said. 'I'm glad you haven't turned your back on me.'

'I never would. I like to think I'm rather more broadminded than that,' he said. 'Besides, we've been friends for a very long time and I'd like that to continue.'

'My troubles are nothing compared to what you must have been through, being away at the war,' she said. 'I suppose you are feeling very happy to leave all that behind.'

'I don't think any of us will ever be able to leave it behind entirely,' he said. 'But, yes, it's very nice to be home.'

'I'm sure.'

'One thing I noticed when I got back,' he said, moving on quickly, 'was how damaged and drab everything is here. I've been in the Far East in the sun so I suppose that's why I noticed it. I didn't realise it would be so scruffy.'

'You noticed it because you can't bloomin' well miss it,' she said. 'The bomb damage is untouched. Nothing has been done at all and rationing is more punishing than ever. I think we all had unrealistic expectations. We thought everything would go back to normal as soon as the war ended, which was obviously not possible. But it's nearly a year and everything is the same as in wartime, except for the bombs, of course, and it's heaven not having those.'

'The war cost us dear, not only in lives,' he said. 'We're in a lot of debt so I suppose the government can't afford to get started on rebuilding just yet.'

'Yes, Beryl was saying something about that the other day,' she told him. 'She's an avid follower of the news and is very well up on current affairs.'

'Still, whatever the state of the place I'm very glad to be back,' he said.

'I can imagine.'

'No place like home.'

'That's right. Anyway, this is where I live,' she said as they reached Beryl's. 'Would you like to come in for a cup of something? I'm sure Beryl wouldn't mind.'

'Thanks, but I'd better get back to the party,' he said, 'as it's been put on for me.'

'Yeah, perhaps you'd better,' she said. 'Thanks for walking me home.'

'A pleasure.'

''Night then.'

'G'night, Liz.'

181

She was feeling pleasantly happy as she went indoors. A night out had done her good. Arthur was such good company too. She had really enjoyed being with him.

Marg came to visit on Monday and was almost bursting with excitement.

'I'm going tomorrow, Liz,' she said.

'To America?'

'Via the transportation camp, yeah,' she said. 'I've been packing for a while because I knew it would be soon but I got a letter this morning.'

'So, I don't suppose I'll see you again then.'

'Well ... no. I've come to say goodbye.'

'Oh Marg,' said Liz, her voice raw with emotion. 'I won't half miss you.'

'Likewise,' said her friend thickly. 'But I am very excited about going.'

'I can imagine.'

Liz was dreading the idea of not having Marg in her life. They had been very close over the years. But her friend wanted this so much Liz was pleased it was happening for her. They wouldn't meet again because ordinary people couldn't afford to go somewhere as distant as the United States.

'I can't stay long,' said Marg. 'I still have the last of my packing to do.'

'Is your Mum going with you, to see you off and say goodbye?' asked Liz.

'Sadly, she can't,' she said. 'There are special trains for war brides and no one else is allowed on them.'

'Oh, that's a shame.'

'Yeah, it is but they are adamant about it,' she said. 'Probably because there are such a lot of us and it's a big job getting us all away. Anyway, it's probably better saying goodbye at home in private.'

It will be painful however you do it, thought Liz, but she said, 'You'll write, won't you?'

'All the time,' she said. 'As soon as I get there I'll write to let you know that I've arrived.'

'Well,' began Liz opening her arms, her voice heavy with emotion. 'All the best. I hope you'll be very happy and I know you will be with Joe.'

'Thanks,' said Marg, tears running down her cheeks. 'I'll just say goodbye to Charlie and Miss Banks and I'll be off.'

A few minutes later Liz, Charlie and Beryl stood at the front door watching her go down the path for the last time. She turned to wave before heading off down the street and Liz had a real struggle not to spoil it for Marg by breaking down. As soon as she'd gone, she let the tears fall. Beryl was looking a bit dewy eyed too.

Chapter Nine

Mick was back working for his old firm but didn't intend to stay for long because he had had an idea that excited him. It would be his route to a more interesting and lucrative way of earning a living without coming out of his trade entirely. It had struck him that there was another side to his line of work other than just fixing electrical systems. There was also the repair and supply of electrified household products. Admittedly not many ordinary people owned any yet, apart from wireless sets, but it was the coming thing. The toffs already had electric toasters and kettles; some even had modern washing machines.

Artefacts of any kind were short at the moment but that would change when the country got back on its feet. Then there would be plenty of scope for a savvy bloke like himself to sell and repair these products. He could offer the goods with a guarantee because he could fix the products himself. He would also take on repairs to customers' existing gadgets so he would still get to use his skills but work in a more varied way. He'd be self-employed, too, and that really did appeal to him because he'd never been good at taking orders and had had his fill of it in the army.

So, how to set about it. Firstly, he'd need somewhere to sell his goods. A market stall would do for starters. He'd ask around as to a supplier and he had kept most of his back pay so that would get him started.

He'd begin with small items; light bulbs and plugs and so on and gradually move on to toasters and kettles and even wireless sets. He could also buy old sets and recondition them for sale. Oh yes, this was an idea in a million and he would start doing some groundwork right away; make a few enquiries about suppliers and market stall rates and so on. Then, when this country began to thrive again, he'd be ready.

He was still living at home, which wasn't what

he'd intended, but he hadn't been able to find accommodation that he could afford. Now, with this new project to think of, he needed all the cash he could get and it was cheaper living at home because he only paid a modest rent. His parents were neutral about it. Go or stay, it was all the same to them.

'Tea break's over, Mick,' shouted one of his mates and he realised that the rest of the lads were all on their way back to work.

'Righto,' he said, getting up and going after them, relishing the prospect of a more interesting way of earning a living.

Liz was feeling low for two reasons. As well as missing Marg dreadfully, she was also worried because Beryl had seemed distant and a little snappy lately and it was most unlike her. Marg had mentioned that the older woman had been bad tempered at work. Liz hadn't noticed anything then but she was aware of it now.

There were two most likely reasons. Either Beryl wasn't feeling well or she was finding it too much having herself and Charlie living here. Both possibilities were a worry to Liz. Obviously she hated to think that Beryl might be ill. But the second and more likely option was equally as troubling because she and Charlie were so happy living here. Beryl in this mood seemed un-approachable but Liz knew she must bring the subject out into the open at the first suitable opportunity.

Her chance came one Sunday after one of Beryl's tasty Sunday lunches.

'I'll do the dishes,' offered Liz. 'You go and put your feet up.'

'At weekends we share the chores, you know that,' Beryl reminded her curtly.

'Exactly,' responded Liz. 'You cooked the meal so I do the dishes.'

'I do not want to go and put my feet up,' she said in such a vicious tone that Charlie started to cry. 'I am not in my dotage yet, thank you.'

'I was just trying to be fair.'

'There's no need to make such a song and dance about it,' she said.

'Sorry.'

'It's all right,' she said coolly. 'But I'll take care of all this. There's no need for you to do the drying. You take Charlie to the park or something.'

In other words, get out of my sight, thought Liz, but she did what the older woman said and left the house.

Ever since she'd had Charlie, Liz had found the park very comforting and now in early summer it was wonderfully refreshing with newly mown grass and flowers and bushes splashing the place with colour.

But today she was too upset to enjoy it. She must tackle Beryl as soon as she got back and ask her if she wanted her and Charlie to leave. It was a sad thought as well as a worrying one. She'd enjoyed her time with Beryl until just recently. Charlie was happy and settled too. But she couldn't stay if it was upsetting Beryl. It wouldn't be fair. It was understandable that she might want her house to herself again. Small boys made a lot of noise and muddle. As well as the personal side of things, it was going to be difficult finding somewhere else to live, especially as her status as an unmarried mother would become relevant again. Living with Beryl, the stigma hadn't existed inside the home.

'There you are,' said a voice. 'Beryl said I would find you and Charlie here.'

'Dora,' said Liz, pleased to see her sister for once. 'Can you do me a favour?'

'Depends what it is.'

'Could you look after Charlie for me for half an hour or so. I need to go home for something.'

''Course I will,' said Dora brightly as she lifted her nephew up and kissed him.

'Thanks, sis. I won't be long,' she said and marched purposefully out of the park.

Beryl was ensconced in an armchair in the living room with her knitting.

'Back already,' she said. 'Where's Charlie?'

'He's in the park with my sister,' she said. 'I came back because I want to talk to you.'

Beryl stopped knitting and looked at her. 'Oh really. You'd better get on with it then,' she said.

'I'll come straight to the point,' she said, trembling inside. 'Do you want Charlie and me to move out?'

'What!' she said, looking shocked. 'What on earth has given you that idea?'

'The way you've been with me lately,' she said hesitantly. 'I know we cause a lot of noise and disruption so I quite understand if you want us to go, but I need to know one way or the other because the atmosphere in the house is upsetting me.'

Beryl stood up, her cheeks flaming. 'Liz, my dear girl,' she began, her voice trembling. 'I love having the two of you here. You've changed my life very much for the better and I don't want to lose you.'

'So why are you being so horrid?'

She held her head. 'Am I really being awful?' she said, her voice trembling on the verge of tears.

'Terrible,' she said. 'The atmosphere in the house has been miserable. But surely you must know that.'

'I suppose I tried not to think about it. I didn't mean to take it out on you.'

'Take what out on me? What's the matter, Beryl? Are you ill? Is that what's wrong?'

'No,' she said. 'That would be easier to deal with.'

'What is it then?' she asked.

The older woman sat down and indicated for Liz to do the same. 'The truth is that being so involved with Charlie has made me think of my own boy and what I have lost.'

'And that is making you feel miserable?'

'Very, but mostly I'm feeling guilty.'

'So, Charlie is causing it.'

'No, of course not,' she said. 'Charlie has nothing to do with it, apart from being a joy and reminding me of what I gave up. But mostly I am wrestling with the guilt of my actions. Supposing they put my boy with a bad family or into an orphanage; they seem such cruel places.'

'I thought you said they were having him adopted.'

'That's what they told me but they would have said anything at the time to shut me up,' she said. 'I was very upset so I was making a fuss.'

'I can imagine.'

'It isn't that I want to intrude on his life or anything like that,' she said. 'But if only I knew he was all right.'

'We can try to find out,' suggested Liz. 'As I mentioned to you before.'

'But if he has been adopted, his new parents might not have told him and my turning up could cause all sorts of trouble.'

'He's a man now and probably had to go away to war so he should be able to cope with finding out he's adopted. But we may be able to find out without his knowledge which would mean we wouldn't be breaking any adoption laws. We could just check with his adopted parents.' Liz looked at her. 'I bet you'd like to see him, though.'

'More than anything, but I'd be happy just to know how he is.' She sighed. 'You'd have thought I would have forgotten all about him by this time, wouldn't you?'

'No. I wouldn't because I'm a mum myself. I know how strong the bond is.' She thought the problem over. 'Do you think you'd feel better if you knew he was all right? Would that be enough for you?'

'I'm sure I'd feel better and I would be prepared to just know and nothing further.'

'Well, I'll help you if you want to try to find him,' she offered.

'Thank you, dear. I'll give the matter some more thought. But people could get hurt and I don't want that.'

'We'd be very discreet.'

'I will think about it.' Beryl looked at her. 'But more importantly I'm sorry I've been taking my personal problems out on you. Please don't ever think I want you and Charlie to leave. The two of you have transformed my life and the only way you will ever leave is when you want to. If I am bad tempered with you again just give me a telling off and I mean that.'

'I wouldn't dare.' Liz was so relieved that all was well between her and Beryl. 'Anyway, I'd better go back to the park. Dora will wonder where I am.'

'I'll see you later then,' said Beryl.

Liz walked back to the park with a spring in her step. Apart from the relief that she didn't have to leave, she'd missed the warmth of her relationship with Beryl. She really was very fond of her.

'You took your time,' said Dora when Liz found her sitting on a seat near the duck pond with Charlie beside her. They were both chewing happily.

'Don't tell me you're sharing your sweet ration with him,' said Liz in astonishment.

'Yeah, what's so odd about that?'

'You never share your sweet ration with anyone.'

'Charlie isn't just anyone, is he?' she said. 'Anyway, what kept you so long?'

'I had something to sort out with Beryl.'

'Such as?'

'Never you mind.'

Dora shrugged and changed the subject. 'Arthur is playing hard to get with me,' she said.

'Is he? How is that?'

'I asked him to go to the pictures with me and he said no, bloomin' cheek.'

'Good for him.'

'Why do you always take everyone else's side and never mine?' she asked.

'I don't always, only when you are in the wrong,' she said. 'You've always been mean to Arthur. He's obviously had enough and good for him. So leave him alone. You're a grown-up now. Too old to mess people around.'

'Arthur seems different since he came back from the war, don't you think?'

'I noticed that he's matured,' said Liz. 'That skinny kid has long gone. I thought he seemed rather attractive now.'

'Mm. Almost fanciable,' said Dora.

'Don't mess with him, Dora, just because you don't have a boyfriend,' Liz warned.

'I've no intention of doing any such thing,' said Dora. 'I couldn't see any harm in a night out at the pictures though.'

'Normally there wouldn't be, but Arthur has always been sweet on you and that shouldn't be encouraged when you're not interested in him.'

'That was years ago, when we were children,' she said. 'There's nothing like that now.'

'I am inclined to agree with you about that, but show him some respect anyway,' said Liz. But she knew Dora would do what she wanted anyway.

'Thanks for looking after Charlie for me.'

'That's all right.'

'I'd buy you a cup of tea and a bun in the café like we used to before the war,' she said looking across at the pavilion-style building that hadn't reopened after the war because of the shortages. 'But you're welcome to come back to Beryl's for one. Her rock cakes are delicious.'

'Okay,' agreed Dora.

Liz hadn't issued the invitation lightly. She thought some lively company would probably be good for Beryl right now.

Liz enjoyed her job at the ice rink. Whilst the evening sessions were adult and a flirting ground for the skaters, her Saturday afternoon shifts were full of noisy children bursting with energy and enthusiasm. Some were less ebullient than others, but they were not nearly so fearful as adults. Liz recalled how frightened she had been on that first visit and how Vic had given her such confidence on the ice. Oh, happy days.

But these were joyful times for the youthful skaters, she thought, as she handed some skates to a young mother with a boy and a girl. This was their time. People who hired skates were usually beginners, the more proficient having acquired their own.

'Let's see how this goes,' said the mother to Liz, out of her children's hearing. 'Their friends have been skating so they want to have a go. They think they'll be doing a figure of eight on their first attempt.'

'Oh dear,' said Liz chattily. 'They are in for a

shock then.'

'I'll say.'

'How are you on the ice?'

'Pretty good. I used to practically live here when I was younger, before I got married,' she said. 'I'll be a bit rusty at first but should pick it up with a little practice. I'll be steady enough to look after those two anyway.'

'Good luck,' said Liz. 'Any problems just give me a shout.'

As the family went off to put their boots on, Liz found herself swamped with nostalgia for carefree days when she came here to have fun, not to work. Fun was of a different nature for her now; it was hearing Charlie laugh and chatter, the smell and feel of him and the way his face lit up at the sight of her. She looked at the clock on the wall and was pleased to see that it was almost time for her to go off duty. She almost yelled 'yippee' with the joy of seeing her boy very soon.

'Oh good, I'm glad you're not late,' said Dora when Liz arrived to collect Charlie.

'Why?' asked Liz.

'Because I'm going out and I want to get ready. Mum has gone to Aunt Mary's because she isn't well. She'll be back soon but she isn't here yet.'

'So, where are you going?'

'To the West End to see a film and have a mooch around with some of the girls from work,' she said. 'There's always a good atmosphere around there. At least we won't be manhunting, thank God.'

'There'll be plenty of blokes about, though,'

said Liz.

'I might be desperate, Liz, but I draw the line at picking up a bloke off the street in the West End.'

'Right I'll leave you to it then,' she said, strapping Charlie into the pushchair. 'Have fun.'

'I'll do my best.'

'We're home,' Liz called in to the house as she opened the door and Charlie went running in.

There was no reply which was unusual because Beryl usually came to meet them. Liz called again as she unloaded the pushchair. When she was greeted with silence she followed Charlie into the kitchen where Beryl was lying on the floor motionless with Dolly beside her.

'Oh my Lord,' said Liz shakily, glad she had taken a first aid course during the war. At least she knew how to take a pulse and other basics.

Having ascertained that Beryl was alive, Liz put Charlie in his pushchair and ran to the telephone box at the end of the street.

Half an hour or so later with Charlie strapped into the seat on the back of Beryl's bike, Liz pedalled furiously to her parents' home. There was no reply to her knocking and the back door was locked. Mum obviously wasn't back from Aunt Mary's yet and Dora had gone out already.

So now what was she going to do? She needed to get to the hospital where Beryl had been taken by ambulance. But she also needed someone to look after Charlie who was tired and needed to be at home. Beryl's neighbours hadn't been in so she'd banked on her mother being home. Oh well, there was only one alternative, she thought, and made her way up the neighbours' front path.

Arthur answered the door.

'Is your mum in?' she asked.

'No, she and Dad have gone to visit relatives,' he replied. 'Can I help?'

'My landlady has been rushed to hospital and I was hoping that your mum would look after Charlie so that I can go to the hospital to see her and find out what's wrong,' she explained. 'There's no one in next door.'

'What's the matter with your landlady?' he asked, looking concerned. 'I hope it's nothing serious.'

'I found her unconscious when I got home from work and I am so worried.'

'It must have been one hell of a shock,' he said. 'But I'll look after him for you.'

'You?'

'Yeah, me,' he said, adding with a smile, 'I'm not as dim as I look.'

'Of course not,' she said as Charlie started to cry. 'But he's tired and he needs his supper.'

'How about I take him to your place where things are familiar to him and give him something to eat and let him sleep when he's ready. I don't know anything about kids but it can't be that difficult, can it?'

'You'd do that for me?'

'Of course I would,' he said. 'If we can somehow get his seat off your bike and on to mine, we'll be on our way. I'm sure a few minutes with a screwdriver will fix it.'

'Oh Arthur, I think you have just saved my sanity,' she said.

'Good, I'm glad about that,' he said. 'Now let's have a look at that seat.'

Two hours or so later Liz got home to find a cup of tea put into her hand and her son fast asleep on the sofa with a pillow under his head and a blanket over him. The cat was snoozing at his feet.

'I found some baked beans so I gave him some on toast,' he said. 'Is that all right? I cut it up for him.'

'Thank you, Arthur, I'm very grateful.'

'No trouble,' he said. 'He's a smashing little chap.'

'I won't argue with you about that.'

'So how is your landlady?'

'Awake and more than a little shaken, I think, though she'd never admit it,' she told him. 'It must be frightening to pass out cold like that.'

'Very,' he said. 'Do they know what caused it?'

'Low blood pressure they think,' she said. 'They don't seem too worried about it, but they are keeping her in overnight for observation.'

'That can only be a good thing.'

'Can I get you a cup of tea?' she offered. 'You gave me one but didn't have one yourself.'

'I made one when Charlie had his supper,' he said. 'I hope you don't mind.'

'Of course not.'

'I'll be on my way then,' he said. 'Let you get the little one to bed.'

'It's Saturday night and you are a single bloke

so are you off out somewhere nice?' she asked casually.

'Meeting some mates for a pint,' he said. 'Then we might go to a jazz club in the West End. If we can get in, that is. There's usually a long queue, though. It's not long been open so everyone wants to go there at the moment.'

'You're a jazz fan then?'

'Only a novice,' he said. 'But I do like the sound of it. It's a bit of a craze with my mates at the moment.'

'I rather like it too,' she said. 'There is such an atmosphere about it. It always sounds deliciously wicked to me; conjures up images of a smoky dance floor and people getting cosy.'

'Perhaps you and I could go to the jazz club together some time,' he suggested on the spur of the moment. 'Or somewhere else if you prefer.'

'What, you and me?' she asked, somewhat taken aback by the idea of a night out with someone she had known all her life.

'There doesn't seem to be anyone else around here,' he said drily.

'Well yeah, that would be lovely,' she said politely, not at all sure if it was quite what she wanted. 'But obviously, I can't make any arrangements until Beryl is better.'

'Of course not,' he said. 'We can do it anytime. It's only an idea. Just let me know if you fancy it sometime.'

'I will do, Arthur, and thank you for asking me,' she said, grateful to him for leaving any next move up to her.

As she saw him off at the front door she experi-

197

enced something that felt oddly like the faint beginnings of excitement and wondered if a night out with him would be such a bad thing after all. But no, she couldn't go out on a date with someone she had known all her life; the spark just wasn't there. He must have given up on Dora and decided to try the second sister. He was a nice bloke though and she liked him a lot.

Arthur headed for the pub, having been home to get washed and changed, wondering what on earth had possessed him to ask Liz Beck out. He was embarrassed by his impulsive invitation and was certain that Liz was too. The poor girl hadn't known where to put herself.

She was an attractive woman, though, with her blonde hair and pretty face. They'd always got on well which was more than he could say for her sister, who had spent much of their childhood tormenting him. He'd had a crush on her and she had used it to get her own way. The crush had ended long before they had gone to senior school, though Dora seemed to be under the impression that it still existed.

Not a good idea to get romantically involved with a neighbour anyway. It was far too close to home. He did like and admire Liz, though. She was strong and independent and kind and caring. But most of all he liked her physical presence. He was a young man so it was bound to come down to basics initially.

Oh well, let's see what the evening has to offer. There were usually some attractive women at the jazz club, he thought, as he went into the pub and joined his mates.

Beryl was very shaken by her collapse.

'It scared the living daylights out of me, I can tell you,' she said to Liz when she was back home again.

'It frightened me too when I came home and found you out cold,' Liz admitted.

'I'm sure it must have done, dear,' she said. 'I'm sorry to have given you such a scare.'

'You couldn't help it.'

'Supposing I'd been looking after Charlie?'

'But you weren't so let's not even think about that,' said Liz.

'Mm,' said Beryl, still seeming worried.

'The chances are it will never happen again so long as you look after yourself,' said Liz. 'They told you that at the hospital.'

'You're right,' she said, visibly pulling herself together. 'It cost me money for the hospital when it wasn't necessary.'

'You needed to get it checked out, though,' said Liz. 'So, it can only be a good thing.'

'Yeah, you're probably right.' She looked at Charlie who was sitting on Liz's lap. 'Oh, I am so glad to be home.'

'And we're glad to have you back,' said Liz who felt as though Beryl had been away for longer than one day; the house had felt sad and empty without her. 'So don't get any ideas of swooning again will you.'

'I certainly will not,' she said emphatically. 'But thinking I was at death's door did get me wondering.'

'What about?'

'That boy of mine,' she said. 'I don't want to go to my grave not knowing what happened to him.'

'Well, when you're ready we'll have a proper chat about it,' said Liz. 'You'll have to give some serious thought to your relatives and who might know something.'

'I'll do that,' she agreed.

'This country is finished,' stated Mick's work-mate in their tea break one day in the autumn.

'That's a bit of a sweeping statement isn't it, mate?' responded Mick.

'It's true though,' said the man, drawing on a cigarette. 'I mean, here we are, the best part of a year and a half since the end of the war and no improvement whatsoever. Not a sign of work being done on the bomb damage and everything is shorter than ever. It's a bloody disgrace. I mean, we've done our bit and risked our lives on the front line and we've come home to nothing but hardship and food rationing. I'm lucky if I can get a packet of fags and I have to search all over London before I find any.'

'I suppose it takes time to put a country right after a war,' suggested Mick.

'This country is broke, mate,' the other man stated categorically. 'That's why nothing's been done. They don't have the dough for it. We're in debt to America, apparently, I read about in the paper the other day.'

'I'm sure the government will sort something out soon,' said Mick optimistically. 'Things always seem to work out in the end.'

The man lowered his voice. 'I'm not waiting around to find out,' he said in a secretive manner. 'I'm off.'

'Where to?'

'Australia,' he said with enthusiasm. 'That's the place to be, mate. Plenty of job opportunities there, not to mention lots of sunshine and good food.'

'I've heard something about it; quite a lot of people are going there,' said Mick.

'They need people to work in their booming industries,' he said. 'They especially welcome tradesman like us. There's an assisted passage scheme. Ten quid, that's all you have to pay.'

'Blimey, that sounds all right,' enthused Mick. 'So, what's the catch?'

'You have to stay for at least two years if you don't like it and want to come back,' he said. 'As I'm planning on staying permanently, that's no problem for me. Now is the time to do something like this, while I'm young and single.'

'So, when are you going?'

'I'm waiting for the paperwork to go through,' he said. 'It takes a while because you get thoroughly checked out. Forms to fill in, interviews, a medical, all that sort of thing. It's quite a palaver but it'll be worth it to live somewhere like that.'

Mick's interest was growing. The situation here in Britain wasn't conducive to putting his work plans in motion, which was disappointing. 'I'm planning on setting up on my own as soon as things improve,' he said.

'You might still be waiting when you're an old

man the way things are going,' he said. 'You could start up on your own in Australia in time. You might have to work for a guvnor for a while because they need trained people, but the wages are good so you might not want all the aggravation of working for yourself.'

Mick's interest was becoming enthusiasm.

'I mean look out the window, mate,' his workmate went on, pointing to the factory where they were doing some maintenance work. 'Dark, cold and raining. They don't have that where I'm going.'

'It's coming up to winter here, mate,' Mick reminded him. 'I expect they have weather like this in the winter.'

'Not as much as here,' he said. 'They have sunshine for a lot of the year. Not like our summers when it always rains. You can absolutely rely on sunshine there.'

'Steady on, mate,' said Mick. 'I love this country.'

'So do I but you can't deny the weather is awful.'

'I suppose so but you don't move to the other side of the world just because the weather is better.'

'It isn't just the weather, mate; it's everything. A better standard of living altogether.'

'You reckon?'

'I do and I have looked into it thoroughly. I've checked everything and all I see is good. I haven't been able to settle properly since I got back from the war,' he told him. 'I heard about this opportunity and decided to find out more about it.'

'What do you have to do to find out more?'

asked Mick.

'You go to Australia House here in London. Only a few stops on the Tube.'

'I might pay them a visit,' said Mick. 'You've certainly given me something to think about.'

Although his manner was casual, Mick was actually very excited as they went back to work. Maybe Australia was the place for him. He had no ties here. He didn't have a steady girlfriend and Mum and Dad wouldn't miss him. So a fresh start in a different country seemed like a good idea. It was certainly worth looking into.

Chapter Ten

Beryl's enthusiasm to trace her son seemed to lose momentum as her collapse faded into the past and her health returned to normal. She liked to talk about the technicalities of finding him and quite often did so. She didn't think they would have any luck with the public records because they had no idea what name he had now and anything connected to adoption was shrouded in secrecy. But she had a cousin living in London who she thought might know something.

'Let's get started then,' suggested Liz.

Beryl turned pale and said she wasn't quite ready, obviously nervous about it.

So Liz decided to leave it to her and not mention it again. Liz didn't mind when they began because she had more than enough to do, especially as the management at the ice rink often wanted her to work extra shifts lately. But, being fond of Beryl as she was, Liz was keen to help her. She suspected that her friend wouldn't rest until she had at least tried to find out what had happened to her boy.

Liz's own son turned two in October and was now a chatty toddler and an absolute joy, full of energy and learning new words every day. Beryl made a birthday cake for him and Dora and Violet came to tea.

His American granny sent him a parcel of treats.

'Isn't it kind of her to send such lovely things for him?' remarked Beryl.

'Very,' agreed Liz. 'I expect she's disappointed not to have her first grandchild living nearby.'

'It's only natural,' said Beryl.

'Oh, I must tell you, Liz,' cut in Dora who hadn't been listening because she had no interest in anything that didn't concern herself. 'Arthur next door has got a girlfriend.'

'Has he?' said Liz, experiencing an unexpected negative reaction to this news.

'Yeah, quite a looker too,' said Dora. 'I saw him out with her in town.'

'Good for him,' said Liz, dismissing her own feelings as ridiculous. 'It's time he found someone nice.'

'I feel discarded,' Dora complained. 'I always thought he was mine.'

'You didn't want him.'

'No, but he was there as a standby.'

'Years ago when you were about six he might

have been,' said Liz. 'But we've all done a lot of growing up since then.'

'Are you saying he isn't keen on me?'

'When we were children he was, very much so. But that was a long time ago. He's been abroad and experienced action in the war. He's a clever man with a good job and certainly wouldn't be short of offers. He won't have been waiting around for you to fancy him.'

'All right. There's no need to bite my head off,' she said. 'Anyone would think you had your eye on him yourself.'

'Don't be so ridiculous,' said Liz. 'He's just a good friend whom I happen to be very fond of. He helped me out with Charlie when Beryl was in hospital and I realised what a nice man he's grown up to be.'

'Makes no difference to me what you think about him,' said Dora.

But Liz knew it did because it was that same old thing with Dora. She put a stamp of ownership on things and people and resented anyone else going near them. Even if she had no interest in them herself.

'That's just as well as he's got himself fixed up with someone else,' said Liz sharply.

'Now, now, you two,' chided Violet. 'Don't spoil Charlie's birthday with an argument.'

'Sorry, Mum,' said Liz and joined her little son in a game with his toy cars on the floor while the cat watched at a safe distance. Charlie's way of showing love towards Dolly was grabbing hold of her wherever his chubby little fingers could get a grip, even if it was her tail.

Liz was cycling home from work at the ice rink one cold and misty evening in December when she spotted Arthur walking home. Instinctively she swung off her bike and joined him.

'On your own tonight?' she asked, leaning her bike against the kerb and hugging herself against the cold.

'Yeah. I've just been to the billiard hall with some of the lads. We like to get together at least once a week.'

'I thought you might have been out with your new girlfriend,' said Liz. 'I heard you are courting.'

Arthur didn't think he could call it that as it was very early days, but the Beck sisters didn't need to know that. For most of his childhood Dora had tormented him; now Liz was doing the same thing albeit that she didn't even realise it. She'd made it very clear that she didn't want to spend an evening in his company so he was making sure she knew that he wasn't available. It was all very childish and most unlike him but that was what happened when romantic feelings crept into your psyche.

'Yes, I am seeing someone,' he said.

'Good for you.'

'How is your landlady now,' he asked, moving on swiftly, 'Any repercussions from her funny turn?'

'There don't seem to be,' she said. 'She's absolutely fine now.'

'And how's Charlie?'

'Gorgeous, thank you,' she said with the softness of tone that always crept into her voice when she mentioned her son.

He felt a pang. He'd enjoyed feeling part of her world for that short time when he'd looked after Charlie. It was something far deeper than when he just fancied a girl. But he said, 'Yeah, I bet he is.'

Noticing the wistfulness in his tone she said, 'Why don't you call round to see him sometime. We're always at home on a Sunday morning. I know Beryl would like to thank you for helping me out when she was taken bad. I've told her all about it.'

He was ridiculously pleased by the invitation. 'I might do that,' he said, hoping he didn't sound too eager.

A gang of noisy youths passed by and became abusive as they recognised Liz. 'Slut,' they called back at her after they had passed. 'Keep away from her, mate. She's got a kid and no husband. She's a right old baggage.'

Without a word, Arthur shot after them and chased them to the end of the street, but they were too fast for him. 'Little buggers,' he said when he returned. 'How dare they insult you like that.'

'Calm down, Arthur,' she said. 'They're just kids.'

'That's no excuse.'

'I've had a lot worse than that,' she said. 'It's best to ignore it even though it isn't easy.'

'It must be horrible for you,' he said.

'It isn't nice but it's the rules we live under,' she said. 'We are meant to be married before we have kids and anyone who disobeys the system is castigated for it and not just by yobbos. A lot of adults have a problem with it too. My father will probably never accept the situation.'

'I know about the prejudice, of course, but that's the first time I've experienced it first-hand.'

'Don't worry about me. I'm one of the luckier unmarried mums,' she said. 'I have somewhere to live with my child. A lot of women in my position just can't cope and they are forced to abandon their offspring. Unless you have a fairy god-mother like Beryl or an understanding family, there is very little, if any, help for women who find themselves in my position.'

'I'm so sorry, Liz,' he said.

'There's nothing for you to be sorry about.'

'I know, but just the same...'

She laughed. 'You soft old thing.'

'Seriously, I think it's terrible.'

'As long as I know I'm doing my best for my boy I can live with it,' she said. 'Yes, it does hurt but I can't let it ruin my life or Charlie's. I am very lucky. Beryl saved me from the gutter and I will always be grateful to her.'

'She sounds like a great lady.'

'You'll get to meet her if you come to the house on Sunday morning.'

'I'll be there,' he said.

The air was cold and the mist sharp to the throat. 'I'll be off then before we both freeze to death,' she said.

'Yes, you get off home,' he said. 'Might see you Sunday.'

'I hope so,' she said and climbed onto her bike

and pedalled off down the street with him watching until she disappeared into the mist.

Beryl and Arthur hit it off immediately which created a lovely atmosphere in the house on Sunday morning. Arthur made a big fuss of Charlie and they all enjoyed coffee and cakes straight out of the oven.

On being complimented on her baking, Beryl said, 'My cakes are nothing like they were before rationing when there was no shortage of ingredients.'

This led the conversation on to rationing and the parlous state of the country in general. Both Beryl and Arthur were quite knowledgeable on the subject.

'The new Labour government don't seem to be doing any better than the last lot, do they,' said Beryl referring to the landslide victory the Labour party had in the general election back in the summer.

'I suppose we have to give them a chance,' said Arthur. 'It takes time and money to rebuild a country after a war.'

'Of course it does,' said Beryl. 'I only hope we'll see an improvement in my lifetime.'

They were all laughing at this when Dora arrived. Her eyes widened when she saw Arthur. 'What are you doing here?' she asked rudely.

'Visiting, if it's any of your business,' he replied.

'Getting your feet well and truly under the table by the looks of it.'

'Dora, don't be so rude,' admonished Liz.

'That's all right, Liz,' said Arthur. 'I'm used to

Dora having a go at me. It's her favourite pastime.'

'Arthur can get his feet under my table as often as he likes,' said Beryl.

'You've wormed your way in then,' said Dora.

'Take no notice of her,' said Liz.

'I'm not,' he said.

But the warm atmosphere had cooled and couldn't seem to be restored. Arthur said it was about time he left and bid them all a hasty farewell.

'Why were you so horrid to him?' demanded Liz after he'd gone and Beryl was in the kitchen.

'I was only mucking about,' she said. 'Arthur knows me well enough not to be offended.'

'He was offended enough to leave.'

'Then he shouldn't be so sensitive,' she said dismissively. 'He's always been a moody sod.'

'Not true at all,' Liz defended. 'You'll never find an easier-going man than Arthur.'

Beryl provided a timely intervention. 'Why don't the two of you take Charlie to the park for some fresh air while I prepare lunch,' she suggested. 'It might cool you both down.'

'Sorry, Beryl,' said Liz getting Charlie's outdoor clothes on and feeling bad about the altercation. She knew that Beryl disliked bad feeling in her house.

'I don't know why you feel the need to be so nasty to Arthur,' said Liz when the sisters headed to the park. 'If I didn't know better I might think it was unrequited love.'

210

'That's the last thing it is,' she said. 'I suppose being nasty to him has become a habit. He's always been there adoring me and it's a comfort seeing as I don't have any success with men.'

'You managed without him when he was away at the war,' Liz remarked.

'Yeah, of course I did,' she said, holding Charlie's hand as they entered the park. 'I must try to stop being so mean to him.'

'I think you should make a real effort,' said Liz. 'He's a lifelong friend. He's a lovely bloke and he doesn't deserve all that abuse you dish out to him.'

'Am I that bad?'

'Yes, you're awful.'

'I just don't seem able to be nice to him.'

There were times when her sister seemed so achingly vulnerable Liz wanted to hug her. But most of the time she was hateful and her next sentence proved that.

'Oh well,' she said airily. 'I am what I am and if people don't like it they can keep away.'

Sadly, that was what they did, thought Liz, but she knew her sister wouldn't listen so she changed the subject.

Violet suspected that George was seeing another woman and she was very worried about it. She wasn't hurt or jealous so much as frightened because she was totally reliant on him. How would she manage if he left her? She had no means of earning a living and very little confidence outside the house even though she put on a show. She tried to tell herself she was imagining things but all the signs were there. He went out all spruced up and didn't get back until late.

Naturally she asked where he'd been and pretended to accept his explanations – a union meeting, a darts match at the pub and so on – because she didn't want to bring matters to a head for fear he would leave and she really didn't think she could manage without him. She had devoted her life to him and relied on him completely. She didn't even know how to change a fuse.

He'd never been a demonstrative man and they had always squabbled a lot. But she thought they had loved each other in their own way and she had felt safe being married to him. Now she was vulnerable and scared. Dora still lived at home but she would fly the nest eventually. Violet had never lived alone as she had left home to get married, so independence was unknown to her.

Perhaps this woman was just a passing fancy. Violet wasn't worldly but she knew that some men were prone to affairs outside of marriage to spice things up. So, she had to hold her nerve and keep quiet. Let it run its course. There was a horrible ache in her heart though.

As the year of 1946 neared its end, Arthur took stock of his life and found it wanting. So he decided it was time he tried to better himself professionally. He currently worked at a local firm of accountants and the clients were all small traders, shopkeepers and self-employed tradesmen. He enjoyed the job but knew he was capable of something more demanding. He was an unassuming man but confident about his work. He'd always been top of the class at school, though he'd much rather have been a whizz on the sports field, which carried much more esteem. But now it was time to concentrate on what he was good at and stretch himself, in one of the big central London accountancy firms perhaps. A challenge was what he needed. So he kept his eye on the jobs in the trade journals and quality newspapers.

Christmas passed pleasantly for Liz and Beryl with Charlie an absolute joy. At just turned two he still wasn't old enough to understand what it was all about but he caught the atmosphere and loved his presents.

It was while Beryl and Liz were making some supper after he was in bed on Christmas night that Beryl made her announcement.

'I've made a decision, Liz,' she said. 'In the New Year, I am going to start looking for my boy. If I don't get on with it now, time will pass and I'll never do it.'

'If you're sure you're ready,' said Liz.

'I'll never be ready because I'm so ashamed of giving him up, but I need to do it.'

'You know we may not be able to find him,' Liz pointed out. 'So best not to build your hopes up too high.'

'I won't even consider defeat,' she said.

'So where do we start?'

'As you'll remember, all of my parents' generation have passed on and I was an only child, but I have cousins. My cousin Maud might know something,' she said. 'I haven't seen or heard from her for years but I have an address in Chiswick. With a bit of luck, she might still be there.'

'It seems a shame that you lost touch,' said Liz.

'Yes, it is rather sad,' she agreed. 'We were friendly enough when we were children, but nothing was ever the same after I got pregnant. Her whole family turned against me so I couldn't wait to distance myself from them all. All they got from me was a Christmas card. I haven't seen any of them since I was young.'

'How sad.'

'Very,' she agreed. 'And the same thing is still happening to girls today, as you very well know.'

'Mmm. I don't know what would have happened to Charlie and me if it hadn't been for you.'

'Well, I was here so let's not think about that.'

'Do you want me to go with you to visit Maud?'

'Yes, please,' she said gratefully.

'Perhaps we could go one evening when I'm not working,' suggested Liz. 'I'll ask Dora to babysit.'

'All right, dear,' she said. 'You go ahead and fix it up.'

They didn't receive a warm welcome from Beryl's cousin Maud, a large, middle-aged woman with deep-set eyes, a pale complexion and grey hair scraped back into a bun.

'If I did know what had happened to your boy I wouldn't tell you,' she said when Beryl had explained the purpose of their visit.

'Oh,' said Beryl nervously. 'Why is that?'

'After all this time you turn up looking for the child you gave away. Not a word for years then

214

when you do come you're after something.'

'I was told to keep away by the adoption people, as I recall,' said Beryl. 'So that's what I have been doing.'

'Until you take it in to your head to try and find your boy,' she said accusingly. 'You've got a cheek.'

'Even after all these years, you still hold it against me,' said Beryl shakily.

'Time doesn't change anything as far as something like that is concerned,' she said. 'You were a disgrace back then and you still are now.'

'That seems a bit harsh,' Liz put in.

'And rightly so,' snapped Maud. 'Not that it's any business of yours.'

'Don't speak to her like that,' rebuked Beryl. 'She's a very good friend of mine.'

'Well, you've both had a wasted journey because I can't help you.'

'I just want to know that he's all right,' said Beryl. 'I want him to know that I didn't want to give him up. That I never stopped loving him.'

'What a load of sentimental claptrap,' Maud burst out. 'If you did love him, which I doubt as he's a stranger to you, you'd leave him alone.'

Normally so indomitable, Beryl seemed to crumble. Such a strong woman, her son was obviously her Achilles heel. She fell silent, her head down.

'Beryl only wants to know if he's all right,' said Liz defensively. 'She doesn't mean him any harm. She doesn't even need to see him.'

'Who are you to interfere in our family business?' Maud demanded.

'I'm a friend of Beryl's and I know how much

215

she has suffered over what she was forced to do.'

'She knew the rules and she disobeyed them so she had to pay the price.'

Liz was thoughtful for a moment. 'You're probably about the same age as Beryl so it's surprising that you weren't more sympathetic to her at the time,' she said. 'The young are usually supportive of each other over such things.'

'We'd been very well brought up,' said Maud haughtily. 'Beryl let the family down. Fortunately for her, the older generation put plans into place quickly and it remained just a family secret. She was lucky that they helped her. They could have thrown her out and let her get on with it.'

'Come on, Liz,' said Beryl, taking her friend's arm. 'Let's go. We are just wasting our time here.'

'Do you think she knows what happened to him?' asked Liz as they waited at the bus stop.

'Yes, she knows all right,' said Beryl. 'I can tell by the look in her beady little eyes.'

'Why won't she help?'

'She has her reasons.'

'Why is she so hostile towards you?' asked Liz. 'It does seem a bit extreme.'

The older woman remained silent.

'What's the matter?' asked Liz.

'The chap who got me pregnant was someone she was sweet on.'

'Oh, Beryl!' she exclaimed.

'I didn't betray her,' she said. 'He wasn't interested in her but she couldn't take that so she made herself believe that I'd stolen him from her. We met him at a dance and she was smitten with him, but it was me he wanted and I was attracted to him.'

'And Maud found out.'

'She found us together,' she said. 'We were canoodling in the alley at the back of our house. He was kissing me goodnight and she saw us. She's never forgiven me.'

'So what happened to him?'

'He moved away from the area and never knew about the pregnancy,' she said. 'Maud blamed me for his going and has never forgiven me.'

'Sounds like a horrible man.'

'No, not at all. He was gorgeous. We were all very young and things got out of hand, that's all. Maud could never see that. She had this romantic dream about him carrying her off into the sunset and was absolutely broken hearted when he left and she found out I was carrying his child. I think that blaming me probably helped her to cope with it.'

Liz was shocked by the story. You just never knew what painful secrets people carried around with them.

'By the way, Liz,' began Beryl as the bus came into sight. 'If it's all right with you, I never want that part of the story mentioned again. Not ever! Not even between ourselves.'

'You have my word,' agreed Liz.

On the bus, Liz asked, 'So, where do we go from here in our search for your boy? Maud's re-action wasn't in the least encouraging, especially as they all turned against you.'

'I'm disappointed but not defeated,' she said. 'But I'll think about it and decide on our next move.'

217

'Okay,' said Liz.

The next morning, a Friday, they found themselves with more urgent matters on their minds when they awoke to freezing temperatures and deep snow covering everything outside.

'You won't be able to get to work, Beryl,' said Liz. 'The buses won't be running in this weather.'

'I'll walk,' said Beryl. 'It will do me good. It will all have melted by the time I come home. These cold snaps never last long in this part of the country.'

As she strode off in Wellington boots, scarves and a bright red knitted hat on her head, Liz was reminded of what an indomitable woman she was.

The snow hadn't melted when Beryl came home from work. More fell, gale-force winds wrought havoc all over that weekend and freezing temperatures continued causing trouble all over the country.

The Thames froze and there was a fuel crisis as snow crippled the roads and railways and coal supplies couldn't be transported to London. As well as affecting people's firesides, it also caused power cuts and long spells without electricity.

Both Liz and Beryl were more concerned about Charlie than themselves. The little boy didn't understand and cried with the cold despite several layers of clothing.

'So much for your cold snap theory, Beryl,' said Liz one night in late February when they sat by a cold and empty fireplace in their outdoor clothes, hugging hot water bottles while they listened to the wireless.

'I couldn't have been more wrong, could I?'

'You certainly couldn't.'

With the weather controlling everything and any journey outside the home being so difficult, the search for Beryl's son was put to one side.

'I hope it warms up soon,' said Liz.

It didn't. Even the arrival of March brought no relief. Beryl fell ill with bronchitis and was in bed for a week on doctor's orders. The thaw didn't come until the end of the month and never had the spring been more joyfully welcomed. People were smiling with relief in the streets and shops.

'Well,' said Beryl one day in April. 'There's no excuse now that the weather is back to normal. The search for my boy is back on.'

'Are you sure you want to do it?' asked Liz.

'I must admit Maud's reaction was a slap in the face but I can't give up yet,' she said. 'I've got a couple more cousins I can go to see.'

'I'll be by your side,' said Liz but she was dreading another response like Maud's. It was heartbreaking to see her friend treated so badly.

The reaction from Beryl's other relatives was disappointing. The first claimed she knew nothing about it. 'It was all very hush hush,' she said. 'They probably didn't want me to know for fear it might give me ideas. I was young then.'

The second and final contact was even more hostile than Maud had been. 'You should leave well alone,' she said. 'It's bad enough what you did back then, the least you can do is leave the

219

boy alone after all this time. As it happens I don't know what they did with him, but if I did I wouldn't tell you. I think he should be left in peace. No good can come from raking up the past.'

'I only want to know if he's all right.'

'It's too late for that so leave him alone,' she said. 'Surely he deserves that much. Think of him.'

'I am. Or I thought I was.'

'You're thinking of yourself even if you don't realise it,' she stated categorically. 'You want to ease your own conscience. You did what you had to back then so let it go and stay away from him. Let him get on with his life.'

'He might like to know that I care.'

'After all these years, I doubt it,' she said.

'Do you know if he survived the war?' asked Beryl.

'I know nothing about him, I've told you,' she snapped. 'No good can come from raking up the past. What's done is done so leave him be.'

'Maybe she's right,' said Beryl as she and Liz waited for the bus home. 'Perhaps I should forget the whole thing.'

'It has to be your decision,' said Liz.

'I thought that I was doing it for him as much as myself,' said Beryl, agonising. 'I thought he might want to know that I didn't want to give him up. That I have never really got over it. But if people are going to get hurt by it...'

'We don't know that they are,' she said. 'It's only your cousin's opinion. It is a delicate situ-

220

ation though, of course.'

'He may not even know he was adopted, in which case he'd be in for a hell of a shock,' said Beryl.

'You'll be speaking to his parents first anyway, won't you,' said Liz. 'So you can decide whether or not to go ahead, depending on what they say.'

'Mm, that's true.' She lapsed into thought for a moment. 'Maybe the fact that there doesn't seem to be a way forward is life's way of telling me to leave well alone.'

'I couldn't say about that,' said Liz because she knew she mustn't influence Beryl.

'I think it will be best if I try to forget about it and leave him alone,' she said miserably. 'I don't have a choice anyway as I don't have anyone left to ask. I suppose my cousins are right. It will be better for him to be left in peace.'

A week later she received a letter from Maud with some very interesting information.

Chapter Eleven

It was a balmy evening, the air infused with the fragrance of spring, and Liz was cycling to work at the ice rink, almost too absorbed in her thoughts to fully appreciate the gentle new season so welcome after the harsh winter weather. Her mind was on Beryl who was agonising over whether or not she should pursue the idea of finding her son, her fragile confidence on the subject having been crushed by the negative opinions of her relatives.

Ironically, she could now go ahead with the search because, surprisingly, Maud had sent the details of the people who had adopted the boy, in the neighbouring area of Fulham, as it happened. Maud had apparently lied to them in the boy's best interest, but had later decided she shouldn't stand in their way even though she still didn't approve. There was no guarantee that the people would still be living there after all this time but it was a strong lead.

Although Liz empathised with Beryl's torment, she felt strongly that she herself shouldn't interfere, though she knew the older woman wouldn't rest until she had at least tried to put things right with her son. The reaction of the relatives had made Liz question her own wisdom in encouraging Beryl, but she would support her friend whatever she decided to do.

'Hello there, Liz,' said someone and slowing down she saw a smart young gentleman in a well-cut suit, carrying a briefcase.

'Arthur,' she said, smiling and pulling into the kerb. 'You're looking very dashing.'

'I wouldn't say that,' he said with his usual modesty. 'But I have to make more of an effort now that I'm working for a big city firm. They are quite strict about the dress code.'

'How is the new job going?' she asked.

'Good, thanks. It's a lot more challenging than my last place but I like to stretch myself,' he said. 'They pay a good salary and make sure that we earn every penny of it. I'm home early tonight.

222

It's often much later.'

'That doesn't sound too good.'

'You have to do it if you want to get on,' he said. 'I lost a lot of years to the war but in a strange kind of way that made me want to succeed even more, especially as I'd been spared when some of my army mates didn't make it.'

'Good for you.'

'I tend to think in terms of a career instead of just a job these days,' he said. 'And that means not worrying about working hours.'

'I see,' said Liz, to whom a career was unknown territory. 'So it will be tuppence to talk to you soon, then.'

'You know me better than that.'

'Just teasing,' she smiled. 'Anyway, you've finished work and I'm just starting. There's an ice show on tonight at the rink. A big one apparently. So, we'll be kept busy.'

'Are you being promoted then?' he asked lightly. 'I imagine the performers won't be hiring skates as they'll have the very best of their own.'

She laughed. 'I'll be showing people to their seats and anything else that needs doing. I'm a bit of a dogsbody there. They know I don't mind turning my hand to anything.'

'You must be a godsend to them.'

'As they are to me,' she said. 'The extra money comes in very handy with a growing boy to clothe.'

'I'm sure it must do,' he said. 'Well I'd better not hold you up then.' He thought for a moment. 'Is Charlie all right, and Beryl?'

'They're both fine.'

'Good. Off you go then to earn a crust.'

'Ta ta, Arthur.'

'So long, Liz.'

She continued on her way, thinking about Arthur, who was quite a dish these days. As well as the smart cut of his suit, he had a new air of confidence about him which was most attractive. She realised that she must be getting over Vic if she was beginning to fancy other men. But Arthur of all people!

It must be nature's way. She was a young woman and she was healing. She had no plans to celebrate the return of her libido but it was rather nice to know that it was there.

The rink was buzzing with excitement as people piled in to watch the show. When she'd been younger Liz had considered ice skating to be a middle-class pastime, until she'd started to come here with Marg during the war. Nowadays young working-class people used the rink for fun as a change from the dance halls.

Tonight the place was packed with all types because skating at this level was such a joy to watch. As the show got underway Liz feasted her eyes on the elegance and skill of the skaters. The beautiful costumes were not diminished because of clothes rationing as skating outfits did not use much fabric. She thought how much Vic would have enjoyed the show and realised for the first time that she didn't feel agonising sadness when she thought about him. It was more a feeling of fondness and nostalgia.

Marg came to mind too. She would have thoroughly enjoyed this spectacle – she loved any sort of a show. Though maybe this would be a little tame for her these days as she was so full of the joys of life in America. Her letters resounded with the wonder of her adopted country. Everything was bigger and better there; the food, the clothes, the houses with their modern gadgets. There didn't seem to be anything about her life in England that she missed.

Liz was pleased for her, of course, but she couldn't help feeling a little hurt as her friend seemed to have lost all interest in things and people here at home. But it was a huge thing she had done so it was good that she had settled so well. Anyway, Liz still had her stalwart pal, Beryl. She was a lady who was going to need plenty of support whether she decided to go ahead with her search for her son or not. Because if she didn't she would never forgive herself and if she did there could be trouble ahead.

Returning to the present, she paid attention to some late arrivals and showed them to their seats, counting her blessings. She had a job, a home, a good friend and a beautiful son. Maybe some aspects of her life hadn't turned out exactly as she had wanted but she considered herself to be very lucky indeed.

Gladys Watson was a forceful woman who wasn't afraid to speak her mind.

'My son is a grown man,' she told Beryl and Liz when they called to see her by prior arrangement, having explained who they were in a letter. 'Quite old enough to make his own decisions. If he decides that he doesn't want to see you, I won't try to persuade him otherwise. Neither will I interfere if he does. I shall tell him you've been looking for him and leave it to him.'

'Actually, I just wanted to know if the adoption worked out and if he's had good life,' Beryl explained. 'I don't actually need to see him if he'd rather not.'

'Surely you'd like to see him?'

'Well, yes, but I don't want to cause any upset,' said Beryl who was unrecognisable as the fierce department head who ruled supreme at the office. Here in this house in Fulham she was acutely vulnerable in the company of her son's adoptive mother.

'Does he know he was adopted?' Liz enquired.

'Oh yes. We told him when we thought the time was right,' Gladys said. 'He didn't seem to take much notice at the time. But we are not a particularly sentimental family so he isn't used to making a fuss about things.'

'Has he ever asked where he came from?'

'Never,' she replied. 'I didn't know much anyway. We heard through a friend that some girl was in trouble and we offered to take the baby when it came as we didn't seem blessed to have any of our own. It was all done very quickly and quietly with a minimum of fuss and paperwork.'

'Yes. I remember how quick it was,' said Beryl sadly.

'He's had a decent life,' Mrs Watson assured her. 'We made sure of that. We are not sentimental people but we did our best for him.'

'Thank you,' said Beryl.

'There's no need to thank me,' she said gruffly. 'We took him on so he was our responsibility, our son, and always will be. I was desperate for a child and it was one fewer baby for the orphanage.'

'What did you call him?'

'Michael, usually known as Mick.'

Beryl nodded. 'So, you'll tell him I've been asking about him?' she said, anxious to leave. 'Please emphasise that I want nothing from him, just to know that he's all right. I couldn't keep him, you see. My parents were very strict and...'

'That's your business and nothing to do with me,' she cut in sharply. 'It's probably best if you give me your address and if he wants to pursue the matter he'll contact you. I won't influence him either way.'

She gave Beryl a used envelope and a pencil and she wrote her details on the back. 'Thanks for seeing us,' she said and Mrs Watson led them to the front door.

'There's just one thing I should mention,' said Mrs Watson as an afterthought. 'Mick is very set on the idea of emigrating to Australia and is quite taken up with that at the moment.'

'Oh,' said Beryl, her disappointment obvious. 'He's going to live there for good?'

'That's the plan,' the woman confirmed. 'Nothing is finalised yet but he's been to Australia House and set the wheels in motion; filled in all the forms and so on. He's very keen to get on with it. You can't blame young people for wanting to go. There's precious little to keep them here whereas Australia is full of opportunities, apparently.'

'Yes, I have heard about the emigration scheme,' said Beryl. 'I hope he decides to get in touch before he goes.'

'I'll tell him you've been asking about him anyway, and leave the rest to him,' she said and Liz detected a little more warmth in her tone.

'She was a cold fish, wasn't she,' Beryl remarked as they walked to the bus stop with Charlie. Beryl had taken the day off in the hope that her son would be out at work and so she could speak to his mother initially to make sure she knew exactly what Beryl intended. It seemed only right. 'Doesn't seem the type who would show much affection to a child.'

'That isn't fair, Beryl. She probably felt threatened by you and was on the defensive,' suggested Liz. 'I expect she thinks you might intrude upon her relationship with her son.'

'That's the last thing I would do.'

'I know that but she doesn't.'

'He's going to Australia so if he doesn't get in touch before he goes I'll never know if he's forgiven me.'

'His leaving will be hard for her too, but she didn't say he was definitely going,' Liz pointed out.

'Mm, that's true. I feel so helpless because there is absolutely nothing more I can do. She might choose not to tell him we were even there and pass my details on to him.'

'I'm sure she will,' said Liz in a definite manner. 'Admittedly she wasn't a very warm person, but she struck me as honest and straightforward.'

'She'll want to protect her relationship with him, though, won't she?' said Beryl. 'It's only natural.'

'Naturally, of course, but I really do think she'll tell him about our visit. So, we'll just have to wait and see what happens,' said Liz as the bus arrived and they moved forward with the queue.

'My mother?' responded Mick to his mother's news, a quiver in his voice despite his nonchalant manner. 'My birth mother was here in this house?'

'That's right,' said Mrs Watson.

'What did she want?'

'To find out if you're all right.'

'Blimey, she's left it a bit late.'

'To be fair, she wouldn't have done it when you were a child in case it unsettled you.'

'I suppose not,' he agreed. 'Anyway, it's just as well I missed her because I wouldn't have wanted to see her.'

'Why not?'

'I don't really know. I suppose there doesn't seem to be much point,' he said. 'You're my mother. I have no need of another.'

'Aren't you the tiniest bit curious?'

'No. Not really,' he said. 'She's just a woman who had me and gave me away.'

'She had her reasons.'

'That doesn't mean I have to want to see her,' he said. 'I mean, what purpose would it serve?'

'For her to make her peace with you, I suppose.'

'There's no need,' he said. 'I don't feel any malice towards her. I am simply not interested.'

'Well,' she said, handing him the envelope on

which Beryl's name and address was written. 'If you do change your mind, here are her details. It's just between you and her and has nothing to do with me. You won't hurt my feelings by contacting her.'

He took the envelope and put it in his pocket without even looking at it.

Liz knew how much it meant to Beryl to see her son and her heart ached for her. At almost three her own boy Charlie was a constant joy and Beryl had missed all that. A crumb was all she wanted; just to see her grown-up son and be able to tell him that she had hated having to give him away.

She was certain that Mrs Watson would give him Beryl's details so there was nothing more they could do. It was up to him now.

Mick Watson was playing darts with a mate in the pub but his mind wasn't on the game.

'What's the matter with you tonight?' asked his pal. 'You're playing darts like a four year old.'

'I'm not that bad,' said Mick. 'Anyway, why would you care? You're beating me something rotten.'

'Exactly,' said the mate. 'I like to win but I also want to have to work for it. What's up? Women trouble, I suppose. When a bloke goes off his darts, it's always a woman.'

It was but not in the way his friend was implying. He hadn't been able to get the woman who was apparently his mother off his mind. He'd felt something when Gladys had told him she wanted to see him; he was physically shaken and he could still feel it now. It must be shock and curiosity, he guessed. What else could it be; the woman was a stranger. Someone who just happened to have given birth to him. Logic didn't come into his feelings. The ache of rejection was too strong.

Maybe he should go and see her to find out what sort of person gave a baby away. If she'd had no one to support her it would have been hard for her to keep him, but even so, how could you hand your own flesh and blood over to someone else and not get in touch for all those years? But even as the thought of paying her a visit played through his mind he knew he wouldn't do it. He had his life sorted. He was back in his old job, having given up the idea of setting up in business in England in favour of a new life in Australia. Things were still in short supply here. He wouldn't stand a chance in business without using the black market. So the sunny opportunities of Australia beckoned. He'd already set the wheels in motion but it would take a while because there were so many applications to process.

So this woman who had given birth to him could go back to wherever she came from. She couldn't just turn up in his life after all this time and expect him to welcome her with open arms. He didn't want any interference now that he was finally home from the war and had plans. She was just a stranger. So why was he having regrets about steering clear? Must be curiosity and he wasn't going to give in to that.

'Are we having another game or what?' asked his mate.

'We're having another pint,' said Mick.

'You won't hear me saying no to that,' said the other man and the two stood companionably at the bar. As the alcohol relaxed him, Mick began to feel better.

'I haven't heard from Marg for a while,' Liz said to Beryl one morning over breakfast.

'She's getting more used to life in America, I expect, and doesn't feel the need to write so often.'

'Too busy enjoying herself more like,' said Liz with a smile. 'She's really taken to life over there. But I hope she gets in touch again. I'm very fond of Marg.'

'The terrible two I used to call you when we all worked together.'

'Those were the days,' said Liz.

'You wouldn't want to go back to them, though, would you?'

'I sometimes miss the company,' admitted Liz, glancing at her son who was busy with his porridge. 'But I love being at home with Charlie and am very grateful to be able to.'

'We're a good team, us three.'

As their adored pet, Dolly, joined them by jumping onto a chair at the table, Liz laughed and said, 'You'd better make that us four.'

'Indeed,' said Beryl, smiling at the animal.

'I suppose later on when Charlie goes to school I might try and change my hours at the ice rink to fit in with him so that I am home when he is,' Liz mentioned.

'Yes, that would probably be better for you. Don't feel you have to, though,' said Beryl. 'The current arrangement can continue for as long as you like as far as I'm concerned. I'm very happy to have him in the evening.'

'Thank you, Beryl.'

She and Beryl had the occasional disagreement but most of the time they got along really well. Liz knew that the older woman was disappointed not to have heard from her son, but she didn't make any fuss about it. Liz felt guilty for encouraging her to look for him as it hadn't had a good outcome, but she had known she wouldn't rest unless she'd at least tried.

Liz thought he probably doesn't want to rake up the past, especially as he's going to live in Australia. He would be looking to the future. Liz stifled her instincts to go back to the Watsons and beg Mick to come and see his mother. This was one occasion when she really must stand back.

'Well, I must be off,' said Beryl. 'I can't have a go at the staff for bad timekeeping if I'm not punctual myself, can I?'

'Not really, no,' said Liz, remembering her days at the office and how she and Marg were permanently at war with Beryl. Life had been so carefree then. Oh, how she missed Marg!

At three years old Charlie was a joy to have around. He had his stubborn moments, but mostly he was chatty and funny with endless energy, which was why Liz took him to the park most afternoons. He could run free and use up some of his vigour there. She enjoyed this stage when he could communicate with her; to her it was more fun than the baby days but she knew

233

some mothers who mourned their passing.

'There's a man at our front door, Mummy,' he announced one autumn afternoon when they were on their way home from the park and had turned into their street.

'I wonder who he is and what he wants?' she said, seeing the stranger and hurrying towards him.

As soon as she saw his face she knew who he was. There was no mistaking those brilliant blue eyes.

'You're Beryl's son, aren't you?' she said.

He looked puzzled. 'How did you know?'

'You have the same eyes as her,' she said, noticing how good looking he was, albeit in a rough sort of way. He was tall and well built with dark wavy hair and those amazing eyes.

'Oh.' It was a new experience for him to resemble someone and it felt odd.

'Beryl is out at work at the moment,' she explained. 'But why don't you come in and have a cup of tea.'

'Are you her daughter?'

'No. Her lodger and friend.' She put the key in the lock. 'But come on in. You might as well now that you are here.'

After a brief hesitation, he followed her inside.

'I didn't imagine her going out to work,' he said after Liz had given him a cup of tea. 'But then I suppose I haven't really given her any thought.'

'Oh yes. She isn't married so has to support herself. She has a good job in a factory office. She's head of department. She used to be my boss.'

She went on to tell him how she came to be Beryl's lodger and friend. 'I was in the same position she had been in when she was a young girl.'

'But you kept your boy.'

She nodded. 'I don't think Beryl ever got over not keeping you,' she said. 'From what I've heard, her family were very domineering and bullied her into giving you up. I think they were quite well-to-do and were worried about the scandal.'

'Really?'

'Yes. If it hadn't been for Beryl I don't know where Charlie and I would be now. He'd probably be in an orphanage and I would be on the streets. She's an incredibly kind lady.'

It didn't seem that way to him. 'Why didn't she keep me, then, if she's all heart?' he said with a nasty edge to his tone.

'Surely you must know how badly unmarried mothers and their babies are treated,' she said firmly. 'You were spared the slur. Now you're an adult it doesn't matter.'

'You make it sound as if she gave me away for my sake.'

'She certainly knew you'd be better off adopted by a married couple.'

'So the fact that she wanted shot of me to save her reputation didn't come into it?'

'Absolutely not,' she said. 'It was all about survival and she didn't think either of you could if she kept you. Her family bullied her into giving you up.'

'But having got rid of me why would she want to come looking for me now?'

'She didn't do it when you were a child in case

it unsettled you. It's against the adoption laws anyway. Now she wants to make her peace with you, that's all. Nothing more,' she said. 'And I must admit I encouraged her. I know it's been eating away at her ever since she lost you.'

'It isn't easy for me to believe that a woman who gets herself knocked up then gives the kid away can be as saintly as you are making out.'

'I didn't say she's saintly,' she said, her voice rising. 'I said she has been very kind to me.'

'You did it though, didn't you?' he said with an aggressive edge to his tone. 'You kept your child.'

She nodded. 'As I have said, I couldn't have done it without Beryl and she didn't have a good Samaritan to help her.'

'What happened to the father of your boy?'

'He was killed in the Blitz,' she said. 'Ironic really. He was an American soldier over here because of the war. He was about to ask me to marry him, apparently.' She paused. 'Sadly, it wasn't to be.'

'Sorry.'

'Yeah, so am I, even now,' she said truthfully; she didn't believe she would ever really get over Vic's death. 'But you just have to get on with it, don't you?'

'You certainly do.' He looked uneasy. 'I'll be honest with you. I'm not sure if I can do the mother and son thing. I wouldn't know where to start. My adoptive mother and I have never been lovey dovey and that's the way we both like it. But, as far as I'm concerned, she is my mum and always will be. She's always done her best for me.'

'Beryl doesn't want anything from you,' Liz

236

made clear. 'Just to make her peace with you. She isn't going to try to be your mother. You only need to see her once if you wish.'

'I can't get past the fact that she gave me away when it wasn't convenient and now wants me back in her life when it suits her. You must admit it isn't really on.'

'She only wants to say sorry; not to have you in her life as such. She knows you have a family.'

'I've been brought up to look out for number one,' he explained. 'My parents taught me that from a very early age. And that is what I do.'

'I'm sure Beryl doesn't want you to change your ways because of her.'

'No. I suppose not. I'm going to live in Australia soon anyway so I won't be around for much longer.'

'As I've said, she isn't thinking of asking you to be a part of her life or anything. So why not let her make her peace with you.'

'Yeah, I can do that I suppose,' he said casually.

'Good.'

He seemed thoughtful. 'So you're her lodger then,' he said.

'Happily, yes.'

'Is she officially allowed to take in lodgers?' he asked in a tone of casual interest. 'Does the landlord know about you?'

'She owns the house so she can do as she pleases,' she explained.

'Owns it?' he said, seeming shocked.

'Yes, she inherited it from her parents.'

His absolute glee was mirrored in his eyes and Liz knew at that point that she didn't trust him.

'Impressive,' he said, having already noticed how well appointed the place was. No cheap tat here. 'I don't know anyone who owns their own property. Everyone in my world just rents.'

'Same here,' she said.

An interruption from her son, who was crayoning at the table, was welcome to Liz because she wanted this meeting to end. 'Is it teatime, Mummy? I'm hungry.'

'Yes, love. I'll make your tea in a minute.' She turned to her visitor. 'Perhaps it would be best if you were to come back this evening when Beryl is at home. Any time after about seven thirty. We'll have eaten by then.'

'Okay, I'll let you get on then,' he said rising. 'See you again later.'

After she had closed the door behind him, she realised that she was trembling slightly. Beryl was going to have to be very careful. Liz had a bad feeling about him. She would keep her views to herself and her eyes wide open for the moment, though. Let Beryl form her own opinion.

Mick was surprised by how small his birth mother was. Being a tall, strapping man himself he'd imagined her to be big and daunting. Instead he found himself faced with a small, apologetic woman with tears in eyes that were the same colour as his. Oh God, he was no good with emotional women. He hoped she wasn't going to start crying. Thankfully she hovered on the brink then seemed to compose herself.

'Thank you for coming,' she said.

'No trouble.'

'When I last saw you, you were a tiny scrap of a thing.'

Oh no, how was he expected to react to a statement like that. 'I suppose we all start off like that,' he said.

'I'm so sorry,' she said. 'That I didn't keep you. I wanted to but it was difficult.'

'That's all right,' he said, as though she'd apologised for spilling her tea. 'I didn't suffer.'

'You had a happy childhood, then?'

He wouldn't go so far as to say that but she needed reassurance so he said, 'Yeah, it was fine.'

'Good, I am so relieved,' she said, visibly shaking. 'Not a day has gone by when I didn't think of you.'

Emotions were being aroused that he didn't know how to deal with and he didn't like it. He wasn't used to this sort of talk and being with someone of the same flesh and blood. Even so, he still couldn't understand how she could have just handed him over and he wasn't ready to forgive her, but he wasn't about to let her know that. There was far too much to gain from this situation if he kept a cool head. As it turned out it was just as well he'd let his curiosity lead him to her door.

'Well I'm here now so we've got some catching up to do,' he said.

'Oh. Yes please,' she said, flushed with delight. 'I want to know all about you.'

'What a lovely young man he's turned out to be,' Beryl said to Liz after Mick had gone.

'Yes,' agreed Liz to keep her friend happy. It was

239

far too soon to give her real opinion. Anyway, she might be wrong about him and she really hoped so.

'He doesn't seem to hold a grudge about my giving him up for adoption.'

'I suppose he understands that you didn't have any option,' she said dutifully.

'Yes, I told him everything and he seemed quite sympathetic.' She was trembling slightly with excitement and pleasure. 'Oh Liz. I am so happy to have him back in my life. So thank you, dear, for encouraging me to find him.'

'That's all right,' said Liz, hoping that they didn't both live to regret it.

'We were just like old friends, straight away,' she said, glowing. 'There's a strong feeling between us. We are both pleased that we have found each other at last.'

'Good.' Liz was happy for her despite her own impression of him.

'I've told him to come around here whenever he feels like it,' continued Beryl excitedly. 'He's going to Australia soon so I want to see as much as I can of him before he leaves.'

'That's only natural,' said Liz, trying to stifle an awful sense of foreboding.

Beryl wasn't the only one smitten with Mick, who became a regular visitor at the house. Dora was full of praise for him too, though there was nothing motherly about her feelings.

'He's absolutely gorgeous,' she said. 'Very good looking but there's a rough edge to him too. I love that in a man. I must get a date with him.'

'You'll have to do some serious flirting then, won't you,' said Liz. 'That shouldn't be a problem since you've had enough practice. But don't be too overpowering and embarrassing or you'll drive him away.'

'As if I would.'

'It has been known,' Liz reminded her.

'All right, don't go on about it,' she said. 'Will he be around at the weekend?'

'I wouldn't be surprised,' said Liz. 'He seems to come any time he can.'

'That's nice,' said Dora. 'It shows how much he thinks of his mother.'

'Yeah,' agreed Liz, wishing she didn't feel so cynical about his reasons for visiting so often.

Chapter Twelve

Liz's mind was distracted from her suspicions about Beryl's son by an unexpected visitor one morning when Beryl was out at work.

'Marg!' she said in amazement when she opened the door to see her old friend standing there. 'How did you get here?'

'Well, I didn't swim,' she said with her old chirpiness then her face crumpled and she flung her arms around Liz in tears. 'Oh Liz, I'm in such trouble.'

'Why? What's happened? Where's Joe?' asked Liz, ushering her inside.

'He's at home in the States.'

241

'Are you back for a visit?'

'No ... for good.'

'You mean ... please don't tell me you've left him.'

She nodded. 'I had to. I couldn't settle,' she said thickly through her tears. 'My homesickness was so bad it was making us both miserable. We thought it would just be a passing thing, but it got worse and spoiled everything. I actually felt physically ill with it at times, Liz. In the end, Dad sent me the money for the fare home. He took it out of his savings and I feel terrible about that too.'

'Did you fall out of love with Joe, then?'

'Oh no, not at all,' she said with emphasis. 'I still love him to bits, but this terrible ache I had for home was ruining both our lives. It reached a stage where I couldn't bear it any longer. I knew I had to come home.'

'Is that why you stopped writing to me?'

'Yeah, I couldn't pretend everything was fine any longer.'

'So, all that stuff about how marvellous it is was lies, then?'

'No. Not entirely,' she said. 'It is a wonderful place. But my heart is here.'

'So, what now?'

She shrugged her shoulders dejectedly. 'I'll have to make a life back here, I suppose. But I miss Joe so much. Now that I'm back I realise just how much he means to me.'

'That didn't override the homesickness when you were there though.'

'No, it didn't,' she said. 'The homesickness

dominated everything and squashed all my other feelings. I was so miserable, Liz.'

'Well, you can't keep sailing across the Atlantic Ocean, that's for sure,' said Liz. 'So, you'll have to try to settle down here.'

'I know,' she said. 'I have to get a job. Do you know if there's anything going in Beryl's department?'

'No, I don't but I'll find out for you. She's very preoccupied with other things at the moment,' she said and went on to tell her about Mick. 'She absolutely adores him.'

'Well, well,' she said. 'Who would have thought Beryl had secrets?'

Liz was about to confide in Marg about her doubts regarding Mick but her friend had quite enough problems of her own. Liz did need to talk to someone about it, though, preferably someone outside of the situation.

'Anyway, Marg,' she began. 'Despite the sad circumstances of you being back I am very pleased to see you.'

'Thanks, Liz,' she said and started to cry again whereupon Liz put her arms around her.

On Sunday morning Liz walked through the suburban streets with Charlie on his scooter, the pavements carpeted with autumn leaves, and knocked at the door of her parents' neighbour. Arthur answered the door.

'Are you busy?' she asked.

'Not especially, why?'

'I need to talk to you.' She looked at her son beside her. 'I'm taking Charlie to the park and wondered if you might join us. Sorry to bother you but it's quite urgent.'

'I'll get my coat,' he said without hesitation, reminding her again what a good friend he was.

It was a glorious morning with a fragrant mist and a feeling of imminent sunshine as they headed off into the park, walking slowly so that Charlie could keep up. She told Arthur about Beryl's son and her own fears about him.

'He might be perfectly well intentioned,' suggested Arthur.

'I know, that's why I need to talk to you about it before I blurt out my feelings and upset Beryl needlessly.'

'What has he actually done?'

'Nothing yet,' she said. 'But he's very sure of himself and he's all over Beryl.'

'Isn't that only natural having been reunited with his mother after all this time?' he said.

'It would be if it was genuine.'

'What makes you think it isn't?'

'His reaction to being told that she isn't short of a few quid, mostly. His eyes nearly popped out of his head when I told him she owned her own house. I could almost feel him working out what was in it for him.'

'Might it just be that you are being a bit too protective towards her?'

'Maybe I am,' she admitted. 'But he's just a bit too full of working-class charm and is overly eager to please his mother,' she explained. 'It seems false. I feel threatened by him.'

'And Beryl?'

'Loving every moment.'

'But you don't think there will be a happy ending?'

'I wish I could say yes, but I really don't think so,' she said. 'God knows what he's got in mind but I'm sure it won't be in Beryl's best interests.'

'Perhaps I should pay Beryl a visit when he's there so that I can judge for myself.'

'Oh, would you, Arthur?' she said. 'I'd be so grateful. He'll probably call round to see her later on. He usually comes to visit on a Sunday morning. You used to come too so it won't seem at all odd for you to call in.'

'No, it won't.'

She had a sudden thought. 'You've not been for ages. Any particular reason?'

He looked at her and seemed about to say something then just said, 'I haven't got around to it, I suppose. But I'll pop over later on this morning.'

'Thanks, Arthur,' she said gratefully.

They spent some time with Charlie, collecting conkers and watching him on his scooter then walked home chatting.

'Any friend of my mother's is a friend of mine,' said Mick, shaking Arthur's hand. 'How do you know her?'

'Through Liz who is an old friend,' he replied. 'She used to live next door to me.'

'Oh well, we're all mates together now, aren't we?'

'We certainly are,' said Arthur, going along with him.

His rough, working-class manner gave Mick a

245

certain charm that made him seem honest to the core. If it wasn't for Liz's doubts, Arthur wouldn't have judged him to be anything less than genuine. But her suspicions made him observe more closely and he could see that he did overdo the friendliness.

'So, what's your line of business, Arthur?' asked Mick.

'I'm an accountant,' he replied.

'He works for one of those big swanky accountancy firms in the city,' said Dora who had been out with Mick a few times and had high hopes of a future for them together.

'Oh really. Should I doff my cap?' laughed Mick.

'You don't have one,' Dora reminded him, laughing too.

'So, what do you do?' asked Arthur with polite interest.

'I'm an electrician.'

'Ooh, a useful man to know.'

'Yeah. There's nothing I can't do with plugs and wires and I've got big plans,' he said. 'I want to set up my own company eventually. Of course, I shall have to start off working for someone else when I'm abroad.'

'He's going to Australia,' explained Dora. 'Unless I can talk him out of it.'

'Plenty of opportunities there at the moment, I understand,' said Arthur.

'Apparently,' said Mick. 'They need people, especially tradesmen like me.'

'So, when are you off?' asked Arthur.

'It will be a little while yet,' he replied. 'There's

a lot of administration to go through the system. You get thoroughly checked out.'

'That's understandable,' said Arthur. 'The Aussies will want to make sure that they get the best people.'

'That's me out of the running then,' said Mick laughing uproariously at his own joke.

Beryl came over to speak to Arthur. 'Haven't seen you for ages,' she said. 'I thought you'd deserted us for ever.'

He couldn't tell her why he'd stopped visiting so he just said, 'I wouldn't do that, Beryl. I've been busy.'

'I heard about your new job,' she said. 'Well done!'

'Thanks,' he replied.

The social interlude continued with Mick doing most of the talking and not seeming to mind Dora's proprietary attitude towards him. He did seem very keen on her, Liz observed. It was a pity she'd finally found someone with reciprocal feelings and he was probably a crook.

'Well,' said Liz in a questioning manner when she saw Arthur off at the front gate.

'He's an entertaining bloke and I wouldn't trust him further than I could throw him.'

'Oh Arthur. What do you think he'll do?'

'Probably nothing, but I can see why you are suspicious.'

'I was hoping you'd tell me I'm imagining things.'

'Look ... he's probably all right,' he said. 'You must try to distance yourself from it.'

'How can I? She's a dear friend.'

'I know but there's nothing you can do at the moment because he hasn't actually done anything and if you let him know that you're suspicious he could turn nasty.'

'I can't just sit back and do nothing.'

'You'll have to for the moment,' he said. 'Keep your eye on the situation and let me know if you see anything dodgy. We're probably worrying unnecessarily. But now that I know about it you have some back-up.'

'Thank you so much, Arthur.'

'You're welcome. Cheerio then, Liz,' he said.

'Bye, Arthur.'

She felt oddly lonely as she watched him stride off down the street.

A week or so later, Liz was cycling home from her evening shift at the ice rink when she saw something that took her mind off Beryl and was such a shock she almost came off her bike. She was waiting for the traffic lights to change when she noticed a couple come out of a pub with arms entwined and totally engrossed in each other. As they walked under the lamppost, she recognised one of them. The woman was a stranger, but the man was *her father!*

Liz was so shaken by what she had seen she stepped on to the pavement and wheeled her bike. What should she do? Her instinct urged her to tell her mother, who surely had a right to know. But she would be so hurt and humiliated. Was there another way to deal with it? Maybe if her father promised to end the affair, Mum could be spared the pain of knowing. But would it be disloyal not to tell her? One thing she did know for certain. She was going to confront her father about it. He wasn't going to get off scot-free!

Speaking to her father without her mother knowing wasn't an easy thing for Liz because her mum was usually home when he was there. Anyway, he didn't like his sinful daughter to be in the house. So she left early for work the following evening and waited for him around the corner from the house with the intention of catching him on his way home.

It was cold and miserable standing there under the lamppost with her bike, her nerves on edge, a mist beginning to float around her. The idea of her father having an affair made her feel sick, her stress increasing as she saw him approaching.

'Hello, Dad.'

'Liz, what are you doing, standing around in the street?' he asked, clearly startled.

'Waiting for you.'

'Is something wrong indoors? Your mother...?'

'Mum is fine ... for the moment.'

'What does that mean exactly?'

'She won't be fine if she finds out what you get up to when you go out of an evening,' she said. 'I saw you with your fancy woman last night. Walking along with your arms around her in public as bold as brass. You are such a hypocrite. All that moralising you did when I got pregnant.'

'This is different altogether.'

'No it isn't,' she said. 'It's worse. You are a

married man; of an age when you ought to know better.'

'So ... what are you going to do?'

'That depends on what you've got in mind,' she said. 'Are you going to leave Mum for this woman?'

'Don't be so ridiculous,' he said. 'I would never leave your mother.'

'So what are you planning?'

'Nothing,' he said. 'It's just a bit of fun.'

'I doubt if Mum will see it that way,' she said. 'It'll break her heart.'

'She doesn't have to know, does she?' he said in a pleading manner. 'I mean, it really doesn't mean anything.'

'It probably does to your lady friend.'

'No, it doesn't,' he informed her firmly. 'It's just a bit of fun for us both.'

'You're despicable,' she said. 'Trying to make out it's nothing much.'

'It isn't,' he said.

'Are you going to stop seeing this woman then?'

'I shall have to now, won't I?'

'How do I know that you'll do it?'

'You'll just have to trust me.'

She gave a dry laugh. 'I lost all my trust in you when I saw you with that woman. I've never liked the way you behave towards my mother anyway, treating her like a servant and never a word of thanks. But this ... this is awful. You're my father for goodness' sake. You ought to know better.'

'All right, you can cut the lecture,' he said. 'I'll stop seeing the woman and you keep quiet.'

'Only to spare Mum's feelings,' she said. 'And

very much against my better judgement. I shall have to rely on you to do your part and end the affair, friendship or whatever you like to call it.'

'Consider it done.' He was obviously relieved. 'Are you coming in to the house?'

'No. I'm on my way to work,' she said. 'Anyway, I'm not welcome, am I? Not a sinner like me.'

'You are welcome to visit any time, Liz,' he said in a serious tone. 'You and your boy.'

He'd changed his tune. That was what fear and guilt did to a person.

She swung onto her bike and went on her way wondering if she had done the right thing in agreeing to stay silent. At least it would save Mum from being hurt.

One thing that remained constant in Liz's life was her love for her son who seemed to get more like his father every day and so was a constant reminder of Vic. She liked that. It reminded her that her beautiful wartime romance had actually happened. Sometimes those happy days seemed so distant.

'You are so lucky to have him, Liz,' Marg said to her one Sunday morning when they were playing ball with Charlie in the park. 'I would have loved a child.'

'I expect you will have one in time,' said Liz. 'You are still a young woman.'

'I meant with Joe,' said Marg.

'Mm, that's more difficult as you're in different countries,' she said. 'Do you think you'll ever be able to get back together?'

'I'm not optimistic because it's such a terrible

251

thing I did to him, leaving like that, and I can't expect him to forgive me,' she said. 'And even if he did find it in his heart, I couldn't go back there to live. It's just too far away, Liz. I felt so lost, so alone, even though I had him and everyone was so welcoming.'

'Might it have been better if you'd had your own place?' suggested Liz. 'Instead of living with his folks?'

'It wasn't their fault; they were very good to me,' she said. 'The blame is all mine because of this thing inside of me, this awful ache of missing home.'

'I think it would have eased off if you'd stayed,' suggested Liz. 'You hear about people getting homesick but it always wears off eventually.'

'So I've heard,' she said. 'But I was in such a terrible state I couldn't see my way through it and I've burnt my boats good and proper now. There's no way back.'

'Are you in touch with Joe?'

'I've tried but he doesn't answer my letters,' she said sadly. 'He was too deeply hurt I suppose. He begged me to stay, to give it a chance. But I couldn't. I was in such a bad way.'

'Anyway, do you fancy forgetting your troubles for a few hours and coming to the pictures with me on my night off?' said Liz. 'They'll have the royal wedding on the newsreel I expect. Princess Elizabeth and that gorgeous prince getting married.'

'Prince Phillip,' she said. 'I saw a picture in Dad's paper, but it's not the same as seeing it on the screen. They probably won't show much but at least we'll see her go in and out of the church. We'll be able to see her dress.'

'I hope so,' said Liz.

'Yeah, I fancy that and I've got some money now that I'm working, thanks to Beryl giving me a job. I'm saving up to pay my dad back for the fare home but a night at the flicks won't cost much,' she said.

'How do you find Beryl as a boss now?'

'She's a different woman to the one I used to work for,' she said. 'She's all smiles and rarely raises her voice these days.'

'That's because she has her son in her life,' said Liz. 'It's changed her.'

'For the better,' added Marg.

Liz wasn't so sure about that but she just nodded and said, 'That's settled about the cinema then. I'll ask Dora if she'd like to come and Mum as well. Beryl won't mind listening for Charlie for me. She always welcomes the chance.'

'The more the merrier,' said Marg, looking a little more cheerful as her mind was diverted from her troubles.

Liz wasn't able to join the others at the cinema after all, because of an unexpected hitch with the babysitting.

'My mother does more than enough for you,' said Mick aggressively to Liz in the living room when Beryl wasn't around. 'You've got a bloody cheek asking her to look after your child while you go out enjoying yourself.'

She was taken aback. 'She enjoys having him,' she said. 'He'll be asleep anyway.'

253

'You're still handing her your responsibility and I'm not having it,' he said. 'So, you will tell my mother that you don't need her after all. That the cinema trip is off.'

'Why don't you tell her?'

'Because she will not welcome my interference so you will tell her yourself and make sure she thinks it's your idea. Tell her you've changed your mind.'

'What makes you think I'll do as you say?'

'Because you know I can make things difficult for you around here if you don't.'

'Oh yeah,' she said defiantly. 'How?'

'My mother is so pleased to have me in her life she will do anything for me.'

'She also has a mind of her own so don't underestimate her,' she said.

'I think you would be wise not to underestimate *me*,' he warned. 'So just tell her your plans for the cinema have been cancelled and everything will be fine.'

'And if I don't?'

'You'd be sensible not to risk it.'

Acutely aware of her responsibility to Charlie and their need for a roof over their heads she shrugged and said, 'All right, I'll do it but I'm not happy about it.'

'Your happiness matters not a jot to me,' he made clear. 'But I'm glad you've agreed to do the right thing for my mother's sake.'

'The princess looked lovely, didn't she,' Beryl said to Liz one evening, brandishing the Sunday newspaper which had a picture of the newly married royal couple.

'Yes, they make quite a handsome pair.'

'It would have been nice for you to see them on the newsreels at the cinema,' she remarked. 'It was a pity your friends decided not to go.'

'Mm,' muttered Liz casually.

'We might have to wait a while for another royal wedding. Her sister Margaret will be next.' Beryl thought for a moment then said excitedly, 'Oh by the way, Mick thinks I should have the telephone installed. You have to wait a while to get it done, apparently, but he said I ought to get on the waiting list. Things are moving again at last after the war.'

'Oh.' Liz was surprised because home telephones were almost unheard of in her circles. She guessed he had an ulterior motive for making the suggestion but couldn't think what it was apart from swank. 'And is that what you want?'

'Ooh, yes,' she said enthusiastically. 'It will be lovely to keep in touch. He said he'll go to the phone box at the end of his street and call me on the days he doesn't come around. Isn't it sweet that he wants to make sure I'm all right?'

'Yeah it will be nice for you.'

'You too,' she said. 'You can use it and have your friends phone you up.'

'Thank you, Beryl,' she said, thinking it might be useful if work wanted to contact her for any reason. She couldn't help but be excited by the idea of a telephone at home even though she suspected Mick had another reason for suggesting it. It was new and thrilling.

Dora thought the telephone was a marvellous idea. 'I'll be able to ring Mick when he's at his mum's from the phone box near us.'

'By the time you've walked to the box you could have come round here.'

'I wouldn't do that,' she said. 'It would seem too pushy unless we had a date. But calling someone on the phone is different. Anyway, it will be fun.'

'Mm, maybe,' said Liz. 'So, things are still going well with you and Mick then?'

'We were made for each other,' she said. 'We're two of a kind. Neither of us is perfect. We both like our own way so the sparks fly quite often. But it's always fun when we make up.'

Despite her dislike of Mick and her suspicions about him she was glad that her sister had found someone who returned her feelings. Liz had seen them together and that was the impression she got. Dora could cope with a bad boy; in fact, it would probably enhance her feelings for him. She'd never been attracted to pillars of the community like Arthur. It was just Beryl that Liz was afraid for. Beryl the tyrant of the filing department had become a shrinking violet in the company of her son.

'Honestly, Liz, you know that I'm with you all the way on the subject of Beryl's ghastly son but I can't see any evil connotations in having a phone installed,' said Arthur when she called to see him on her way home from work one evening to keep him up to date. 'Are you sure you're not getting a bit paranoid about Mick? I mean what possible harm can a phone do?'

'None, I suppose,' she said. 'It just seems a bit unnecessary and an extra expense for Beryl.'

'She can probably afford it,' he suggested. 'She has a good job and probably has a fair bit of dough behind her if her parents were well off.'

'Even so...'

'Liz,' he said, sounding stern. 'You need to calm down. You're getting into a state about this bloke when there is no reason. I know we don't trust him but you mustn't suspect his motives for every single thing he does. More ordinary people will have a phone put in as things gradually get better in this country.'

'But things aren't better, are they?' she said. 'Rationing is worse than ever. Business people and the well-off have a phone in their house; not ordinary people like Beryl.'

'Perhaps he doesn't want to come to see her as often so if she has a phone he can call her to save the journey.'

'Oh yes, that might be it,' she said brightening.

'Anyway, there's probably a hell of a waiting list so it will be ages before she actually gets the phone installed.'

'Hm.'

'So calm down and try to get along with the man until he does something that really is out of order, and I've no doubt that he will. Then, together, we will sort him out.'

'You're right,' she said. 'Sorry to have bothered you with it.'

'You could never bother me, Liz,' he said. 'I just don't want you getting into a state unnecessarily.'

'I know, Arthur.'

She wanted to feel his arms around her, to luxuriate in his closeness. But he never made any sort of move in that direction. So she just said, 'I'd better be on my way.'

'Will you be all right on your own?' he asked. 'I can get my bike and come with you, if you like.'

'Of course I'll be all right,' she said. 'I'm used to being out on my own after dark.'

'I won't insist then because I know it will annoy an independent woman like you.'

'Absolutely,' she said. 'So, I'll say goodnight then.'

'Goodnight, Liz.'

''Night Arthur.'

She hurried to the gate and swung on to her bike, feeling almost tearfully lonely.

Liz took Charlie to the ice rink one afternoon to show him where she worked and it proved to be a rather emotional interlude because the child was very taken with it and keen to go on the ice and the whole thing brought his father back to her so strongly she had tears in her eyes.

'Not today, Charlie,' she said. 'But one day when you are a bit bigger we'll come here and I'll take you on the ice.'

'Tomorrow?'

'No, not tomorrow,' she said. 'But one day soon. I promise.'

Not normally a difficult child, today he decided to make a fuss, refusing to leave the place and demanding to go on the ice. In the end, she had to literally drag him out. Even though she was angry and embarrassed she couldn't help think it rather strange that he had taken such a liking to the place where his father had been happiest.

Christmas was a disappointment to Liz this year because Mick joined them in the afternoon and the easy, homely atmosphere she had enjoyed with Beryl on previous Christmases was notice-ably absent. Although Mick made a minimal effort to keep his feelings hidden, probably so as not to upset Beryl, it was obvious to Liz that he didn't enjoy having a child around.

'How did your parents feel about you deserting them on the big day, Mick?' she asked.

'As long as they've got plenty of booze in they're not bothered if I'm there or not,' he said. 'So, I thought I'd get on my bike and come over as there's no public transport.'

'And we're very glad you did, aren't we, Liz,' beamed Beryl.

'Of course,' she said politely, hating every moment of his company but deciding that she wasn't going to allow it to spoil things for Charlie or Beryl.

The little boy was so enthralled with his new toys and the festive atmosphere that he didn't seem to notice Mick's coldness towards him, which became more noticeable with every drink Mick had, and he certainly knew how to consume alcohol. After tea when he went into the kitchen to help himself to more beer Liz followed him, leaving Charlie happily playing with Beryl.

'I'd appreciate it if you could be a little less hostile towards my son,' she said.

'Why should I?'

'Because he's a little boy and it's Christmas Day.'

'He's spoilt.'

'It's Christmas Day so of course he's getting a little indulged,' she said. 'Today is the time for children.'

'You should put him to bed out of the way,' he said. 'Give us all some peace.'

'How dare you!' she said. 'He's as good as gold and this is his home.'

'Not for much longer,' he said.

'What do you mean by that?'

He looked at her, his bright blue eyes heavy from the booze. 'I've been meaning to have a word with you and now is as good a time as any.'

'A word about what?'

'I'll be moving in here soon.'

'Oh. Beryl hasn't said anything.'

'She doesn't know yet, but she'll be thrilled to have me around all the time,' he said. 'She can't get enough of me as you've probably noticed.'

'But why would you want to move in here?' she asked, dreading the thought of having him around all the time.

He shrugged his shoulders. 'A classier part of town, a nicer house, to be with my mother, take your pick,' he said, his tone slightly mocking.

'Is this just until you go to Australia?' she asked.

'No, it will be permanent,' he said. 'I've changed my mind about emigrating. I wouldn't want to leave my mother now that I've found her, would I?'

His sarcasm was scathing but she managed to hang on to her rising temper. 'I see,' she said.

'Well I suppose there's room for one more.'

'There will be plenty of room for me because you and your kid won't be here,' he said.

'What do you mean?'

'I'm not living in a house with a lodger and her noisy kid,' he said. 'So I want you out.'

'I think your mother might have something to say about that,' she said.

'You will tell her that you want to move out because you've found somewhere better.'

'She won't believe me because there are no better places at a price I can afford.'

'Tell her that you want to move in with your family, then,' he suggested.

'She knows that's the last thing I would ever do.'

'I'll leave it to you to work something out then because I want you out of here and Mum must think it's your idea.'

'And what if I won't do as you say?'

'I shall tell her you've been coming on to me and that's why I want you out,' he said.

'She won't believe you.'

'She thinks I'm God's gift and I can do no wrong so I believe she will,' he said.

Liz knew with a sinking heart that this was true.

'But I've got nowhere to go,' she said.

'Your problem, I'm afraid,' he said. 'You had a lucky break with my mother. Time now to face up to the real world.'

'What's your game, Mick?' she asked. 'Are you planning on taking over your mother's life completely to get at everything she owns?'

'I am simply looking out for her,' he said. 'You've

261

sponged off her for long enough.'

'I have never sponged off her,' she denied. 'I always pay my way. I suspect that is more than you will do.'

'Insults won't make me change my mind.' He was calm because he knew he had the upper hand. 'You can stay on here for another week or two then I want you and your kid gone.'

She knew he had made up his mind and she wouldn't give him the satisfaction of begging him to let her stay. But for the second time in her life she faced homelessness and she was terrified!

Chapter Thirteen

'Oh Liz, that's terrible,' said Arthur when she knocked at his door the next day and told him what had happened. Dora was playing with Charlie next door. 'You were right about that son of Beryl's. I'll go around there and sort him out right away. He's not getting away with this.'

'No, Arthur, please don't do that because it might make things difficult for Beryl. It's best to go along with him for the moment.' She had been awake for most of the night worrying about her plight. She'd got used to security for herself and Charlie, thanks to Beryl's good nature. Now they faced the prospect of some overpriced, scruffy room with very few facilities, or a hostel. She would also have to get her hours put up at the ice rink as the job of housekeeping for Beryl would stop the day she moved out. Mick would see to that. Then there was the problem of getting Charlie minded while she was out at work. Oh dear, it all seemed too much but she must try not to panic. 'Apart from my own personal problems, I'm worried about what his ultimate aim is for Beryl. He wants me out of the way and he's moving in with her. So he's obviously got something definite in mind.'

'A scheme to get hold of her money and he doesn't want you around in case you scupper his plans.'

'Exactly, and I won't be there to protect her from him if he turns nasty,' she said. 'I know Beryl is under his spell at the moment but she's a very intelligent woman. If she realises she's being conned before he's finished the job he'll turn on her and I won't be on hand to help.'

'Depends how crafty his scheme is,' he said. 'She might not realise until she's signed everything over to him then he won't turn nasty because he'll be gone.'

'Oh Arthur.'

'Don't panic. This is all just speculation.'

'But it's very likely to happen and we're helpless to stop it.'

'Not completely. We can both visit regularly to keep an eye on things.'

'Mm, that's true.'

'I presume you haven't told Beryl you're leaving yet.'

'No. It's Boxing Day and I don't want to spoil it for her so I'll leave it until after the holiday,' she said. 'I'll have to make up some story about why

I'm moving out. He's ordered me not to tell her he's asked me to leave. I know that if I don't do as he says he'll make things bad for Beryl somehow.'

'Will you move in with your family?'

'Dad won't have me living there; the fallen woman and the illegitimate grandson,' she said. 'So I don't know what I'm going to do yet. I've been too worried about what that crook has in mind for his mother.'

'You have to think of yourself and Charlie, Liz,' he said, concerned.

'I know, but as it's Boxing Day there's nothing much I can do today,' she said.

'Shall I ask Mum if you can stay with us?'

'It's kind of you, but no thanks, Arthur,' she said. 'It would be too humiliating for Mum, my living next door. Don't worry, I'll work something out.'

A silence fell then, 'Let's all go to the pantomime at the Chiswick Empire this afternoon,' he suggested spontaneously, hoping to take her mind off her problems for a few hours. 'My Boxing Day treat for us all. You, me, Charlie and Beryl. It will cheer us all up and Charlie will love it.'

'What a lovely idea. Mick won't be coming to Beryl's today. He's going out with Dora. I heard him telling Beryl so she won't feel as if she has to stay at home to be with him. But how can I go out enjoying myself when I'm about to become homeless? That would be really irresponsible.'

'It won't cost you anything because I'll be paying and it will give you a break from the worry so you might feel better able to cope afterwards. So, I can see nothing irresponsible about it.'

'Have you got tickets then?'

'No, but I'll be at the theatre as soon as the box office opens,' he told her. 'I can't promise the greatest seats in the house at such short notice, but I'll do the best I can. You need some light relief, something I suspect has been missing this Christmas.'

'Charlie has enjoyed it and that's the important thing, but it hasn't been the best Christmas for me because of Beryl's ghastly son.'

'Let's make sure it finishes on a high note then, shall we?' he said, smiling persuasively.

'That will be lovely, Arthur. Thank you,' she said, touched by his kindness.

'I'll do my very best to get tickets,' he said. 'And if we aren't lucky I'll think of something else for us to do. Christmas wasn't much fun for you, but Boxing Day will be better and that's a promise. You are not going to stay at home fretting. I'll make sure of it.'

'Not a word to Beryl about my accommodation worries,' she said. 'Not yet.'

'I won't breathe a word.'

The seats weren't the best in the house, being at the back of the stalls on the end of the row, so they only had a side view of the stage. But the show and the atmosphere were fantastic. It was everything a pantomime should be; dancers in sparkly costumes, women dressed as men and vice versa, silly jokes, a pantomime horse, lots of songs and plenty of audience participation, especially for the children.

As the applause rang out for the finale, Liz realised that she had thoroughly enjoyed it and was feeling better; the tension knots in her stomach had eased so that she felt stronger and more able to cope with the problem.

'Thank you, Arthur,' she said as they walked back to Beryl's for tea. 'I've had a lovely time. I feel a bit more human now.'

'Good, I enjoyed it too,' he said. 'I think the adults appreciated the show more than the kids.'

'The children don't understand the grown-up jokes.'

'Just as well as some of them were a bit near the mark.'

'I can never quite see why they have such saucy jokes in a kid's show.'

'To keep the adults entertained as they paid for the tickets, I suppose.'

'That'll probably be it,' she said smiling.

They had cold meats and pickles, Christmas cake and mince pies for tea, everybody chatting about the show. The difference in the atmosphere without Mick was tangible to Liz. Beryl was happy and relaxed as she had been before her son had come into her life. Arthur stayed until after Liz had put Charlie to bed then she saw him off at the door.

'I would ask you to come out for a drink with me tonight but I think it might be pushing it with Beryl to ask her to babysit on Boxing Day,' he said.

'What about your girlfriend?' she asked.

'That's finished,' he said. 'It never really got started. It was just a few dates.'

'Oh, I see,' she said feeling ridiculously pleased. 'I'm sure Beryl wouldn't mind listening for Charlie, but I won't bother her tonight if you don't mind. I haven't had much time with her over Christmas because of Mick so she might welcome a little of my company while he isn't around. But thank you ever so much for mentioning it. It's kind of you.'

'I wasn't just being kind, Liz,' he said. 'I really enjoy being with you.'

'Likewise, so can we do it another time soon, Arthur?' she said smiling. 'I'd really like that.'

'Me too,' he said, becoming more besotted with every meeting. But now wasn't the time to blurt it all out. Not while she had so much on her mind.

Arthur's efforts to take Liz's mind off her troubles must have had an effect because she felt calmer as she got into bed. She was able to think more clearly and suddenly she knew exactly what she had to do to save her son and herself from homelessness. It was the last thing she wanted but she had a duty to Charlie. If there was any other way to save them from some bug-ridden lodgings she would do it, but there wasn't so she had to forget her own feelings and get on with it.

It was bitter cold with a promise of frost as Liz stood on the corner under the lamppost the next day in the early evening. This was one of the most belittling things she had ever had to do and she didn't like herself one bit. But there were times in life when you had to grovel.

'Oh no, not again,' said her father gruffly as he came into sight and she approached him. 'What do you want this time? You've got nothing on me. I've finished with that woman.'

'I need somewhere to live, Dad,' she said. 'I need a home for Charlie and me.'

'You're not moving in with us,' he stated firmly. 'I said you could visit. That is all.'

'But it's the family home, Dad, and I wouldn't ask if there was any other way,' she said. 'For myself I can rough it, but I don't want Charlie having to live in some awful place.'

'You lost any right to live with us when you got yourself in trouble,' he said.

'I know that but I'm desperate.'

'Oh ... well it's your own fault.'

'I don't know how you can be so heartless,' she said.

'You brought it on yourself.'

'I shall have to see what Mum thinks about it,' she said.

'Your mother would never go against me.'

'She might if she found out what you get up to when she thinks you're out playing darts.'

'That's all finished, I've told you,' he said gruffly. 'It was nothing; just a silly lapse.'

'I doubt if Mum will think it's unimportant,' she said. 'Anyway, that doesn't alter the fact that it happened. If she were to find out you'd be the one in the street, not me.'

'You wouldn't tell her.'

'I'd rather spare her from knowing, it's true, but I have a child to look after and I have to find a home for us,' she said. 'If I had any alternative I

268

wouldn't be asking, believe me. The last thing I want is to live in the same house as you with your mean-minded ways, but I have no other option. Surely you wouldn't see your grandson on the streets?'

'He's no grandson of mine.'

That hurt more than any insult her father could throw at her. Her lovely boy disowned by his grandfather! 'He is, whether you like it or not,' she said. 'But I can see that I shall have to ask Mum if we can move in.'

'I pay the rent so she has no say in it.'

'She more than earns the right to a say, the way she looks after you with never a word of thanks.'

'It's her job.'

'She didn't sign up to be a skivvy when she married you,' she said. 'But as you're not pre-pared to help me I shall ask Mum if I can move in and I'll have to be quick because I am on my way to work. There'll be enough time for me to say what I have to, especially about your recent carry-ings-on.'

Propping her bike up against the kerb, she walked towards the house.

Her father caught up with her. 'All right, you can move in,' he said quickly. 'But you must keep that boy of yours in order. I don't want a lot of noise about the place.'

'He's three years old, Dad,' she reminded him. 'Of course there'll be noise.'

'Well, don't let him run wild then.'

'My son is not a hooligan,' she said firmly. 'Will you tell Mum, or shall I?'

'I'll tell her as you've got to go to work.'

'And, Dad, there's something else...'

'Oh gawd, what now?'

'I'll need to ask Mum to look after Charlie for me while I'm at work in the evening. I know she'll love to do it but I don't want you making a big fuss about it.'

'There'll be no fuss.'

'Thanks, Dad,' she said and went on her way.

She hated herself for doing that to her father but she had Charlie to think of. Her mother and sister would be delighted to have him around so he would feel loved even though his grandfather wanted nothing to do with him. She felt it was a backward step for herself personally. You were supposed to leave home for good when you grew up; not come home when things went wrong. By traditional standards she hadn't made a success of her adult life. But she had her dear Charlie and compared to that all else paled into insignificance.

Beryl was upset to hear that Liz was leaving.

'Is it something I've done?' she asked, her eyes wet with tears. 'I know I've been a bit preoccupied with Mick lately. Have I upset you?'

'No, absolutely not, Beryl. It's just that Mum could do with a bit extra towards the rent,' she fibbed.

'I will really miss you.'

'And I you, but Mick is moving in soon so you'll have plenty of company and you'll be glad of the extra space.'

'There will always be room for you and Charlie in this house no matter who else is here,' she said. 'Remember that and if you ever want to come back you'll be more than welcome.'

'Thank you, Beryl. That means a lot to me,' she said. 'And I'll keep it in mind.'

'It won't be the same without you and Charlie,' she said sadly. 'I shall miss you terribly.'

'Beryl,' began Liz in a serious tone. 'My time here has been absolutely wonderful. I have loved every moment and I'm sad to be leaving. But all good things come to an end. I shall visit often so you haven't seen the last of me.'

'I hope you mean that.'

'I do, Beryl,' she said with feeling. 'You'll get fed up with me popping in so often.'

'Never,' she said.

'So, when is Mick moving in?' she asked quickly as emotion threatened.

'In a week or so, apparently,' she said.

'You must be delighted to be having your son around all the time.'

'Yes, of course,' she said. 'I've told him he'll have to abide by my house rules though. To keep his room tidy and no loud noise late at night.' Her eyes filled with tears suddenly. 'Oh dear, I shall miss you so much, Liz, you and Charlie.'

'And we'll miss you,' said Liz thickly. 'But I'll visit all the time, I promise. And we're only a short walk away.'

'Yes, I realise that, but it won't be the same,' said Beryl sadly. 'It really won't.'

The next morning Beryl stood wet eyed at the front door as Liz walked down the path. When Liz turned to wave, there were tears in her eyes too. She felt so angry with Mick for making this

271

happen and worried too about what he might do while she wasn't there to keep an eye on things.

'Nice to have some young company in the house again,' said Dora when Liz and Charlie had moved in. 'As well as unlimited access to my gorgeous nephew.'

'Glad you approve,' said Liz lightly, but she knew that her time in this house had come to an end the day she had moved out under a cloud. She had simply outgrown it and now felt alien to her family, the odd one out, resentful of the house rules. This was her family home, but she'd felt much more loved and at ease at Beryl's house. Anyway, she was of an age when she needed independence, a home of her own. But this was all she had so she had to make the best of it and be grateful. It certainly beat shabby lodgings or a hostel.

Liz visited Beryl every weekend with Charlie and sometimes called in briefly of an evening when she wasn't working.

'Are you checking up on me or something?' asked Mick when Beryl was out of earshot.

'No. Why would I do that?' she lied.

'You're here so often you needn't have moved out.'

'I didn't have any choice, did I?'

'Shush,' he said. 'We don't want my mother to hear such things.'

'I don't know what your game is, but I know you have something in mind for Beryl and it won't be for her benefit,' she blurted out.

'You need to watch what you say,' he said. 'I could have you done for slander.'

'You won't though, will you?' she said. 'Because you have other, more lucrative plans.'

'You should treat me with more respect, especially as we might be related one day.'

'How?'

'I'm courting your sister...'

'You're not serious about her, are you?'

'I am as it happens,' he said. 'She's my sort of woman. None of this good-girl stuff with Dora. We're two of a kind. We both like our own way and fight to get it. Neither of us care much about upsetting people. She isn't the easiest of people to get on with, but neither am I so we understand each other. There's no shortage of arguments but we always make up.'

'So, as you have such a strong relationship, you won't mind if I tell her about my suspicions about you then?'

'I don't mind in the least,' he said. 'I'm sure she'd be as amused as I am. Dora enjoys a good joke.'

'Don't underestimate her,' she said. 'She's selfish but she isn't stupid. When she finds out what you're really like she'll soon send you packing.'

'She knows what I'm really like,' he said. 'I have never tried to pretend that I'm a saint. And she can't get enough of me.'

Liz gave an exasperated sigh. 'I've had enough of this. I'll have a cup of tea with Beryl then be on my way.'

'Good,' he said. 'And you can tell that mate of yours, Arthur, to stop calling as well.'

'You don't mean that.'

'I bloody well do,' he said. 'I don't want to see either of you here again.'

'But we are Beryl's friends.'

'And I'm her son,' he reminded her. 'So guess who is more important to her?'

'Respect that and be good to her then.'

'Have I ever been anything else?'

'Not that I've noticed – not yet.'

'Mind your own business and leave my mother and me alone,' he said.

'Not possible I'm afraid,' she said and went to join Beryl in the kitchen where she was making the tea.

Not only was Dora in thrall to Mick, so were Liz's parents.

'They can't get enough of him,' she confided to Arthur over the garden fence later that same day when Mick had come to call for Dora and was being given a royal welcome by her parents. 'He's all sweetness and light to them. You wouldn't know it was the same man that I was speaking to earlier. Oh and by the way, he told me to tell you to stop calling on Beryl.'

'Not on your life.'

'That's the stuff,' she said. 'I told him I shall continue to visit her too.'

'Good.'

'Dora is absolutely besotted with him,' she went on. 'But somehow they are right together. They are as selfish as each other but it seems to work, despite their many arguments. I'm not worried about her because she's a match for him.'

'Yes, I think she probably is.'

'No regrets that you've lost your childhood sweetheart, then?'

To Liz's surprise he seemed a bit rattled. 'How much longer do I have to be reminded of something that ended when I was a little kid?'

'Just joking, Arthur.'

'I should hope so.'

A familiar call came from the back door. 'Mummee,' cried Charlie. 'Are you coming in soon?'

'Coming now.' She turned to Arthur smiling. 'My life isn't my own. Bye for now. See you soon.'

She was too busy attending to her maternal duties to notice that Arthur didn't look happy.

For all that Liz hadn't wanted to move back in with her parents, something rather wonderful came out of it – her mother's relationship with Charlie. She had always been good with him but now that he was around all the time she became something of a supergran and couldn't do enough for him. Liz had never thought of her mother as a particularly patient woman, but she had endless patience with Charlie. Her tolerance levels outshone everyone else's and the two of them enjoyed each other enormously.

She was firm when necessary but mostly she was a soft touch. This rather lovely relationship meant that Liz could go to work with an easy mind and when asked to do extra hours she could do so without agonising. Her father didn't take much notice of his grandson. It was almost as if to do so would somehow sanction his daughter's status as an unmarried mother. But sometimes she noticed him grinning at something Charlie had said or done so she was hopeful.

'It's all worked out all right for you, then,' remarked Marg when she called one day. She hadn't been told the real reason Liz had left Beryl's because Liz thought the fewer people who knew the truth about Mick the better at this stage. Anyway, Marg was still very preoccupied with her broken marriage.

'Yes, as it happens,' she said. 'So, what's the latest from the United States?'

'Joe is answering my letters again,' she said seeming relieved. 'I've told him I'll go back. He's trying to raise the money for my fare.'

'The man is a saint.'

'Yeah I know. But what if I still can't settle?'

'You'll have to make sure you do,' said Liz who would have given a lot to be married to Vic. 'You married the man for better or worse after all.'

'You think I'm being selfish.'

'I'm trying not to judge you,' said Liz.

'I know if I go again there will be absolutely no turning back,' said Marg. 'That's what scares me. But I'm determined to make a go of it this time. What do you think?'

'I'm saying nothing,' said Liz. 'It's your life and your decision. But what's so great about it here in England anyway? We've got bomb damage, rationing and everything needing a lick of paint. At least in America there's plenty to eat and nice things in the shops to buy.'

'I can't tell you the answer to that,' said Marg

emotionally. 'Unless you leave England for good you won't understand.'

'Oh. Well as I'm not likely to go further than Southend on a day trip, I'll just have to take your word for it.'

'Yes, you will.'

'He can't come here, I suppose?'

'He has a good job there,' she said. 'It would be madness to give that up.'

'Whereas if you go there you wouldn't need a job because he'll support you.'

'Exactly.'

'I'll have to get used to missing you all over again,' said Liz.

'Likewise,' said Marg.

Liz wondered how she would have felt about leaving England if Vic had lived. It seemed so exciting and glamorous when you heard about the GI Brides going to America to live. But Marg's experience had shown her that it wasn't always that simple.

Liz and Arthur continued to visit Beryl often despite Mick's objections. But nothing untoward happened and Beryl seemed fine.

'Do you think we might have misjudged Mick?' Liz asked Arthur one day in spring.

'I wish I could say yes, but I think he still needs watching,' he said. 'I enjoy going to see her anyway so I won't stop no matter how much he dislikes it.'

'Me too,' she said. 'I wouldn't dream of not going but everything seems to be okay there.'

'Long may it stay that way.'

Sunday was always a good day to visit Beryl because Mick went to Fulham to see his drinking pals and have lunch with his parents so Beryl was on her own. One Sunday morning when Liz went to see her and approached the house, she saw something that stopped her in her tracks. An estate agent's For Sale board!

'Why, Beryl?' she asked. 'Why on earth would you sell the house that you love, where you grew up?'

'Because Mick and I are going to buy a place together,' she said. 'But I have to get rid of this first to get access to the money I'll need for my share.'

So, this was it. Mick had made his move. Quite how he was going to get his hands on the money his mother got from the house, Liz didn't know but she was certain that was his purpose. It wouldn't be difficult to persuade her to transfer her funds to him if she thought it was for a property. He didn't want to buy a house with her; just to get his hands on her money.

'So where are you thinking of going?' Liz asked.

'Not far because of my job,' she replied. 'But Mick thinks this house has too many bad memories for me; you know my getting pregnant and then having to give him away. It wasn't nice and it all happened while I lived here. I was sent away to have the baby but this was my home.'

'But there are good memories too, surely,' said Liz. 'Like when Charlie and I lived here, for instance.'

'Oh yes, that was lovely, but there has been a lot of sadness here too, when I was younger. Besides I've never done anything exciting and this will be. Don't you think?'

'Well I suppose it could be,' said Liz. 'But it will be a massive upheaval too.'

'It's time I did something a bit daring,' she said. 'I've been in a rut all my life.'

'Moving house will be a huge change for you,' suggested Liz, not wanting to pour cold water on the idea, but worried about her friend.

'Mick will take care of everything so I won't have to worry about a thing,' she said. 'He said he will do all the packing-up and see to all the removal arrangements as well as the actual sale; the money and everything.'

'The money?'

'Yes, he'll do all the negotiations and make sure the money comes in,' she said. 'We are going to have a joint bank account for the house. He'll transfer his funds into it and when the money from the house comes that will go in with it. So, we'll be ready to proceed with a new place. As soon as we get some interest in this house we'll start looking at property.'

Beryl's money would go in to the bank account and disappear along with Mick in Liz's opinion. But what could she say? How could she stop her friend from losing everything and having her heart broken when she was so thrilled about it?

'It's all a bit sudden, isn't it, Beryl?' she mentioned cautiously. 'Might it be a good idea to think about it some more before going ahead?'

'What is there to think about?' she said. 'I have

found my son and he wants to buy a house with me. That's what I call a happy outcome.' She gave Liz a warm smile. 'I have you to thank for this and I'm very grateful, dear. If you hadn't encouraged and helped me to look for him I would never have found Mick and had such happiness.'

Liz said nothing.

'So thank you, dear,' Beryl went on. 'You've been such a good friend to me. I really hope you will be a regular visitor in our new place.'

'You can rely on it,' said Liz, trying not to spoil the moment for Beryl by looking too horrified.

'We'll have to stop it somehow,' said Arthur.

'But how?' asked Liz who popped next door to see Arthur as soon as she got home. 'She's thrilled to bits and sees Mick's plans as a sign of his commitment to her.'

'I can't understand it,' he said worriedly. 'Beryl is an intelligent woman who holds down a responsible job. How can she be so taken in by him?'

'She wants to believe well of him, that's how,' she said. 'She lived with the guilt of giving him away for all those years. So the fact that he seems to have forgiven her sufficiently to want to buy a house with her, as she thinks, has made her so happy, all common sense has flown. And, of course, she doesn't see what he's really like because he makes damned sure of it.'

'Once he's got her money, she won't see him again,' he said. 'There will be no new house.'

'That's what I think,' she said. 'But what can we do to stop it from happening? If we were to tell her of our suspicions she wouldn't believe us.'

'You're right. But we'll have to stop it going ahead somehow,' he said. 'Even if it means telling her stuff she doesn't know and won't like, such as him forcing you to move out and trying to stop us visiting.'

'He'd just deny it.'

'Mm, you're right,' he said. 'So the first thing to do is for me to have a few words with him.'

'Oh Arthur, be careful.'

'I'm a match for him,' he said.

'I know, but he probably has tough mates.'

'Don't worry about me,' he said. 'Anyway, I'm not going to start a fight with him. Just ask him what he's up to and let him know that we'll be keeping an eye on things. I shall ask him where he is going to get the money for his share in this supposed house purchase since he doesn't have a property to sell himself.'

'How will you manage to speak to him without Beryl hearing?' she asked.

'I'll catch him in the pub at the end of Beryl's road,' he said. 'I've seen him going in there of an evening on my way home from work.'

'Shall I come with you?'

'No, I'll do this on my own, man to man.'

'Good luck with it then,' she said.

'Can I buy you drink?' Arthur asked Mick when he found him standing at the bar in Beryl's local.

'Why would you want to do that?'

'Just wanted a chat, actually.'

'Oh yeah, and what could we possibly have to say to each other?'

'The fact that Beryl's house is up for sale.'

'So, what business is that of yours?'

'Beryl is a friend and I'm looking out for her.'

'She's got me to do that.'

'Apparently you are going to buy another property together,' said Arthur.

'Yeah, so what?'

'You're paying half each.'

'That's right.'

'So, Beryl will pay her share with the money she'll get from the sale of her property,' Arthur began. 'But you live with your parents so how are you going to pay your share?'

Mick turned pale with fury. 'What business is it of yours?' he demanded.

'None personally, but as a friend of your mother's I see it as my duty to look out for her.'

'You're well out of order, mate,' said Mick. 'What happens between me and my mother is none of your business.'

'You don't have the money, do you?' said Arthur. 'There'll be no other house. Once you've got the money for the one she's sold you'll be off with it.'

Mick took a swallow of his beer. 'That is a serious accusation,' he said.

'It's a serious matter.'

'Yeah, and if you value your health, you'll stay out of my business.' His eyes were bright with fury. 'This is a serious warning. If you approach me again, I shall involve the police and have you done for harassment.'

'And if you steal your mother's money I'll make sure the police know about it.'

'Oh, go and play with your numbers,' he said. 'That's what you do for a living isn't it? That's what all accountants do. A few sums and charge people a fortune for doing it.'

'If you say so,' said Arthur, managing to stay calm. 'But just so you know, Liz and I will be keeping an eye on things at your mother's.'

'I might have guessed Liz would be nosing around.'

'She's Beryl's friend. Of course, she'll look out for her.'

'Oh, go away before I really lose patience and give you a hiding.'

He turned his back on Arthur and engaged in a conversation with the barman.

'Until someone actually puts an offer in for Beryl's house, she's safe isn't she?' said Liz, having been told about Arthur's meeting with Mick.

'Until she actually completes and money changes hands she's safe. Trouble is, it's a nice, well-maintained house so there will be no lack of interest.'

'I feel so helpless but when things progress, we'll have to have a straight talk with Beryl,' she suggested.

'I don't think she'll hear a word against Mick,' said Arthur. 'He's got his feet well and truly under her table.'

'We'll have to make her listen somehow,' said Liz. 'But there's no need to say anything just yet.'

'Thank the Lord for a breathing space,' he said and they both giggled nervously.

Dora was in high spirits when she got home from her date with Mick one night in May.

'Guess what,' she said to Liz who was having a cup of cocoa at the kitchen table, their parents having gone to bed.

'Something good by the smile on your face.'

'Really good,' she said. 'Mick and I are going away a bit later on in the year.'

'For a holiday?

'I'm not sure, but I'm pretty certain it will be for longer than that,' she said. 'Mick just told me to be ready to go at short notice because he'll need to get away. I don't know when or how long for. I'm just excited to be going anywhere with him.'

Liz froze. They would be disappearing into the sunset with Beryl's money. 'Did he say where you'll be going?'

'No, he didn't,' she said. 'He hasn't decided yet. I like that in a man. Impulsive, lives for the moment.'

'Isn't that a bit annoying that you don't know exactly when or where? I mean, you'll need to get things ready and how can you arrange for the time off work?'

'I don't care about any of that,' she said. 'Once I know when, I'll tell them I need time off and if they argue I'll leave.'

'That's a bit drastic.'

'Not really. I work in a grocery shop. I'm not on the career ladder at Harrods,' she reminded her. 'There's plenty of other shop jobs around. We still have rationing but there's no shortage of work, not in my line anyway.'

'You'd lose your job for Mick then?'

284

'Like a shot,' she said. 'I'd do anything for him. This is the first time I've been lucky in love and I'm going to hang on to him no matter what. He has plenty of faults and so do I, but he's the man for me. He wants me to go away with him and I'll go, no matter where it is or why we're going.'

'You have got it bad.'

'Yeah, I have and I'm enjoying every moment.'

Liz realised with a sinking heart at that moment that it would make no difference to her sister's feelings for Mick if she was to know the truth about him. She'd stay with him no matter what and there wasn't a thing Liz could do about it.

Chapter Fourteen

It was Sunday afternoon and Beryl was sitting in the armchair in her living room quietly sobbing, the cat dozing on her lap. There had been several potential buyers viewing her property over the weekend and she knew she must end this charade before it went any further.

She couldn't leave this house, the only home she had ever known, and it was time she stopped lying to herself about it, *and about everything.* Mick didn't have any money to put towards their supposed joint venture; the whole idea was just a way of getting his hands on hers. When she'd allowed herself to be honest she had seen the plan for what it was from the moment he had suggested it and had never believed that he had any intention of raising the cash for his share. But she had refused to fully accept the truth because it had been such a lovely idea; reunited mother and son making a new start together.

The reality wasn't easy to take but it was time she faced up to it. What had she expected anyway? A devoted, loyal son when she had abandoned him, given him away to take his chances without his mother to love and guide him? Their only tie was a biological one which she felt but he obviously didn't. It was understandable as she hadn't been there to see him grow up and to set him on the right path.

Whether the reason for his plan was revenge, to pay her back for deserting him, or plain and simple greed she didn't know. But whatever the motive she had to tell him the whole thing was off and as soon as he got back to the house she would get on and do so. She guessed that she would lose him but she would have done that anyway when he went off with her money. At least this way she would still have a roof over her head. The whole thing was deeply painful though.

Arthur had been having a Sunday afternoon kickabout with some mates in the park and as he walked home he was thinking about Liz and how he could change the nature of their relationship. Or at least tell her how he felt about her. They had these special moments when he was sure his feelings were reciprocated but, afraid to break the spell, he had let these times pass without comment. Now it was time he brought things to a head. If the answer was no, then he would stop agonising and get on with his life, though he knew it wouldn't be easy.

At a more practical level, he wondered if Liz had been to see Beryl today. He intended to go when he'd been home to change. He'd give Liz a knock on the way. If she hadn't already called to see their friend they could go together and, maybe, on the way home he would broach the subject so much on his mind.

Dora was always fed up on Sundays because Mick went to Fulham to visit his parents and catch up with his mates so she didn't see him until the evening. This meant she was stuck at home with her boring family all day.

'Can I take Charlie to the river to see the ducks, Liz?' she asked, keen to get out of the house.

'Of course, if he wants to go,' Liz said amiably. 'I'm going to pop over to Beryl's so a trip to the river with you will be more fun for him. I'll call for Arthur on the way.'

As it happened Liz met Arthur about to knock at her door so they headed for Beryl's together.

'So, are you telling me that you are not selling the house after all?' said Mick furiously. He had come home early and been told of Beryl's decision.

'Yes, that's right.'

'What's brought this on?'

'I forced myself to face the truth.'

'Are you saying that you don't want to move, then?' he asked angrily.

'It's more that I don't want to be left homeless while you go off with my money.'

He attempted to look puzzled. 'What are you talking about?' he asked.

'You know exactly what I'm talking about.' She was sad and tired. Coming to terms with this had broken her heart and exhausted her. 'I would have given you money, within reason, but to invent a scheme to take all I have is pure evil.'

'Well, yeah, I suppose it is,' he said, not bothering to deny it as she was on to him. 'But I reckon I deserve some sort of compensation as you gave me away so that you could get on with your comfortable life.'

'What comfortable life?' she said. 'I've always worked hard for every penny. And giving you up for adoption was the most heart-breaking thing I have ever done, I've told you that several times. But I had no way of keeping you and you'd have hated me for it if I had. Being known as a bastard wouldn't have been nice.'

He shrugged carelessly.

'One thing I would like to know and would appreciate your honesty,' she began. 'Was the money your only incentive in this scheme? Or did you want to punish me?'

'I'm not twisted. I don't go looking for revenge or hold grudges. I saw the chance of getting my hands on some dough so I went for it. It's as simple as that,' he said gruffly. 'Unlike you, I have always had to work for every penny. I am never likely to inherit a house.'

'Does the fact that I'm your mother mean nothing to you then?' she asked.

'How can it when I don't know you?' he said. 'You turn up out of the blue and I'm expected to come over all sentimental. How am I supposed to have feelings for a complete stranger?'

'I did give you the gift of life,' she reminded him.

'Mm... I don't really know how I'm supposed to react to that. I'm just an ordinary bloke. Not a man of words,' he said. 'But thank you for that.'

She nodded. 'Did you move in here to try to get to know me or just to set your plan in motion to rob me of my money?'

'You don't need me to answer that,' he said. 'You know it was the second.'

She gave a sharp intake of breath, the pain almost unbearable. 'Yes, I suppose I do,' she said, almost in a whisper.

'Look,' he began and at least he had the decency to look a little ashamed. 'You've known about me since my birth. Until you appeared in my life I knew nothing about you. When I was told that I was adopted I didn't ask who my real mother was because I wasn't interested. It came at a time in my life when I was growing up and had all sorts of new feelings to cope with and I suppose that was enough, so I put it out of my mind and moved forward with the life I had. That was my way of coping with it, I suppose. When you came looking for me, I didn't feel anything for you. How could I when you were a complete stranger?'

She nodded. 'At least you've been honest about something,' she said.

'I've never lied to you about that,' he said. 'I've never pretended to have feelings for you.'

'No, I don't suppose you have.'

'And while I am being honest, there are a

couple of things you need to know,' he began. 'I forced Liz to move out. She didn't want to.'

'Oh,' she gasped. 'Why did you do that?'

'I thought it would be easier to put my plan into action without her nosing around,' he said. 'I also tried to stop both Arthur and Liz from visiting you.'

'Oh Mick!' She was shocked.

'Yeah, pretty low, I must admit. They didn't take any notice anyway, but I did try.' He cleared his throat. 'So I suppose I'd better pack my things.'

'Where will you go?'

'Back to Mum and Dad's to start with but it's time I was off their hands,' he said. 'I'm too old to still be living at home. But there is someone I need to see before I do anything else.'

'Dora?'

'Yeah.' He paused. 'Look, I know it probably won't be much consolation, but I'm sorry for what I had planned and that it didn't work out as you hoped between us.'

She nodded and there were tears in her eyes.

'I must be a huge disappointment to you.'

'I only came looking for you to see if you'd done all right. I didn't have any expectations.'

'Just as well.'

'Yes.'

There didn't seem to be anything more to say so he left the room and met Liz and Arthur outside the door, who had heard every word.

'The back door was open because of the sunshine,' Liz explained.

'As it happens I'm pleased to see you both,' he said. 'Mum needs you just now and I know you'll look after her.'

'Course we will,' said Liz.

'It's true what they say. There's no fool like an old fool,' said Beryl to Liz and Arthur after Mick had left the house.

'You're no fool, Beryl,' said Liz. 'You just wanted to believe in a happy ending, that's all.'

'At least you know that he's all right,' said Arthur. 'You said you were always worried in case things hadn't gone well for him. Now you know that he's a survivor.'

'I'll say he is,' said Beryl. 'As long as he's all right, blow everybody else. But I don't believe he would have actually gone through with the plan to steal my money.'

Liz and Arthur exchanged glances.

'That's something we'll never know,' said Liz. 'Let's just be thankful that it didn't happen.'

'Yes,' sighed Beryl. 'I'll never forget him though and I hope he keeps in touch once this has all blown over and he's had a chance to think about things. He will always be welcome here.'

As a mother herself Liz could understand her feelings. She knew that the love she had for Charlie now would continue into his adulthood, even when he grew up and flew the nest. She also knew it was unconditional.

'I'll be lost rattling around in this house on my own,' said Beryl. 'I've got used to having lodgers.'

'I'd love to come back but Charlie is used to it where we are now and I think Mum would be hurt if we left, especially as my father is growing fond of his grandson, even though he isn't ready to admit it yet,' said Liz.

'I quite understand Liz,' said Beryl. 'Maybe I'll do it properly next time I take lodgers. I could have the upstairs made into a proper flat with its own kitchen. To give everybody more privacy. There's such a drastic need for more housing at the moment and I don't need the whole house.'

'What a good idea, Beryl,' approved Liz.

'Excellent,' added Arthur.

'Time for tea I think,' said Beryl managing a smile.

'I'll put the kettle on,' offered Liz.

When Liz and Arthur set off for home, he led her into the park and found a quiet corner.

'Why have we come in here?' she asked.

'Because this situation between us has gone on for far too long,' he said, turning to her. 'I don't want to be your friend, Liz. It isn't enough.'

'You certainly took your time.'

'You too?'

'Of course,' she said. 'I was beginning to think you'd never get around to it.'

'When you've known someone all your life…'

'Stop talking, Arthur,' she said, putting her arms around him.

Later that same day before heading back to Fulham, Mick called at the Watsons' and asked Dora to go for a walk with him.

'What's all this about?' she asked as they headed for the river. 'I wasn't supposed to be seeing you until tonight.'

'I have things to say to you.' They crossed the

road and found a riverside bench. He turned to her. 'I'm a bad lot, Dora. Not a good person at all. I had plans to steal my mother's money and I have broken her heart.'

'Oh Mick,' she said. 'That's awful.'

'I know,' he agreed. 'She guessed what I had in mind and put a stop to it.'

'That's a relief.'

'Yeah, it is to me too, in a way,' he said. 'It would have been a hell of a thing to live with.'

'I presume you've moved out then.'

'Yeah, I've left my stuff at a mate's place and I'll go back to Fulham later on.'

'So, I don't suppose you'll see Beryl again.'

'I'm hoping to. When the dust has settled, I'll go to see her and try to make my peace with her, if that's possible. It might take a while because she's been so hurt and I feel awful about it,' he said. 'I may not be able to be the son she'd like me to be, but I could try to be a friend.'

'So you do have a good side then.'

'I'm not sure about that but, apparently, I have a conscience.'

'Is that it then?' she asked. 'Is that what you had to tell me so urgently?'

'No, there is more.'

'Oh gawd. What else have you done?'

'Nothing, but I don't know what to do with my life, whether to go abroad or stay here, whether to set up in business or stay as I am.'

'Yeah, so what...'

But he cut in. 'There is one thing in my life I am sure of. I love you, a lot.'

'Oh,' she beamed. 'I feel the same about you.'

'We are good together.'

'So, is this your idea of a proposal?'

'I suppose it is.'

'Are we getting engaged then?'

'Yeah, if you want to,' he said casually.

'Of course I want to,' she said. 'Who else is going to put up with me?'

'Exactly.'

'There's no need to agree so quickly.'

'Oh, come here,' he said putting his arms around her.

'Not so fast,' she said. 'What about a ring?'

'I haven't got one yet because I didn't plan this,' he said. 'It was a sudden decision.'

'I want a ring.'

'You'll have your ring,' he said.

'When?'

'At the weekend, we'll go and choose one.'

'Okay,' she said. 'You can kiss me now.'

Liz left early for work the next evening and called in to see Marg who had just got home from work.

'Arthur and I are courting,' she announced happily. 'It's official.'

'About bloomin' time too,' said Marg smiling and hugging her. 'You've been fancying each other for long enough. I'm so pleased for you, Liz.'

'Thanks,' she said. 'Who would have thought that Arthur and I would get together?'

'He's a very attractive man, especially since he got back from the war.'

'I know and he's mine.'

'I've got a bit of news of my own as it happens,' said Marg.

'Oh?'

'I'm going back to America next week,' she said. 'It's all arranged.'

'I shall miss you.'

'Likewise,' said Marg. 'But I'm determined to make a go of it this time. I'm going to concentrate on making Joe happy. It was all about me last time. If I'm homesick I'll just have to put up with it and hope it will eventually wear off.'

'That's the right attitude,' said Liz. 'I think you'll be all right this time.'

A year or so later, Liz left the ice rink for the last time as an employee. Now that she was married to Arthur and they were settled into the top floor of Beryl's house, which was now a lovely flat with its own kitchen, she didn't need to work of an evening and they liked to spend the time together. Charlie had started school and she missed him a lot during the day. But he would be having a brother or a sister soon so Liz would have plenty to occupy her when the new baby arrived.

The rink would always be special to her because of Vic, but it was time to move on now with her life with Arthur. When Charlie was old enough she would bring him here and tell him what a whizz his dad had been on the ice. If he wanted to try it himself she would encourage him. His American grandma still sent him a parcel for his birthday and at Christmas so he was aware of his US connections. Liz planned to make sure of that as he grew up, with Arthur's full support. But now she felt warm inside at the thought of going home so she got on her bike and pedalled off into the night.

Beryl was delighted to have Liz and Arthur living upstairs with Charlie. It had been worth the effort to have it made into a proper flat because they all had more privacy. Her lodgers spent quite a bit of time downstairs with her, though. They seemed to enjoy her company and she certainly liked to see them.

Mick visited regularly, sometimes with his wife Dora, who was a good influence on him in that she didn't let him have all his own way, mostly because she wanted hers. But somehow or another, they got along.

Beryl could never forget what Mick had planned to do to her, but she had learned to live with it. Whatever the others thought of him she knew he would never try to cheat her again. Other people perhaps. But not her. Maybe they would never be like a normal mother and son but he was trying and that was more than she'd ever hoped for. So, one way and another she was happy. Dolly jumped on to her lap and she fondled her, smiling.

'Very quiet isn't it, George, now that the girls have married and left home,' said Violet one evening.

'Not half,' he said. 'We can hear ourselves think now.'

'Mm. I miss them, though.'

'Let's go out,' he suggested.

She looked at him in astonishment. 'But you always go to the pub to see your mates,' she said.

'Maybe it's time for a change,' he said. 'You

need to get out more.'

'Where would we go?' she asked.

'Anywhere you fancy; the pictures, the pub. We could even see if we can get in for a show,' he said.

'Blimey, George, what's come over you?'

'The kids have left home,' he said. 'So we are free to do as we please. Let's make the most of it.'

Violet looked at him. He would never admit it, but he'd grown fond of his grandson and was always keen for the children to visit. He had been a little more respectful towards her lately, too. At first, he'd been furious when she'd taken a part-time job in a local shop, but she'd stood her ground and he didn't seem to mind now.

So what if he'd had a bit of a fling a few years ago. She could never quite forgive him, but it had obviously fizzled out and he did seem to be making more of an effort lately.

'We could go for a drink at one of the pubs by the river,' she suggested.

'Yeah, all right,' he said. 'Whatever you fancy.'

'I'll get my coat,' she said, smiling.

We do hope that you have enjoyed reading this large print book.

Did you know that all of our titles are available for purchase?

We publish a wide range of high quality large print books including:
Romances, Mysteries, Classics
General Fiction
Non Fiction and Westerns

Special interest titles available in large print are:
The Little Oxford Dictionary
Music Book
Song Book
Hymn Book
Service Book

Also available from us courtesy of Oxford University Press:
Young Readers' Dictionary
(large print edition)
Young Readers' Thesaurus
(large print edition)

For further information or a free brochure, please contact us at:
Ulverscroft Large Print Books Ltd.,
The Green, Bradgate Road, Anstey,
Leicester, LE7 7FU, England.
Tel: (00 44) 0116 236 4325
Fax: (00 44) 0116 234 0205